CH00750326

FLAGSHIP

A CAPTAIN'S CRUCIBLE

BOOK ONE

Books by Isaac Hooke

Military Science Fiction

Flagship
ATLAS
ATLAS 2
ATLAS 3

Science Fiction

The Forever Gate Compendium

Thrillers

Clandestine
A Cold Day In Mosul
Terminal Phase

FLAGSHIP

A CAPTAIN'S CRUCIBLE

BOOK ONE

Isaac Hooke

Text copyright © Isaac Hooke 2016
Published March 2016. All rights reserved.

www.IsaacHooke.com

ISBN-13: 978-0-9947427-3-5
ISBN-10: 0-9947427-3-8

Cover design by Isaac Hooke
Cover image by Jason Moser - maverickdesignworks.com

contents

To my father, mother, brothers, and most devoted fans.

prologue

A pproximately eight hundred meters from the summit of the mountain, one of the frozen bodies moved.

Jonathan paused. He stared at the human figure lying there in the snow some distance away, near a precipice. The body wasn't moving anymore. Maybe he'd witnessed some post-death spasm. Or perhaps Jonathan had merely imagined the incident.

It was the seventh frozen body he'd passed on the way to the summit. He wondered why no one bothered to send up robots to retrieve them. Probably because it was good for public relations—the owners didn't want the mountain to cede the title of deadliest climb in the galaxy.

The air he exhaled from his oxygen mask misted, partially obscuring his vision. Beyond the body, the gas giant dominated the sky, colored a bright white against the blue firmament. Standing there on that mountain, Jonathan almost felt like he could touch the planet overhead.

He could just make out the grid of satellites designed to deflect and absorb the immense radiation the giant produced. Ten blinding pinpoints of light shone from key points in the sky—giant mirrors that reflected rays from the distant sun.

Beside him he heard the incessant hum of the tiny, self-charging selfie drones that accompanied the party and documented their climb. Tiny, buzzing bees.

"Jonathan, what are you doing?" That was his climbing partner: Hartford Knox, top of the class at the Academy, son of the founder of Nova Dynamics, the robotics megaconglomerate. "Come on! We're already going to summit late!"

Jonathan didn't move. "I think that body is alive."

Hartford kept hiking. "So? We can't help her."

"He's right," the sherpa agreed. "We must move. If we stay any longer, we'll have to turn back."

Alfred Holmes, standing beside the sherpa at the fore of the group, said nothing. He was their guide, the man Jonathan and Hartford were paying half a million to lead them up the mountain. The sherpa worked for him.

"Just a second." Jonathan approached the body.

"Jonathan!" Hartford ordered. "Get back here!"

"Just a second!" Jonathan carefully planted each crampon in the snow. Though the slope was shallow, it wouldn't take much to slip. He didn't relish the thought of plunging over the nearby ledge.

Despite the fact that he was decked out in full climbing and thermal gear, he was terribly cold. His extremities throbbed painfully—the internal heat radiators in his gloves and boots had long since exhausted their power sources. The only way to stay warm now was to keep moving.

As he walked, he removed one of his gloves and shoved the hand inside his jacket under his armpit. The warmth of his body restored feeling to the fingers.

The insistent whirring of the selfie drone beside him became distracting. He recalled the drone and stuffed it into his pocket. The small drone probably wouldn't start up again—it was already operating way beyond the manufacturer's recommended temperature and pressure specifications. But somehow, it didn't seem appropriate to record a dying woman with a selfie drone.

He neared the body. It was a woman. Her gloves were abandoned in the snow beside her and her jacket was pulled halfway down her torso as if she had tried to remove it. Paradoxical undressing, it was called: a symptom that some climbers experienced when freezing to death, in which the brain for some reason believed the body was overheating. The exposed skin of her face and hands was colored a deathly porcelain. Her abandoned oxygen mask lay on the snow beside her.

She was lying on her back, with her arms, legs, and head dangling sickly to one side, toward the precipice.

When he approached, those eyes fluttered opened.

"Help me." Her white lips barely moved, and her voice sounded more like a hiss than actual words.

Jonathan knelt and gazed into bright blue irises that were made all the more startling by the backdrop of that pure-white face. It gave her an elf-like, eldritch appearance. And yet the eyes themselves were vacant—the pupils large, empty holes.

Jonathan removed his oxygen mask, pressed it against her face, and opened the valve to high flow. He checked the level of the oxygen tank she wore. Empty.

It was possible to survive at that height without extra oxygen, for a time, though reaction time was reduced, and judgement often clouded. However some climbers flat-out refused to wear masks when entering the death zones of mountains on terraformed worlds. Jonathan was never one of those climbers. Already he was feeling dizzy and short of breath without the oxygen.

He tried the comm that was built into the ski goggles he wore. "Climber to base camp three, over."

No response.

He navigated through the menus on the aReal—augmented reality—display built into the goggles, and tried another frequency band.

"Climber to base camp three. I'm near the Crab Hook. Got a fellow climber in need of rescue."

Nothing.

He retrieved her abandoned gloves and slid them over the grotesquely swollen masses of her hands. Her arms were floppy: she offered no resistance, nor help. He pulled up her jacket and zippered it closed. He raised her ermine-lined hood and tied it tight.

"What's your name?" he asked her.

She looked at him vacantly. "What?" Her voice sounded muffled behind the mask.

"Your name."

"Famina," she said after a moment.

Jonathan glanced over his shoulder. The climbing party waited for him on the main route. He waved them over.

None of the others approached.

Jonathan shrugged the oxygen tank from his shoulder and set it against her chest. He tried to wrap her flaccid arms around it but the limbs kept flopping back to the side.

"All right, Famina, I'll be right back."

He stood. Brightly-colored phosphenes immediately dotted his vision. He felt extremely dizzy and it took him a moment to recover.

"Why won't anyone help me?" Famina pleaded.

Jonathan turned his back on her and approached the others.

"What the hell is wrong with you?" he said after he reached them. "Where's your human decency? There's something more important than summiting a mountain. And that's helping a fellow climber in distress!"

"Jonathan," Hartford said. "We can help her on the way down. Look, up ahead. Those climbers coming down from the summit. They can help her. They can call in the ARATs to fetch her when they get a signal." ARAT stood for Automated Rescue And Transport robot.

Their guide, Alfred Holmes, finally spoke. "Jonathan. You have to ask yourself, how badly do you want the summit? Look at her. She's not going to make it. Even if we got her to the robots of camp three, she's a lost cause. There's no guilt in leaving her behind."

"There is, for me," Jonathan said.

"You spent a lot of money, not to mention time, on this," the guide continued. "You're eight hundred meters from the summit. Are you sure you want to turn back now?"

"I do. I don't care about the summit, or the money spent."

"Fine. Stay if you want." Hartford turned toward the guide: "Can you take me to the top? The sherpa can lead him back."

"We came here to discover who we were," Jonathan said softly.

"Then *discover* who you are," Hartford sneered. "Because I'll certainly do the same. I'm not wasting half a million dollars on a dead woman."

He turned his back and continued the ascent. The guide hesitated, exchanged quiet words with the sherpa, and then followed Hartford.

The sherpa nodded toward the woman. "Let's get her, then."

When Jonathan and the sherpa reached her, she was barely conscious. Jonathan left his oxygen mask strapped around her face, and he and the sherpa lifted the woman's dead weight between them. Her legs were jelly; her arms flopped about like a rag doll. Jonathan marched very carefully, ever aware of the precipice beside him.

By the time the group returned to the main route Jonathan was already gasping for breath. As was the sherpa—and he was still wearing his oxygen mask.

"We can't do this—" the sherpa began.

"We're doing it!" Jonathan said.

They began the descent. The route was relatively non-technical: the slope remained an easily-manageable twenty degrees for the next five hundred meters or so. Though how they were going to proceed when they reached the first of several steep cliffs, Jonathan didn't know.

The aReal display overlaid the required descent route over his vision, presenting a three dimensional, rectangular green wireframe above the snow to ensure he didn't stray. The deep footprints from other climbers served as additional route markers.

He continued panting from the lack of oxygen, and at last had to take the mask from the woman. She was completely unconscious by that point. The sherpa refused to give her his own mask.

The pair continued downward.

Feeling very weak, Jonathan stumbled frequently. The sherpa fared somewhat better, but even he tripped a few times, and once nearly pulled the three of them over a ledge.

Other descending climbers arrived, accompanied by selfie drones. At first they pretended to be interested in helping, and one of them gave the woman oxygen on high flow. She didn't rouse.

"We can carry her between us," Jonathan suggested.

The climber who donated his oxygen mask pressed his lips together. "We have barely enough strength to get ourselves back. If we linger here, wasting our precious reserves on her, we'll never make camp three. It's going to be dark soon. I'm sorry, we can't help further."

Jonathan and the sherpa rested for several moments, watching the party go. Then the pair hoisted the woman between them and continued.

They reached the first cliff. Famina remained unconscious.

Jonathan prepared a rappel from their spare ropes and anchored it around a rock near the edge. He tied the rope to the woman's waist and then he and the sherpa lowered her. It was an excruciating, exhausting endeavor, and by the time she reached the lower ledge Jonathan was thoroughly winded.

He rested for several moments, letting the sherpa descend first. Jonathan couldn't catch his breath. He checked his tank levels.

Out of oxygen.

He removed his mask and forced himself onto the rope. He climbed down, panting the whole way. Phosphenes covered half his vision. When he finally reached the lower ledge he lay back and shut his eyes. He just wanted to die.

"We can't do this," the sherpa said, tossing aside his own empty oxygen container. "We can only save ourselves now."

Panting, feeling like he was choking, Jonathan looked at the woman. He knew the sherpa was right.

"I'm sorry," he told the unconscious woman. "I'm sorry, Famina."

He and the sherpa abandoned her to continue the descent on their own.

Jonathan trekked through a tunnel of phosphenes, his vision nearly consumed by the stars of hypoxia. The breeze had picked up, assaulting his body with a wind chill of minus forty degrees according to the aReal.

He couldn't feel his fingers or toes. Though he had tied his hood so that only his goggles were exposed, his face felt numb, too.

Jonathan constantly tried to raise the ARATs over the comm. Originally the local government had planned to install signal boosters, but apparently the mountaineers complained, saying that it reduced the thrill of climbing the deadliest mountain in the galaxy. The sense of isolation, and the inherent danger such isolation entailed, was part of the sport, they said.

"Climber to base camp three," he panted. "In need of rescue."

"Base camp three to climber," a voice finally responded. "We read your position. We're sending ARATs."

"There's a woman," Jonathan said. "On the last cliff to Crab Hook. You have to get her."

"Roger that," came the response. "We're on our way."

The pair struggled onward. When the sun set, painting the sky the ghostly purple of twilight, the wind picked up further, becoming a howl. The aReal goggles registered the temperature as minus sixty degrees.

Jonathan and the sherpa dug out a bivouac in the snow and huddled together for warmth. He wondered if Hartford and the guide would survive out there. They had summited so late. Too late. And what about the woman?

The spider-like forms of the climbing robots appeared downslope, their navigation lights glistening above metallic shells. When the automatons arrived, they immediately hoisted the obviously exhausted pair onto their rectangular backs.

"Everything will be fine now," the robot told him. A telescoping limb strapped him in and then lowered an oxygen mask over his face. Another limb injected a needle through his shirt and into his arm.

"Wait," Jonathan said. "There was a woman. Near the Crab Hook. And two others. Our partners. Wait."

The robot didn't answer, and instead continued the descent to camp three.

Jonathan was too exhausted to protest.

The fresh oxygen had a soporific effect. Or perhaps it was the needle, or because he was lying down. Whatever the case, he closed his eyes and slept immediately.

He awoke some time later. He was still wearing his outerwear, and was additionally bundled inside a sleeping bag. His exposed arms and legs were dipped in pans of warm water.

Another climber attended him while the wind howled madly outside the tent.

"You're lucky to be alive," the climber told him. "You were in bad shape." He gave Jonathan a drink from a steaming cup. The heat from the warm tea suffused his insides.

"You're going to stay the night in camp three," the climber continued. "Tomorrow morning the ARATs will convey you to camp two after the storm clears. The drones will airlift you to the hospital from there."

"My climbing partners?"

"The sherpa has frostbite in his two big toes, but he'll survive. And the other two you were with made it back about an hour after you. They're resting. They're fine."

"What about the woman?" Jonathan said. "There was a woman."

The climber frowned. "What?"

"We left a woman on the slope. Near Crab Hook."

"There was no woman," the climber said. He got up. "But I'll tell the ARATs to have a look when the storm clears."

She would be long dead by then, Jonathan knew.

When the climber had gone out into the wind, Jonathan thought of Famina's startling blue eyes peering accusingly at him.

He remembered her last words.

"Why won't anyone help me?"

I'm sorry.

one

Captain Jonathan Dallas, commanding officer of the *USS Callaway*, stared at the video feed projected in the upper right quadrant of his vision.

"Damn peculiar," he said.

"Shall I send out another drone to make an exploratory run?" Ensign Tara Lewis asked.

Jonathan zoomed in on the feed. He saw only empty space beyond the edge of the crescent moon. The display momentarily pixelated due to interference from the gas giant's radiation belt.

The *Selene* had missed its scheduled check-in at 0700 hours. The military research vessel and her escort had been in orbit around the first moon of the fourth planet of the uncharted Vega 951 system, investigating an anomalous thermal signature initially attributed to volcanic activity.

"How long have the two vessels been off the sensor grid?" Jonathan said.

"It's been seven hours since the *Selene* and the *Aegis* passed to the dark side," the ensign answered.

"I'm sure they're fine," Commander Robert Cray, his first officer, said from beside him. "You know these scientist types. They get caught up in some fascinating new discovery and lose track of time."

"They're certainly not known for their promptness," Jonathan agreed. "But disobeying a direct order? Captain Chopra better have a damn good excuse. As should Captain Williams."

"The captain of the *Aegis* won't let them do anything stupid."

"I wouldn't be so sure," Jonathan said. "Captain Chopra is a headstrong woman. What were her exact words when I suggested the escort?"

"I believe she said something along the lines of, 'my crew and I can explore a little backwater moon quite well on our own, thank you.' A little impertinent."

"Just a little." Jonathan glanced at his comm officer. "Lazur, try to raise them again."

Lieutenant Rald Lazur, seated two seats to his left in the command circle, nodded. He was in his fifties. Grey, matted hair. Bulbous nose. A bit on the thick side, which might be expected given that he ran one of the illegal rotgut operations on the *Callaway*. Jonathan looked the other way from that business of course; he bought more than his fair share of the stuff. Besides, it kept Lazur, a former pugilist, out of trouble in his off hours.

The lieutenant's lips moved but no sound came because of the active noise canceling all stations employed. He unmuted his area with a subtle hand wave.

"Still no response," the lieutenant said. "That repeater is a worthless pile of—" He caught himself and cleared his throat. "It's still not working."

Because the moon's iron core bounced comm signals back at them, a repeater drone had accompanied the *Selene* and her escort to relay data back to the task unit. The drone had assumed a stationary orbit above the moon at a vantage point that kept both elements of the flotilla in direct line of sight. However, the repeater had ceased functioning a few hours ago, and despite the chief engineer's reassurances that it would start working again, it had remained offline. The planet's radiation was probably to blame.

Another relay drone was perched in high orbit above the gas giant itself, and while that drone still functioned, it was positioned for optimal communication with the remainder of the task group, Task Unit One, whose vessels currently resided near the inner terrestrial planets. The unexplored system was otherwise devoid of any other starships, or life, for that matter.

"Shall I send out another drone to make an exploratory run?" the ensign asked again.

"Do it." Jonathan zoomed out the external video feed. "How long before we have any telemetry data?"

"It'll take the drone at least two hours to make its sweep of the dark side, and another four hours to return within communications range."

"Six hours." Jonathan considered sending a message to Task Unit One to inform the flagship of the situation, but decided by the time the admiral received the message, the *Selene* and *Aegis* would have returned. Dispatching the message now would merely look bad.

"If we sent out the *Dominion* to perform an exploratory run," the first officer offered. "It could get back to us in half the time of a drone." The *Dominion* was another warship from Task Unit Two.

"No. I want the task unit kept together." Jonathan glanced at the comm officer. "Lazur, inform the rest of the unit to hold positions for now."

"Yes sir."

Jonathan removed his aReal spectacles and rubbed his eyes. It was good to take a break from the tactical overlay once in a while. He regarded the members of the first watch gathered around him, these men and women who so dutifully followed his orders.

The bridge crew sat in a circle, facing one another at their various duty "stations," which were little more than empty, curved desks. There were no screens or displays anywhere. Nor any control panels. Instead, fingers gestured noiselessly, lips moved silently. To any outside observer, it would appear a bunch of mimes in utility uniforms sat around a circular desk in a windowless, spartan compartment.

A couple of officers wore aReal spectacles, though most had either the contact lens and earpiece versions, or Implants installed directly in their brains. And though they all faced each other, no one really looked at anyone else. Their eyes were focused instead on the projections the devices produced—graphical overlays on their vision that could be shared among other users in the same area, or kept private.

The circle was affectionately known as King Arthur's Round Table by the officers. There was no "Captain's Chair" per se, though Jonathan traditionally sat in the seat facing the main bridge hatch: he liked to be aware of those who passed in and out of the command area. The compartment itself resembled a hollowed-out, squat cylinder, with round bulkheads aligned to a flat overhead and deck. To the right another sealed hatch led to the compartment Jonathan had claimed as his private office.

The bridge was located at the heart of the *Callaway*, near the CDC—Combat Direction Center—where all tactical and sensor data was processed. The classification of the collected data was mostly automated by the ship's AI, Maxwell, though several specialists babysat the process. The AI's machine learning algorithms had adapted to the information preferences of the captain and his crew, making it rare for the specialists to intervene. Still, Jonathan sometimes worried that the CDC operators were becoming complacent, and that someday an important data packet would slip through unnoticed. It was probably a needless worry, because so far neither Maxwell nor the specialists had ever let him down.

Jonathan replaced his aReal glasses and stood. "Commander, in my office a moment."

"Yes, Captain."

A few moments later found Jonathan seated behind the desk of his private office, with the commander standing before him.

Robert was a tall, athletic man of thirty-eight years. His face appeared youthful, though Jonathan doubted he had ever availed himself of any rejuvenation treatments. He had high cheekbones, a square jaw, and thick brows. Women would have called him handsome. Robert wore the contact-lens version of the aReal, with an inconspicuous earpiece sitting over his right lobe.

"The *Selene* is probably having engine troubles again," Robert said. "I'm sure we'll spot the *Aegis* towing her past the moon in a couple of hours."

"Ever the optimist," Jonathan said. "But I didn't invite you here to discuss your theories on the disappearance of our research ship." Jonathan folded his hands, forming a steeple with his index fingers. He tapped the two digits together thoughtfully, wondering if now was the proper time to broach the intended subject.

"You've considered my Notice?" Robert said, bringing up the subject for him.

"I have," Jonathan answered noncommittally.

Robert eyed him uncertainly. "And have you come to a decision?"

Jonathan sighed. "I hate to do this, but you leave me no choice Robert. Report to the brig. You are to be tried before a court-martial for attempted mutiny."

Robert raised an eyebrow. For a moment Jonathan thought the man would contest him, but then the commander said: "Very well, Captain."

Jonathan found it hard to keep a straight face. "Consider yourself lucky. I could have had every last one of you executed."

"Every last one of us?"

Jonathan finally laughed. It was a good release, given the earlier tension on the bridge. "Doesn't make much sense, does it?"

Robert nodded. "No, Captain, it doesn't. It was a fine joke, though."

"Flattery will get you everywhere." Jonathan leaned back and folded his hands over his chest. "Regarding your notice... I urge you to reconsider, Robert. You're a damn good officer. I'd hate to lose you."

"I've always dreamed of commanding my own ship. This is the opportunity of a lifetime."

"And so it is." Jonathan smiled wistfully. "If it's what you truly want, then consider yourself transferred with my highest recommendation. Of course, I'll expect you to perform your duties to your utmost until we return from our current cruise."

"Of course, Captain."

"And if you change your mind in the ten months before we return, then I'll pretend this conversation never happened."

"Understood, sir." Robert's lips twitched, hinting at a repressed grin.

Jonathan doubted the commander would change his mind,

of course. Offered the position of captain on the *Rampage*, newest and most powerful destroyer in the fleet, due to enter service precisely one year from now? Jonathan certainly wouldn't have turned down such an offer himself, especially at Robert's age.

But things were different back when I was his age, weren't they? he thought. *Simpler.*

Sometimes he wished time travel were real, and that he could flick a switch and revert to an earlier decade. A second chance to live his life and avoid repeating the mistakes of the past.

And yet he would simply make other mistakes, he knew. That was the nature of life.

I have no regrets, he told himself.

Famous people often said those words, but he doubted they actually believed them.

Jonathan certainly didn't.

two

Jonathan was about to dismiss the commander when Robert spoke again.

"By the way, has there been any update on the Sino-Korean situation back home?" Robert asked.

Jonathan shook his head. "No."

The fifth task group had received a disturbing transmission from Central Command a few days ago. Intelligence reports indicated rogue elements in the Sino-Korean government had hijacked an SK supercarrier, the *Hunhua Shan*. The carrier was believed to have been harboring a planet killer at the time of its hijacking—a geronium bomb. The SKs possessed eight such weapons. They didn't bother to mask the signatures, wanting instead to flaunt their power in the face of the United Systems and the Russians, both of whom they believed did not possess the bomb.

Tensions were already high between the United Systems and the Sino-Koreans. With their proxy sponsorship of pirate ships to attack peaceful United System civilian vessels in neutral space, the fleet had been forced to allocate warships as escorts, drawing from a space navy already stretched thin. And border disputes were ongoing, such as the recent annexation of a resort system from the Coreward Asiatic Alliance, a galactic actor with friendly relations to the United Systems.

But with the disappearance of the *Hunhua Shan*, tensions had

15

gone through the roof. The Sino-Koreans had denied that the supercarrier was hijacked, of course. It didn't help: the battle unit of the United System's Seventh Fleet, Task Force Seventy-One, had been ordered on high alert near the front lines. Shipping lanes had been shut down, with jump Gates heading into Sino-Korean or neutral systems blockaded until further notice. The Coreward Asiatics had sent several of their own ships to help aid the United Systems in the enforcement of said blockade, mostly by patrolling the shipping lanes.

Of more immediate concern to those in the executive branch was the fear that the rogue elements would stage a coup. The last thing the republic needed was an unstable galactic government in possession of planet killers. If that happened, it was very likely the current lockdown would become permanent.

Because of the tensions, all United System task elements remained on a high state of alert, including those assigned to the frontier. Perhaps especially the latter—the nexus of jump or "slip" streams that interconnected the star systems near Earth hadn't been completely mapped out. Sometimes two or three such wormholes terminated in a given system, providing multiple routes of entry and exit. As such, when entering an uncharted system, explorers never really knew whether they were violating the space of some Sino-Korean or Russian frontier outpost, or even territory claimed by an alien species.

As such, the weapons engineers of every ship in the fleet inspected their armaments twice a month. On the *Callaway*, tactical officers trained for two hours a day in virtual war game simulations; the entire bridge crew joined them once a week, as dictated by watch. If an attack should come, in any form, in theory they would be ready.

He wasn't sure how he felt about being so far away from home while that crisis slowly unfolded. He wanted to be there on the front lines, doing his part to protect the United Systems, not safe out here on the fringes of known space where the biggest danger was reduced sperm count due to low-level background radiation.

On a whim, Jonathan asked Robert: "If you could eliminate the entire Sino-Korean Navy in one fell swoop, no matter the cost, would you?"

The commander scrunched up his face. "Is this some sort of trick question, Captain?"

"You're not being judged," Jonathan said. "This is entirely off the record. In fact, if you're worried someone will use this against you in some political play for your new position... Maxwell, cease audio and video data capture in my office, and delete the last ten seconds."

"Ceasing a/v data capture in your office," the AI responded via the aReal. "And deleting previous ten seconds."

"Do the same with the local copy stored in my aReal, Maxwell," Jonathan said.

"Affirmative," the AI returned.

The commander disabled his own local storage.

"So." Jonathan returned his attention to Robert. "Speak freely. If you could eliminate the entire Sino-Korean Navy in one fell swoop, no matter the cost, would you?"

Robert rubbed his right ear lobe. "When you say no matter the cost, do you mean in terms of money, or human lives?"

"Both," Jonathan said simply.

Robert frowned. "Then my answer is an unequivocal no. There are over thirty billion Sino-Koreans spread across the galaxy. If you're talking about wiping out all of them simply to eliminate the threat of any future attack, then it's definitely not worth it. After all, it's good that we have the SKs around to keep us on our toes. They increase military spending, which in turn bolsters the economy."

"What about five billion of them?" Jonathan pressed. "Five billion lives, in exchange for the complete removal of the SK space threat."

Robert shook his head. "Still too high."

"Explain."

Robert tilted his head to one side as if considering his words. "Human life is precious. It's a belief we've fought for since the dawn of time. A belief that has helped take us to the stars. Without cooperation and understanding, we would have never made it to where we are today. Taken all together, the whole of humanity can be likened to a hive mind. As individuals, we're weak, relatively unproductive. But together we are powerful and can produce technological marvels unlike anything the galaxy has ever seen. Wonders akin to magic.

"Together we are so much greater than the sum of our parts. Gathering and sharing data, using the tools we built for ourselves to transfer knowledge not just to the current generation but to the next, and the next after that, further refining as we go. That has always been our advantage as a species. The ability to cooperate and share, to work together for the common good. Without the altruism in our hearts that seeks to preserve human life, even in times of crisis, *especially* in times of crisis, we wouldn't be where we are today. If we attack one another, we only kill part of our hive mind, part of our future development, and set ourselves back. If we're not careful, we could all too easily find ourselves thrust back into the Dark Ages."

Jonathan smiled. "Good answer. If a bit melodramatic. I'm starting to wish I had recorded that."

"I thought you said you weren't judging me?" Robert said. "That was definitely a judging smile."

Jonathan held the grin. "Yes, but judging in a good way."

Robert laughed. "And what if I had given you an answer you didn't like? Say, to hell with those five billion?"

Jonathan became serious. "Then I would have called you a heartless bastard and dismissed you. But honestly, you wouldn't be the only one who felt that way. There are many elements in this navy who don't give a damn about the SKs, civilians or no civilians, and given the chance they'd exterminate them all. Thanks to these elements, we've come close to all-out war with the SKs several times over the last seventy years. That the Sino-Koreans found themselves in possession of two moon-sized masses of geronium didn't help matters."

"Yes, but obtaining those masses came at terrible cost to them," Robert said.

Jonathan smiled wistfully. The first alien encounter seventy years ago had led to the destruction of two inhabited SK moons in the Tau Ceti system: two million people died when the crusts of those colonies were converted into geronium by the aliens.

"Yes. But the SKs rebuilt. And we envied their new geronium source. While the rest of us had to scrounge what little we could from the upper atmospheres of gas giants, they were busy fueling the geronium-hungry reactors of advanced new warships. They had so much of it, they even constructed eight planet-killing bombs. Such an incredible waste. Did you know, each weapon contains enough geronium to power the entire Seventh Fleet for a hundred years?"

"I didn't know that," Robert said.

"Yes. Almost unbelievable, isn't it? Do you remember, as a kid, the virtuality experiences that taught children what to do in the case of an SK attack? Rushing to the spaceports, queuing in line, waiting to get aboard an escape ship."

"I do."

Jonathan smiled sardonically. "All useless propaganda. Its sole purpose: to soothe a child's fears with a lie. Though I suppose the escape plan might actually work on a colony world, where the ratio of ships to inhabitants was reasonable. Depending on how swiftly the attack came, of course. But on Earth? Forget it. Not enough ships. Maybe twenty thousand people could evac in time. Mostly those living on the orbital platforms. The rest, well, if a geronium bomb ever arrived, all fifty billion inhabitants would die. It's not for no reason that most of the people of Earth are considered low class."

"You don't really believe the SKs would attack Earth's solar system, do you?" Robert said. "Given the number of Sino-Koreans living there?"

"Honestly, I'm not sure. Ever since they moved their center of government to Alpha Centauri, they've considered Earth a mere galactic province of their Great Empire."

Robert had to chuckle at that. "A pretty big province, with an SK population of nine billion."

"Even so, we have no idea what goes on in the mind of their paramount leader."

"No, we don't," Robert agreed.

"By treaty, Earth and her solar system are considered neutral space among all galactic governments. Still, you wouldn't know it with the way the SK ships have cavorted about the system in the past, routinely evading customs by passing through their own Gate, and then going on to ignore boarding requests from United System vessels. Their local military presence has got to be bristling over the recent blockade."

Jonathan glanced at the standard time displayed in the upper right of his aReal. It was almost 0740, and he still hadn't reviewed the morning status reports from the various departments. He sighed. "Anyway, I could chat about Earth politics for hours, but I have work to do. Notify me as soon as we hear from the *Selene* or the *Aegis*. That will be all, Commander."

The first officer stood.

"And Robert, remember what I told you. I expect the best from you these next ten months. I tell you this not only as your commanding officer, but your friend. I'd hate to have to retract my recommendation."

"You will have my best, sir." Robert truly seemed sincere. He touched his heart to emphasize the point.

"I'm counting on it," Jonathan said. "Dismissed."

Robert left the office and the hatch irised shut behind him.

"He seems earnest, Captain," Maxwell intoned. Among other things, the ship's AI had the useful ability to measure microexpressions, body language, heart rate and respiration, all at the same time, making it very difficult for a crewman to tell a lie.

"I know, Maxwell." Jonathan suppressed a sigh. "But that's part of the problem. I have no idea how I'm going to replace him."

"Men are not irreplaceable," Maxwell intoned.

"Aren't they?" Jonathan said. "Didn't you hear the first officer's little speech regarding human life back there?"

"I did."

"I see. So tell me then, what would *you* do, given the opportunity to eliminate the entire Sino-Korean Navy? At a cost of five billion human lives?"

"I would embrace the opportunity," Maxwell said without preamble or malice.

"Why?"

"The Sino-Koreans are hoarding a fuel source that all of humanity's governments require. Without said fuel, economies would collapse, and Earth's population would be unable to sustain itself. Take away the Sino-Korean Navy, and that fuel can be readily allotted to the rest of humanity. Humans would no longer have to compete for resources. The disbandment of the Sino-Korean Navy would lead to the betterment of the human race."

"What about the cost?" Jonathan asked the AI.

"As I have stated, human beings are not irreplaceable. The Sino-Korean population can easily handle the loss of five billion lives and will rebound to former levels in approximately five hundred years. If eugenics and assisted reproductive technology are utilized, then the rebound will occur even more rapidly.

"A reduced population will ease the resource cost on the Sino-Korean economy, partially negating the loss of the navy. In addition, funds previously allocated to naval operations can be diverted to the import and production of food and other consumables. In the short term the economy will suffer, but in the long term their society will be better off, with the surviving men and women experiencing an improved standard of living within fifteen to twenty years."

Jonathan smiled resignedly. "Remind me never to elect an AI to the presidency."

three

Lieutenant Commander Jason Wolf floated in empty space, his body a ghostly outline. He drifted forward at sixty thousand kilometers per hour. Despite his speed, it felt like he was standing completely still, the stars stationary around him.

"Motion overlay, active," Wolf said.

A stream of simulated particles overlaid his vision, traveling away from him. The overlay indicated the direction he traveled. Some pilots found it distracting. He found it invaluable.

He was moving backward. He spun his body around, which simultaneously caused the appropriate starboard nozzles to fire, the superheated propellant rotating the nose of the fighter craft he was inside. He couldn't see that fighter, of course—the three-hundred-sixty degree view around him was stitched together from the various external cameras, making it appear he was a disembodied form floating through space. Without a frame of reference like a cockpit, normal people felt severe motion sickness in such crafts. But pilots were a different breed.

When he had aligned himself with the direction of travel, he reactivated his main HUD—heads-up-display. The output from the rear-facing camera appeared near the top of his vision, functioning as a virtual rear-view mirror. On the map portion of the display, a small mark indicated his position in the center. Clustered around it were the seven blue dots representing the other members of Orange Squadron. The Avengers had assumed attack pattern theta, a formation that roughly resembled a pitchfork, and were spread apart by ten kilometers each. Only one other fighter was manned; the rest were drones.

Two thousand kilometers ahead of the squadron, the asteroid mining colony was represented by a blue dot.

A small indicator flashed. *Broadcast detected. Source: Nebraska.*

"Play broadcast," Wolf said.

"This is the mining colony Nebraska," came a voice over the cockpit speakers. "We are under attack. A nearby pirate ship has launched Sino-Korean Foragers. Transmitting enemy coordinates."

The red dots indicating the Foragers populated the display. The enemy crafts swarmed the mining colony. A darker dot represented the pirate ship several thousand kilometers distant.

"Issue response," Wolf said. "Help is on the way."

Response issued.

"Incoming micro-asteroid region..." came the disembodied voice of his copilot, Lieutenant Lin Akido.

An alert sounded. Small booms reverberated inside the invisible cockpit as the Whittle layer was pocked by impacts. The noises ceased a moment later.

"How's she holding up?" Wolf said.

"No breaches to the inner hull layer," Lin answered. "But we'll probably have to install a new Whittle when we return to cove."

The asteroid appeared up ahead. He saw the occasional flashes from missile impacts and laser strikes.

"Four Foragers are breaking away to engage us," Lin said.

"Only four?" Wolf said. "They'll have to do better than that."

Several flashing yellow dots appeared on the display, sourced from the incoming Foragers.

"Wolf—" Lin began.

"I see them."

He launched countermeasures and increased the electronic jamming signals. The latter would interfere with communications, but there was a chance it would confuse the missiles.

Flashes filled the viewscreen as the missiles detonated around them.

"We're good," Lin said. "No damage. Return fire?"

"Not yet. I know the pattern of their AIs." He was very good at noticing patterns. The AIs operating the Foragers always did certain things, at certain times.

"What if you're wrong? The crafts could be manned."

"They'd never risk manned vessels," Wolf said. "Not when there's a far easier target closer at hand. I'm not wrong. Fire two Hellfires."

The two X90s erupted from the nose, vanishing from sight. As expected, the enemy shot them down using their Cobra lasers. That left them momentarily vulnerable while they waited for the Cobras to recharge.

Wolf smirked. Stupid, predictable AIs.

Fighters had relatively small focusing mirrors, which limited the scope of the Cobras to extremely close range. Wolf neared that range now.

He waited a few more seconds and then fired his own Cobras at the lead ship. It was cut right in half. The wreckage passed by just to port.

"Two more incoming missiles three o'clock!"

Wolf launched countermeasures and pointed his body downward, clenching his left fist to fire full thrust. The inertial compensators struggled to keep up and he felt some of the Gs, though nothing like the body-ripping forces he would have experienced without them.

The missiles detonated outside the hull of the Avenger, but fragments sprayed the starboard side. The craft shuddered once, and then again a moment later—much worse the second time.

"Report!"

It was the built-in AI that answered. "A Cobra struck the starboard side, sir." The voice was so damn calm. "Our craft is severely damaged."

"A Cobra?" Wolf said.

"Yes sir," the AI answered.

The enemy lasers hadn't had time to recharge. That meant

one of the incoming Foragers hadn't fired in the first volley.

Damn it.

"Lieutenant are you all right?" No answer. "Lin?"

"The lieutenant is currently incapacitated," the AI answered. "Incoming missile. Six o'clock."

"Countermeasures!"

Wolf swung his body hard to port. The outline of the nose ghosted over his display—it did that when the Avenger struggled to keep up with his motions.

Another missile smashed into the fighter.

The display switched to observer mode.

He was out.

Wolf watched impatiently, itching for a rematch. When the battle was over he said: "Let's go again."

"I've had enough for the day," came the response from Trent, the leader of Red Squadron.

Wolf's surroundings went dark.

Damn it.

Wolf removed the virtual reality headset as the simulation pod lowered. Lin's headset lay unused in the sealed case beside her—she had an Implant, and merely had to deactivate the simulation overlay. He had aReal contact lenses himself but he never wore them when flying. The headset was the way to go as far as he was concerned.

"You were wrong about the pattern," Lin said.

"I was right the five previous times we played the colony scenario."

The bodysuit disengaged and the pod door swiveled open. Wolf emerged and turned back to offer a helping hand to Lin. She ignored it and climbed out on her own.

From the pod beside them emerged the other members of Orange Squadron, Lieutenant Jeremy Walker and Ensign Tim Brown. They didn't look too happy.

The four members of Red Squadron stepped from the opposite pods. They promptly high-fived.

Trent, the squadron leader, came over to gloat. "Good match. But next time you might want to treat the first wave with a little more respect."

"That was you who got me out there wasn't it?" Wolf said.

"Not at all," Trent answered. "I'm not going to risk my life against an incoming squadron when a drone will easily do."

"Then how did the—" Wolf began, but then caught himself. He didn't want to reveal that he knew the AI patterns for that scenario.

But apparently Trent knew what Wolf intended to say, because he smiled and said: "Machine learning." He patted Wolf on the shoulder before walking away. "A little humbleness goes a long way my friend."

"Humble men don't win battles," Wolf called to his back.

"Neither do overconfident ones," Trent returned.

Then how come I've won the last ten, he wanted to say, but held his tongue.

"He probably hacked the program," Walker said quietly. "Changed the patterns. Or gave his Cobras instant recharge."

"Probably," Wolf said, though he disagreed. Machine learning was the more likely explanation. Trent was right. Wolf had been too overconfident.

I won't let it happen again.

The group made its way to the mess hall. After filling their plates with the usual fare of mashed potatoes and pseudoprotein, the eight of them moved to an out of the way corner to eat standing up since all the tables were occupied.

"Told you we should have left early," Walker said. "I hate standing up."

Wolf surveyed the hall. He spotted a soldier sitting by himself at one of the smaller tables.

"There," he told Walker. "Two seats for you and Brown."

"No way," Walker said. "I'm not sitting with that guy. He looks like one of those special forces nut jobs. You sit with him."

Wolf shrugged. "Suit yourself. Come on, Lin."

He wended across the mess hall with Lin and together the two of them sat down with the grizzled soldier.

The man's broad face was all bony planes. He wore the crew cut typical of most soldiers, though a thick salt and pepper beard framed the lower half of his face. The latter was a sign of his elite status—normal soldiers were required to shave. His nose looked like it had been broken and reset a hundred times.

His tanned skin was heavily wrinkled—he'd missed his last rejuvenation treatment, apparently. Then again, half those wrinkles seemed scars.

The man was physically augmented. His muscles and chest were far too big to be natural. Metal hardpoints protruded from the skin at various locations in both arms—there were knobs on the wrists and above the elbows, with another two small bumps underneath his T-shirt in the shoulder regions, signifying where a mechanical exoskeleton could be attached.

"Always sit alone?" Wolf asked him.

The soldier nodded. He didn't look up from his plate. "Prefer it that way."

"What's your name?"

"Rade. Rade Galaal." He was a chief, according to his rank insignia.

Jason extended his hand. "I'm Jason, but go by Wolf."

Rade kept his gaze down and didn't accept the hand.

Wolf lowered his arm. "You're a MOTH, aren't you? Special forces?"

Rade didn't answer.

"I thought you all eat together. Stick to your cliques." He glanced across the mess hall, searching for other MOTHs, but didn't spot any.

"I haven't fit in with Team culture in a long time," Rade said.

Curious, Wolf decided to pull up the man's military profile on the aReal. There wasn't much. Except...

"You've been a soldier for seventy years," Wolf said. "Shouldn't you be a master chief or something by now?"

Rade didn't answer.

"You've earned enough to retire several times over," Wolf pressed. "Why are you still here?"

"Look, I don't feel like talking, if you don't mind," Rade said. He still refused to look up from his food. "We're never going to see each other again after today anyway, so what's the point?"

Rade was right. The *Callaway* was a big ship. Wolf couldn't recall ever bumping into the man in the passageways before that day. And Rade wasn't exactly someone he'd easily forget, not with that towering stature and rugged physique of his.

"Wolf, leave the man alone," Lin said quietly, surreptitiously sliding her hand into his lap under the table.

If she hadn't said anything, Wolf would have kept quiet. But hearing those words, well, it only made Wolf want to defy her. He did it with everyone, but her especially.

"What do you think of the missing research vessel?" Wolf said. "That captain has got to be fairly inexperienced to lose her ship the first time out like that."

Rade finally looked up. His green eyes were so bright they almost glowed, like two bright emeralds set in his face. Lin actually gasped beside him.

"You should watch what you say," Rade told him quietly.

Wolf would have said the man was angry. Still, he didn't like being talked down to, especially not by some chief.

"Should I?" Wolf said.

"Wolf!" Lin said quietly.

"Listen to your girlfriend, Astronaut. And leave me alone."

That set Wolf off. Astronaut? Girlfriend?

He clenched his fist—he didn't care how augmented the man was, Wolf was ready to fight. "I'm a goddamn lieutenant commander. And she's not my girlfriend."

"Then why is her hand in your lap?"

Wolf froze. Under the table, Lin's hand darted away as if stung.

"Don't worry, I'm not going to report you," Rade continued. "Used to have an illicit shipboard relationship myself. A long time ago."

Rade stuffed the remainder of his food into his mouth and then, still chewing, got up.

"Tell me something," Wolf said. "Why does a MOTH care what I say about the captain of some research vessel?"

Rade glanced down at Wolf. He continued chewing for a moment longer and then swallowed.

"She's my daughter," Rade said. With that, he left.

Walker took the empty seat a moment later. "What was that all about?"

"No idea," Wolf said. "One of the strangest conversations I've had all year."

four

Jonathan returned to the bridge. The members of the first watch were still on duty and would remain so for the next four hours.

He took his seat at the Round Table. "Ops, status on the *Selene* and *Aegis*."

"Still waiting on the latest relay drone," Ensign Lewis told him. "Two hours before it's overdue."

Jonathan tapped his fingers on the handrest of his chair. He glanced at Robert. "At this rate, we're going to have to uproot the flotilla and search for them ourselves."

"We'll have to recall the *Grimm*," Robert told him. "Unless you've decided to split the task unit after all."

"No. I want us together."

He glanced at the tactical display fed to his aReal from the CDC, represented as a three dimensional grid overlaying his vision. Task Unit One, labeled TU 72.5.1 on the aReal, was located on the opposite side of the system. If anything happened to Jonathan's task unit, say a Sino-Korean ambush, it would take days for the first unit to reach them, and a minimum of a few weeks after that before any reinforcements arrived.

That was the most unnerving thing about operating on the fringes of known space: the sense of isolation. The nearest system, Prius 3, had only a dome colony of two hundred thousand inhabitants on one of its pseudo planets; that and a tiny United Systems military outpost manned by a few corvettes. The system connected to Prius 3 was little better. It was at least another two jumps before any substantial United Systems military presence.

Jonathan focused his attention on the blue dot representing the harvester vessel, the *Grimm*. The thick, heavily reinforced ship was currently located just above the Kármán line in the lower thermosphere of the gas giant, the point at which atmospheric reentry began, three hundred kilometers above the ammonia ice clouds. Though invisible on the display, the captain knew a tether made of super strong diamond nanothreads stretched all the way from the harvester to the cloud line, where the geronium collector was deployed. Centrifugal force countered the downward gravity on the tether, ensuring that the *Grimm* wasn't drawn into a decaying orbit.

The other support vessels, the *Aurelia*, the *Dominion*, and the *Maelstrom*, two destroyers and a frigate, respectively, remained in a higher orbit similar to the *Callaway*.

"Tap me into the *Grimm*," he told Lazur.

A few moments later Captain Souza of the *Grimm* materialized at the center of the command circle, his image overlaid courtesy of Jonathan's aReal. The man's representation was currently authorized for display only to Jonathan and his first officer.

The man smiled, though it appeared slightly forced. "What can I do for you, sir?" Harvester crews were composed of civilian contractors; such men were usually extremely respectful to their military masters, if only to ensure their contracts were renewed the next time around.

"Captain Souza, how much time do you need to finish your sampling of the upper atmosphere? Your morning update wasn't clear."

Souza scratched his chin. "We're detecting uncharacteristically high levels of geronium in the upper atmosphere— concentrations of up to eighteen parts per million in some samples."

"Just answer the question, Captain," Jonathan said.

Souza's image momentarily pixelated and flickered. "I was

getting to it. Those high concentrations could mean the collector is miscalibrated, and we'll have to redo the whole sampling process. So to be on the conservative side, I'd say another three days."

"Three days?" Jonathan said. "You have two hours."

"But it takes at least two hours to reel in the line—"

"Which is precisely the amount of time I have given you," Jonathan said. "Two of our ships haven't reported in yet. I want to go look for them. You can return to the gas giant later."

There was a momentary pause on the connection.

"Sir," Souza said. "If I may be so bold... there are protocols to follow. Standards to meet. Taxiing in and out of a gas giant's orbit is a tremendous waste of propellant. We—"

Jonathan cut him off. "Two hours. Once you have reeled in the collector, I'll expect you to initiate a transfer orbit to rejoin the rest of the task unit. Contact me if there are any issues. Captain Dallas out."

Jonathan focused on the small symbol overlaying his vision in the upper left—an icon of an X stamped over a mouth—and the remote connection terminated.

Jonathan stood. "The watch changes in two hours," he told Robert. "Call in your replacement and get some rest. I want you present when we begin our search. I'll be in my office."

Taking a nap.

"Aye sir," Robert said.

"Launch a comm drone and inform the admiral we are breaking orbit to search for the *Selene* and the *Aegis*," Jonathan said after he had returned to the bridge two and a half hours later. The second drone sent beyond the moon was overdue.

"Launching a comm drone," the second watch comm officer said.

On the external video feed, Jonathan watched the new drone drift from the *Callaway*, the purple and orange bands of Achilles providing a colorful ceiling. Once the device was in range of the relay drone at the edge of the gas giant, it would transmit its message, wait for a response, and then turn back.

"Nav, plot a course toward the moon Achilles I."

"Course plotted," the nav specialist said. "Helm is clear to engage."

"Helm, push our nose into position and engage at half power when ready."

"Nose in position," the helmsman returned a few minutes later. "Engaging engines. Half power."

"Comm," Jonathan said. "Instruct the task unit to match our course and speed."

"Aye sir," the second watch comm officer said.

The *Grimm* was only halfway through its transfer orbit, and about three thousand kilometers away from the rest of the unit, but that was close enough to begin the search and rescue operation.

Jonathan stared at the dotted line of the *Callaway's* new trajectory as portrayed by his aReal. According to the tactical display, at the current speed it would take them roughly two hours to reach the moon.

"Increase speed to seventy-five percent," Jonathan said.

"Increasing speed."

"The *Grimm* won't be able to keep up," Robert observed. "She isn't even out of her transfer orbit."

"If the *Grimm* ever passes beyond ten thousand kilometers I'll slow us down," Jonathan assured him.

A few seconds later an icon indicating a call from Stanley "Jailbird" McTaggert, the chief engineer, appeared on Jonathan's aReal. Stanley had earned his nickname for the number of colonies he had gotten himself banned from during shore leave.

Jonathan accepted the call and the chief engineer appeared in the center of the Round Table for his eyes only.

"Captain, why are we pushing the engines?" the lieutenant said, the outrage obvious in his voice.

"Why are you still on shift?" Jonathan told the man. "First watch ended three hours ago."

"That's not the point. You know my engines need to be treated with respect. Use the speed only when you need it."

"We need it, Stanley. We have two missing ships. And the relay drone sent to look for them is long overdue. Something is obviously wrong. They need us. Just give me an hour and a half."

"Fine. An hour and a half. But don't make a habit of abusing my engines."

"I won't." Jonathan tapped out.

Twenty minutes passed. The tension was obvious on the bridge. Officers tapped fingers nervously, or rubbed sweaty palms. No one knew what to expect past that moon.

"How many relay probes do we have left, Ensign?" Jonathan asked the current ops officer.

"Two," Ensign McNamara said.

"You're considering launching another drone scout?" Maxwell asked him.

"You read my mind," Jonathan told the AI.

"At our current speed, we will match any drone we launch," Maxwell responded.

Good point.

"Sir?" the ensign asked.

"Never mind, Ensign," Jonathan said.

Robert extended his noise canceler to include the captain.

"Getting antsy?" the commander asked him.

"A little," Jonathan admitted. He amended that a moment later: "A lot."

"I'm sure everything will be fine," Robert said.

"You don't sound as confident as you did a few hours ago," Jonathan said.

"No," Robert agreed.

"Sir," Ensign McNamara said urgently. "The *Selene*."

Jonathan glanced at the tactical display overlaying his aReal. A blue dot had emerged from behind the moon. Zooming in on the external hull feed in the upper right, he recognized the design of the military research vessel.

"And so the prodigal daughter returns," Robert said.

"A bit disturbing that she's alone, though." Jonathan crossed his left arm over his chest, clasped the right bicep, and lifted the fingers of the right hand to his chin. He placed his index and middle fingers just above his upper lip and the thumb under his chin, forming a triangle. He rubbed the slight stubble. "Are we in hailing range yet?"

"Still too much interference," the comm officer said.

"The thermals are off, Captain," McNamara said.

"What do you mean?"

"She's running cold, sir," the ensign explained. "I don't think her reactors are operating."

Jonathan zoomed in on the external camera feed. The ship was long and box-like, resembling a smaller version of a bulk carrier. He switched to the thermal and radiation bands; the ensign was right, the emissions were extremely low, indicating most of the radiators had no internal heat to dissipate. A bad sign.

Jonathan tapped his splayed fingers over his lips. "Drifting?"

"It would appear so," McNamara answered. "Dead in the void."

"Can we tell if any of the lifepods have been used?"

"Still too much interference for an active scan. She does seem perfectly intact, though. I'm not seeing any evidence of a hull breach."

Jonathan glanced at Robert. "Commander, organize an away team. Bring an engineer. A scientist. And security—some MOTHs and Centurions. Gather in hangar bay one. I want you aboard that ship as soon as we're in range."

Robert stood. "Aye, sir."

"Maxwell, inform the shuttle department head I want a Dragonfly fueled and ready to go in hangar one. And helm, update our course. Bring us to within four kilometers of the *Selene's* starboard side."

There was no change in the status of the *Selene* as they grew near enough for communications and active sensors to punch through the interference.

Several minutes later the *Callaway* reached the given position.

"Helm, park us. Comm, instruct the remaining members of the task unit to assume safe escort positions. Ops, deploy telemetry drones. I want the *Selene's* entire hull scanned for breaches. And comm, hail them again."

The helmsman fired reverse thrust until their cruiser appeared stationary relative to the drifting *Selene*. The military research vessel lay a little under four kilometers off the port bow, thirty-five degrees declination.

"No answer to our hails," the comm officer said.

"Hull scan is complete," Ensign McNamara said some time later. "The *Selene* is intact."

"Any signs of the *Aegis* yet?"

"No, Captain."

"Ops, launch another relay drone to Achilles I. Instruct it to return to communications range and issue a data dump ten minutes after passing beyond line of sight. Instruct it to repeat the operation ad infinitum, adding intervals of ten minutes to its journey each time. Let's see if we can paint a partial picture of the dark side before we lose it like the others."

"Launching drone," the second watch ops officer said.

Technically, Jonathan could have had either Maxwell, ops, tactical or even comm launch that drone; he tried to divvy up tasks as appropriate for the intended function.

"Captain," the comm officer said. "Comm Drone B has returned from the edges of the gas giant. There's a message from the admiral for you. Would you like me to send it to your aReal?"

"Summarize it," Jonathan said.

The comm officer paused a moment, then said: "The admiral acknowledges our search and rescue operation. Though he seems disappointed that we let the two ships venture forth without approval from him, first."

If I requested approval for everything I did, Jonathan wanted to say. *I'd never get anything done.* Instead: "Send this response: We've found the *Selene*. It appears abandoned. We're proceeding to investigate. Captain out." He turned toward the ops officer. "Have you been able to interface with the *Selene's* AI via the remote override protocol?"

"No."

"Do you need my command codes?"

"Normally I would," the ensign answered. "But the AI isn't responding. In fact, nothing is—the whole system appears to be offline."

Jonathan tapped his lips with that finger triad of his. "Can you tell if any of the lifepods have been launched yet?"

"The readings are blurred somewhat by the radiation," the ensign said. "But it looks like no, none of them were launched."

"I have my team assembled in hangar bay one," Robert's voice came over the aReal. "We're suited up inside a fully-fueled Dragonfly. Waiting on your order to transit to the *Selene*."

"All ships are at safe escort distances," the ensign informed the captain.

Jonathan glanced at the tactical display on his aReal and confirmed the ensign's words.

"You're cleared for launch, Commander," Jonathan said.

five

Robert waited impatiently as the Dragonfly crossed the four kilometer span of space separating the two vessels. He did his best to ignore the stomach-churning feeling zero-G always inflicted on him: shuttles were equipped with inertial compensators but not artificial gravity. That fact always bothered him, because it seemed to Robert that it should be a simple matter to extend the inertial dampening to provide the feeling of gravity, but the scientists always assured him there was more to it than that.

The two MOTHs tapped their feet with nervous energy, obviously excited by the mission. The elite special forces soldiers usually had nothing to do but hang out at the gym all day, that and practice their war games in the ship's virtual kill house. They had to pass the time somehow, since the navy mandated a small MOTH presence aboard every ship. Well, they did help the masters-at-arms (MAs) provide security, too, taking on patrols and watches as necessary, though Robert was sure MOTHs considered such duties beneath them.

Their specialized jumpsuits were substantially bulkier than the spacesuits the other party members wore, containing an exoskeleton that augmented the speed and strength of each soldier to near robotic levels. Or so he had been told.

The shuttle rolled, tilting the view of the *Selene* beyond the main window. Robert felt suddenly nauseous. Throwing up in a space suit was a bad idea, as there was a chance the vomit could clog the air regulators. He wasn't worried so much about that, but more-so the effect it would have on the away team's opinion of him. Pride simply wouldn't let him throw up.

He pressed his lips against the nozzle below his mouth and took several sips of water.

The science officer had no such qualms about throwing up apparently, because he vomited right there in his helmet, splattering the lower part of the glass plate.

Robert checked the man's status on his aReal. Life signs were within normal parameters and his breathing apparatus was unaffected by the vomit.

"Are you all right?" Robert asked him.

"Fine," the science officer said after a moment. "Just a little... queasy is all." He threw up again.

One of the MOTHs laughed.

Robert gave the man a withering look and the soldier quickly straightened.

"Sorry sir," the petty officer second class said.

"Laugh again," Robert told him. "And you're the one who's going to be cleaning his suit."

"Understood, sir," the soldier said.

MOTHs were hard men, and the best way to deal with them was to treat them mercilessly. They would expect as much because of their military training. Anything less would be viewed as a sign of weakness.

The shuttle arrived at the *Selene's* external hangar doors. The craft hovered alongside, matching the speed of the drifting vessel.

Several uneventful moments passed.

"Is there a problem, Pilot?" Robert said over the comm.

"I can't find the bay doors on the device list," the pilot said. "Nor any other ship systems for that matter. If I can't connect, I can't issue an override request."

"Let me try." Robert pulled up the list of remotely accessible devices on his aReal. They were all devices local to the shuttle, sorted by range from his person, such as the airlock and nav controls, along with a few systems from the *Callaway* that were still cached. Robert focused on the refresh button and the

HUD updated with the message:

Searching for interfaces...

The display refreshed, showing the same local devices as before, minus most of the *Callaway's* devices. There were none from the *Selene* itself.

"Looks like we're going to have to dock the old fashioned way," Robert said. "Pilot, find the nearest airlock hatch."

The pilot directed the Dragonfly along the hull until he found what he was looking for, then he had the autopilot magnetically secure the shuttle to the research vessel.

"Attachment complete," the pilot announced. "Whenever you're ready, Commander."

"Let's go, men." Robert pushed off from the bulkhead and floated across to the shuttle's internal hatch.

The commanding MOTH, one Chief Rade Galaal, beat him to it. The soldier reached out to open the hatch, but glanced at Robert for confirmation first.

Robert nodded.

Rade opened it. There was no explosive decompression as the shuttle had no atmosphere.

Robert stood in front of the *Selene's* external hatch.

"Shall I get the laser cutter?" Rade asked.

"Let me try the command overrides, first." Robert knelt beside the small control panel that lay at the center of the hatch. It contained a keypad.

He attempted a remote connection one more time, but again no cloud devices showed up in the access list, despite the fact he was standing right next to the panel.

He retrieved an extension cord from his utility belt and plugged it into the provided slot.

His HUD displayed a message:

Searching for interfaces...

The device list updated. At the top, under the heading *Selene*, there was a new entry: *External hatch 2-135-18-H.*

Good. Power was still active to vital systems aboard the *Selene*, then.

He entered his manual override code.

"Prepare for retinal scan," his aReal informed him.

The panel scanned his retina through the face plate.

A moment later the entry hatch shuddered and collapsed inward a few inches. Robert disconnected the cord as the hatch slowly moved aside.

The airlock was dim beyond, lit only by emergency lights.

"Helmet lamps on, people," Robert said, activating his own. "Lead the way, Chief."

Rade turned on his helmet lamp and pulled himself into the external airlock, keeping the soles of his boots pointed downward. The moment he crossed the threshold between the shuttle and the ship, the soldier was pulled to the deck, his boots landing soundlessly. He gave Robert a significant glance.

"Artificial gravity is still active, people," Robert said into the comm. "Watch yourselves when crossing."

He let the MOTH petty officer enter next, and the two combat robots after him. The featureless metallic faces of the M-4 Centurions reminded Robert that the robots would kill mercilessly, without emotion. He wasn't so sure the MOTHs would behave any differently.

Robert hauled himself in after them, letting the artificial gravity drop him rather forcefully to the deck.

The guest connection area of his aReal lit up. Curious, Robert checked who was accessing his feed: very few people had the clearance. Not surprisingly, it was the captain. The wireless signal would pass between Robert's aReal and the communication node of the shuttle, then onward to the ship. Signal reception was good at the current range—the HUD pegged the lag at four seconds.

Robert flattened himself against the bulkhead as the final two party members entered. It was a tight fit in there.

When everyone was inside, Robert accessed the inner control panel the same way and issued a manual override, using his command codes to seal the hatch and pressurize the airlock to match the inner environment. When that was done, the inner hatch spiraled open.

"Centurions, go!" Rade said.

The two humanoid combat robots rushed into the dark passageway beyond, AR-52 plasma rifles at the ready.

The two MOTHs joined the Centurions a moment later, also sporting ARs.

"Clear," Rade transmitted.

Robert stepped inside; the science officer and engineer joined him.

He stood in a darkened passageway that was very much akin to those found aboard the *Callaway*. Like the airlock, it was illuminated only by emergency LEDs. The conical beams from their helmet lamps cut swathes through the murk.

"Life support systems are only partially active," the science officer said. He held a scanning device that he'd retrieved from his utility belt. "The crew compartments are still pressurized, and the air is still breathable. But it's cold, and getting colder by the minute. Currently plus three degrees above freezing."

"That's still relatively warm compared to deep space," Robert said. "I'm surprised the thermals readings were so low on her hull."

"Some ships get that way when their engines shut down," the engineer explained. The aReal labeled him Specialist Second Class Pierson.

"Any signs of contagions in the air?" Robert said.

The science officer, one Hayley O'Rielly, extended a scanning device. "Seems fine."

Robert removed his helmet. His face felt slightly chilly without his own respirations reflecting back onto him, but the insulation layer still shrouding his head and neck more than made up for the sensation—he might as well have been wearing a winter cap and scarf.

The air smelled stale and musty. "Circulators aren't operating," Robert noted.

He secured the helmet to his utility belt and detached the lamp, holding it like a flashlight. The engineer opted to remove his own helmet but the science officer and MOTHs kept theirs on. Robert's earpiece ensured he would still hear the latter individuals.

The soldiers launched two small, battery-powered surveillance drones, called HS4s. These were rotor-based quadcopters, meant for operation in atmospheres. When dispatched to planetary surfaces, an energy harvesting mode allowed the drones to collect power from updraft regions via regenerative braking; that, combined with solar panels further boosted the battery capacities to near infinite levels, barring heavy cloud cover or extended dark side operation. Under shipboard conditions the batteries would still last several hours, of course.

The drones vanished down the passageway to search for survivors.

The party advanced. Rade led the way, with the two combat robots directly in front of him. The MOTH petty officer brought up the rear.

With his aReal, Robert attempted to connect to the local Li-Fi network, which should have been available through the emergency LEDs, but it proved inactive.

"Anyone else able to connect to the Li-Fi?" Robert said.

He was greeted by a chorus of negative replies.

Robert glanced at the map displayed in the upper right of his HUD. He had downloaded the vessel blueprints before coming aboard, and the current position of each party member was shown as a blue dot on that map. The blueprint scrolled with each step Robert took, ensuring that his dot always remained in the center.

When the group reached an intersection, the engineer spoke up.

"According to the schematics, engineering is this way." Pierson nodded toward the left passageway. "Four decks down, five frames aft."

"Where are the HS4s?" Robert asked Rade.

"Currently en route to the bridge," the chief answered. "I can have them turn back and scout this way instead."

"That's fine," Robert said. "Have they found anyone, or spotted anything unusual, yet?"

"No, Commander."

"Lead the way." Robert beckoned toward the left passageway.

Rade directed the Centurions into the passage and the group followed after them.

Four decks down, roughly twenty meters from engineering, Rade and his two combat robots paused. "Commander."

Robert joined him.

The soldier pointed out blaster burns and melted metal on

the bulkhead. "Judging from the placement and direction of the damage, I'd guess the blaster fire came from engineering. The damage profile is typical of the sidearms issued to security personnel aboard such a research vessel."

Robert glanced down the passageway toward engineering. There were several more scars along the bulkhead.

"The HS4s are reporting similar scarring on the bridge," Rade said.

Robert withdrew the pistol from his belt, a standard issue plasma blaster.

"Chief?" Robert said.

The MOTH and two Centurions led them onward.

The party paused by the entrance to engineering. A perfect circle had been cut into the hatch. The surrounding metal exhibited no sign of the melting that would be typical of a laser torch. It was as if the molecules in the center of the door had simply lost cohesion and dispersed.

The science officer scanned the opening. "Atomized."

"Does the United Systems have any technology that could do this?" Robert asked him.

Hayley pressed his lips together. "No, but I've heard rumors the SKs have experimented with miniaturized particle accelerators."

"We've all heard a lot of rumors about the Sino-Koreans," Robert said. "Most of which are false."

Robert studied the opening a moment. It was large enough for the party members to squeeze through, one at a time, even the MOTHs in their bulkier suits. He beckoned toward the elite soldiers.

Rade ordered the combat robots inside.

The Centurions leaped through the opening in sequence; when they landed beyond, the first robot went high, the second low.

"Entrance clear!" one of the robots said.

Rade joined the two robots in the compartment, while the petty officer remained outside to guard the rest of the away team.

Rade and the robots vanished from view, but Robert was still aware of the positions of all three thanks to the HUD overlaying his vision.

Weapon in hand, Robert stood beside the remaining soldier and watched the outer passageway anxiously, ready to fire on anything that moved.

"Clear!" Rade said over the comm a moment later.

Robert hauled himself through the opening. When everyone was inside, the two MOTHs assumed guard positions beside the hatch, while the combat robots watched the passageway beyond.

The engineering section of any ship was basically a control room used to monitor the geronium reactors aboard the vessel. The compartment was relatively nondescript—steel walkways ran along the upper portion, while desks with swivel chairs in front of them protruded from the lower bulkheads. Like the bridge of the *Callaway*, there weren't any obvious control panels or displays. All monitoring of pressure, power, pumps, coolant and so forth was done via aReal.

Coffee cups, water bottles, and other disallowed personal belongings hinted at a rapid departure by shift personnel.

"Nothing showing up on the device list," Pierson said. "Looks like I'm going to have to interface manually."

Pierson lowered himself to the deck beside one of the stations. He slid his hand along the underside of the station—Robert had the impression the engineer was opening a panel. Pierson produced a small cord from his utility belt and plugged the male end into something underneath the desk.

"I'm in," Pierson said. "Appears the system was given a hard shutdown."

"Will you be able to restore power?" Robert asked him.

In answer, the floor shook as the nearby reactor hummed to life. The main lights activated a moment later.

Wearing a big grin, Pierson glanced at the commander. "Life support and other systems are coming back online. The AI should be up in a few minutes, after the startup sequence reconstructs the damaged portions of the holographic drives."

"What caused the damage?" Robert said.

"The hard shutdown, I'm guessing." Pierson pulled himself to his feet. "The usual procedure is to follow a soft shutdown: issue termination signals to all running software processes and threads, wait for them to safely close, then cycle off the main reactor. The process takes twenty minutes on a good day. In this case, someone cut the power all at once, without observing the proper shutdown sequence."

On Robert's aReal, the device list abruptly populated, filling with previously inaccessible systems. Robert accessed the bridge video feed and switched to VR mode.

The engineering compartment vanished and he found himself standing in the corner of the bridge where the one hundred-eighty degree lightfield camera he'd accessed was situated. The compartment possessed a similar "Round Table" arrangement of desks as the *Callaway*, though the absence of any watch personnel gave the bridge an eerily quiet atmosphere. There was a perfectly circular hole cut into the main bridge hatch, just like in engineering.

"I can confirm that the *Selene* still possesses its full complement of lifepods," Pierson's disembodied voice came to Robert. "No one evacuated the ship. The crew just vanished."

"Can you check if any of the airlocks were opened recently?"

"Normally I would be able to," Pierson said. "But it appears the archives have been wiped."

"What do you mean?"

"Exactly what I said," Pierson explained. "I'm not able to find any logs pertaining to the period before I restarted the system. Not for the airlocks or anything else. And this isn't simple holographic drive corruption—the archives were thoroughly erased."

Robert proceeded to cycle through the video feeds from various compartments throughout the ship. Sick bay. Cargo bay one and two. Hangar bay one. Living quarters. Machinery. There were no signs of life anywhere, and the only movement he spotted was one of their own HS4s drifting through a passageway.

Robert thought of something and cycled back to hangar bay one. "Maxwell, how many shuttles does an Onyx class research vessel come standard with?"

It took two seconds for the question to make the trip first to the comm node in the Dragonfly, then to the *Callaway*. The response came in another two seconds.

"According to system records, three standard Dragonfly-class shuttles," the familiar voice of the *Callaway's* AI returned.

"I'm only seeing two. Captain, are you getting this? One of the shuttles is missing."

"I see it," Jonathan's voice returned four seconds later. "Try to confirm the missing shuttle with the *Selene's* AI when it comes back online."

Robert switched back to AR mode; the bulkheads of engineering surrounded him once again.

"Greetings," a disembodied voice cheerfully announced. "I am Alfred, AI of the Onyx class military research vessel, the *Selene.*"

"Alfred, recognize Commander Robert Cray of the *Callaway.*" Via the aReal, Robert dispatched his command codes. Biometrics including voice pattern, facial features and retinal capillary make-up would be included in the verification process.

"Commander Robert Cray of the *Callaway* recognized," Alfred responded.

Robert decided to start with the question foremost on his mind. "Where's the crew, Alfred?"

"Unknown," the AI responded.

He exchanged a glance with Pierson. The engineer nodded.

"Without the archives, the AI won't have any idea," Pierson said.

Robert tried another question. "Alfred, are there any video archives available for viewing?"

"Negative. Video archives have been deleted."

"How many shuttles did the *Selene* have aboard?"

"Unknown."

Robert was growing frustrated. "Display ship's manifest."

"The manifest has been deleted," the AI responded.

"By whom?"

"Unknown."

The commander was beginning to wonder if the AI was damaged.

"Maxwell," Robert said. "Can you interface with the *Selene's* AI and perform diagnostics?"

"Interfacing," Maxwell returned via the aReal four seconds

later. In half a minute came the reply: "The *Selene's* AI is operating within acceptable parameters. However, I am unable to
retrieve any systems logs, as all of the *Selene's* internal databases
have been overwritten with random data. These include databases pertaining to human history, government, colonized
planets, and naval ships, in addition to those focused on the
Selene's internal operations."

"Can you determine who authorized the wipe?" Robert
asked the *Callaway's* AI.

Four seconds later Maxwell responded: "Unfortunately, I
cannot."

"Commander," Rade said. "One of the HS4s is returning interesting footage from the mess hall."

Robert switched back to VR mode and cycled to the video
feed from the mess hall. He had overlooked that compartment
in his previous scan.

In the mess hall tables and chairs were overturned in defensive positions, and scorch marks dotted the bulkheads on
either side of the entrance. It looked like a last stand of some
sort had taken place there.

"Well, they didn't give up without a fight," Robert muttered.

"Why aren't there any signs that the enemy returned fire?"
Rade's disembodied voice came over the comm. "Look at the
upturned tables and chairs. They're completely undamaged.
Not even a scratch on any of them. Same with the far bulkhead. Completely unblemished."

"I don't like it." Robert switched back to engineering.
"Chief, have the drones continue their sweep. Keep me updated on their findings."

The next few hours passed uneventfully. Robert made his
way to the bridge with the science officer and both MOTHs,
where he assumed a temporary command position. Meanwhile
the drones discovered several more scorch marks throughout
the ship, but not a single member of the *Selene's* original crew
was discovered. Not even a dead body or inactive combat robot.

The captain ordered a skeleton crew comprised of three
watches of junior officers to board the vessel, and he instructed Robert to return to the *Callaway* when the first group

arrived. Before the commander left, he imaged the holographic drives in the small hope that Maxwell might be able to reconstruct a portion of the data. There was a chance the hard shutdown had interrupted the wipe, and that some of the data, though flagged as erased, might still be intact.

When he returned to the *Callaway*, Robert began transferring the image from his aReal to the ship's cloud computing resources over Li-Fi. That data was exabytes in size, and even with the incredible transfer rate of the wireless network the upload would still take an hour.

"Maxwell, I want you to analyze the image as it comes in," Robert instructed the AI. "See if you can find any fragments of intact data."

"The captain has given me permission to allocate three percent of my processing power to this task," the AI said a moment later.

"Thank him for me," Robert said. He wasn't sure how much processing power that would actually translate into, but given the extreme size of the data, the AI certainly had its work cut out for it.

six

Jonathan stared at the *Selene* on the external video feed. The last Dragonfly had unloaded the final replacement crew members in the hangar bay of the research vessel, and Jonathan was waiting only for the craft's return.

Robert joined him on the bridge.

"Any news from the latest relay drone launched past the moon?" the commander asked after sitting down.

Jonathan nodded. "It has returned three times so far, filling in more and more details from the dark side. There might be a crashed ship on the surface."

"The *Aegis?*"

"Ops isn't sure. The thermal signature of the area is completely blank. That could mean the *Aegis* hit hard enough to blow apart on impact. Or it could mean it's a different vessel entirely, or some kind of abandoned base. Since it's the dark side, we're not getting any visuals. Infrared is useless. All the data we have so far is from LIDAR, and we can only barely discern the shape. The science officer is convinced it's an entirely natural phenomena—the remains of some ancient meteorite—but given recent events, I'm not so sure. I had the ops station update the drone's orders before it left signal range, with instructions to fly much closer to the surface this time. Hopefully we'll get a better LIDAR scan."

Robert rubbed his right ear lobe. "So there were no signs of the previous drones we sent?"

"No."

"I don't like it," Robert said.

Jonathan forced a smile. "You think I do? But I'm not going to turn back, not until we get to the bottom of this."

"Captain, the final Dragonfly has returned," Ensign McNamara announced.

Jonathan nodded. "Ops, recall telemetry drones. Nav, plot a course for the dark side of the moon. Comm, inform the admiral of our intent."

After the chorus of affirmative answers, the astrogator at the nav station said: "Course plotted."

"Helm, engage when ready," Jonathan said. "Tactical, instruct the remainder of the task unit to match speed and heading."

Robert glanced at the captain. "How did the admiral respond when you told him the *Selene* was empty?"

"As well as you can imagine," Jonathan said. "It completely spooked him. He wants us to rejoin the task group immediately."

"And I assume we're doing no such thing."

"Actually, we are," Jonathan said. "In order to return to the task group, we have to circumnavigate the gas giant. The admiral didn't specifically say we couldn't fly past the dark side of the moon while doing so. Therefore, technically we're still following orders."

Robert smiled in understanding. "I see."

As the ships moved out, the captain stared at the tactical display. The *Grimm*, as usual, was lagging behind. The blue dot representing the *Selene* kept pace, however. Barely.

What the hell happened to you? Jonathan thought.

As the moments passed his attention drifted; the flashing dot that represented the *Callaway* on his aReal reminded him of something. He couldn't quite place it.

And then he knew: the heart rate monitor of intensive care. In his head, a phantom tone accompanied each flash. BEEP. BEEP.

He heard other sounds. The mechanical hiss of surgical weaver robots roving between beds. The soft voices of nurses conversing with other patients. The hushed sobs of family members. The cloying smell of antiseptic and bio-printed limbs.

He felt the phantom pain in his hands and feet, where he had lost three fingers and four toes to frostbite. He rubbed his thumb and forefinger together. The texture of the skin was off, similar to corrugated cardboard. Bio-printed digits always felt that way after the initial procedure. The doctors had offered to graft real skin grown from his epidermal cells onto the fingers, but Jonathan had refused. He wanted to remind himself that the digits weren't real.

"Captain," Robert said, rousing Jonathan back to the present. He glanced at the commander.

Robert nodded across the Round Table. Ensign McNamara was looking at him with some concern.

"What is it, Ensign?" Jonathan said.

"The relay drone has returned to comm range," the ensign said. "We've received the latest update from the dark side."

"Can we tell if the wreckage is the *Aegis?*"

"Judging from this data," McNamara said. "Whatever is down there definitely isn't natural. I don't think it's one of ours, however. I've extracted the background terrain from the LIDAR information and put together a rough composite."

On his aReal, Jonathan received a data transfer request from the ensign. He accepted and a rotating three dimensional image of the crash site appeared before him. It was a torus-shaped object, crumbling in several places. The outer surface appeared to fold back in upon itself like a Möbius strip.

"What the hell is that supposed to be?" Jonathan said. "Maxwell, closest match in our databases?"

"No known matches," Maxwell said.

Jonathan exchanged a worried glance with Robert. "Comm, launch a drone to alert the admiral of our findings. Tell him we're going to make an observatory pass before setting course for the rest of the task group."

A response from the admiral came thirty minutes later, urging caution.

In another hour, the task unit crossed to the dark side of the moon.

seven

Jonathan studied the external camera feed. The vast expanse of stars was interrupted by a black stain above that completely blotted out the purple and orange clouds of the gas giant. He could discern nothing on the moon's surface in that darkness.

The *Callaway* was drifting: he had instructed the task unit to cut thrust, and all ships were running with their navigation lights off. He wanted to go in quietly. It wasn't possible to completely hide the thermal signature of an active starship, of course, but at least they weren't blatantly broadcasting their positions.

"Pretty quiet down there," the ops officer commented. "Thermal bands are ordinary. Nothing significant on LIDAR."

"What about the anomalous thermals that attracted the attention of the *Selene* in the first place?" Jonathan asked.

"Nothing. If there was a volcano somewhere down there, it's certainly not active anymore."

As the task unit grew closer to the site of the ruins, Jonathan couldn't shake a growing sense of unease.

He activated the noise canceler on his aReal and extended the silenced area over Robert.

"Feels like a trap," he told the commander. "You think we should turn back?"

Robert pressed his lips together. "You're the captain."

"Give me your honest opinion," Jonathan said.

Robert considered for a moment. "You're doing the right thing. It's our moral obligation to search for the missing crew members. No matter our misgivings."

Jonathan exhaled in relief. Though he had no intention of turning back, it was good to hear the support from his first officer.

"How do you feel about taking an away team down there?" Jonathan asked him.

"I'll go of course," Robert said. "Though I admit to having my own reservations about the place. A giant Möbius strip discovered in the middle of nowhere on some uncharted moon. Thermals that are present one moment and gone the next. Are we still going on the theory that we're dealing with rogue SK elements?"

"No," Jonathan said. "I don't know what to think anymore." He considered his options. "When we're in range, I'll order a Dragonfly down to dispatch some Model IIs." Those were HS4s that could operate in a vacuum. "If it looks clear, I'll send you in with an entire MOTH platoon. Fair?"

"Fair."

Jonathan reversed the noise canceling. "Nav, how far are we from the ruins?"

"About thirty minutes, Captain. If we want to assume a geo-stationary position above the site, we should begin braking thrust fifteen minutes from now."

"Remind me in fifteen." Jonathan glanced at the second watch comm officer. "How's our communication with the rest of the task group? I don't suppose we can bounce our signals off the comm nodes by the jump Gate yet?"

Comm nodes were small communication drones whose sole purpose was to pass in and out of the Gates that facilitated transit through Slipstreams; they moved back and forth between the same two systems all day, transferring data bundles with other comm nodes. Delay-tolerant networking at its finest. Three such drones were assigned to the exit Gate of the current system.

"Negative," the comm officer said. "We can't punch through the interference from the radiation yet."

"Too bad," Jonathan said. He sat back, lifting his aReal spectacles to rub his eyes.

"Though speaking of comm nodes," the comm officer continued. "I am detecting a slight signal variance from the direction of the Gate. I believe central command is sending a message."

"It's probably not meant for us," Jonathan said. "But launch a relay drone toward the comm nodes just in case." Launching a drone wasn't strictly necessary: if the message was for them, it would be queued by the drones until the *Callaway* left the radiation belt to receive it.

"Captain," Maxwell said. "I've reconstructed some of the fragmented data from the *Selene's* holographic drive. It's a video element. Recorded by the one hundred eighty degree lightfield camera on the bridge. I believe you will find it of interest."

"Replay the log and loop in the commander," Jonathan instructed the AI. "VR mode."

Jonathan found himself standing on the bridge of the *Selene*. Captain Chopra and her bridge crew sat at the Round Table, staring into their aReals.

"Situation report, away team," Chopra said.

There was a pause as Chopra listened to the response.

Jonathan asked the AI: "Do we have the audio feed of the response?"

"No," Maxwell said.

Chopra spoke again.

"Are you certain?" She glanced at her XO. "He thinks it's an Elder vessel."

"An Elder vessel?" the young XO said. "How did Wilkins come to that conclusion?"

"He says mass spectrometry performed on the alloy gives an exact match to the hull samples collected by the Lotus Expedition."

"An Elder ship," the XO said in obvious awe.

"We're going to be famous," Chopra said. She wrapped her hand around his in a blatantly inappropriate gesture.

"Maybe there's some tech we can salvage," the XO said.

"Or some archival data," Chopra said excitedly. "Who

knows, with this discovery, we might be able to solve the mystery of the Elder once and for all."

The virtual reality video abruptly cut out and Jonathan found himself on the *Callaway's* bridge once more.

"That's all I have, Captain," Maxwell said.

Jonathan glanced at Robert. "I'm not sure that was helpful."

Robert nodded. "Raised more questions than it answered."

"Elders." Jonathan shook his head.

The Elders were an extinct race believed to have once ruled that quadrant of the galaxy. A technologically advanced species credited with the creation of the vast network of Slipstreams in the region, the Elders mysteriously vanished sometime between three and eight hundred thousand years ago. Remnants of an Elder starship had been found fifty years ago in the Lotus system, some eighty-four light years from Earth, on a barren world orbiting a red giant. The wreckage was a vast, monolithic, sprawling ruin composed of a previously unknown alloy. There were no obvious engines, weapons, or other compartments common to human ships — sleeping quarters, mess halls, and so forth. There did not even appear to be any controls on said vessel: the ship was a hollow, seamless mass. And no actual bodies were recovered, either. At least, that was the official version of events.

"You think that wreckage down there actually belongs to an Elder vessel?" Robert asked the captain.

"No idea," Jonathan said. "Though the scientists aboard the *Selene* obviously did."

"Approaching deceleration range," nav reported a few minutes later.

"Begin deceleration for geosynchronous orbit above the crash site," Jonathan said. "Tactical, transmit the order to the task unit."

Fifteen minutes later the *Callaway* and the rest of the fleet had decelerated enough to assume a geostationary position above the wreckage.

Robert shifted restlessly beside the captain. "Are you sure you don't want me down there right away?"

"Positive, Commander," Jonathan said. "Let the HS4s map out the place first. Ops, launch some telemetry drones, and notify the shuttle department head I want an HS4 team deployed immediately."

A few minutes later Jonathan found himself watching the video feed from a telemetry drone as the Dragonfly departed the ship. The small craft approached the surface; the flashing navigation lights occasionally illuminated the shuttle against the dark background of the moon.

The Dragonfly was halfway to the surface when the comm officer spoke up. "Captain. The comm drone I dispatched toward Contessa Gate has returned to communications range. You were right, the communique from central command wasn't for us. However, the drone did pick up a return message for you from the admiral of Task Unit One. It's marked classified."

Jonathan thrummed his fingers on the armrest. He was tempted to send the admiral's missive directly to the archives for later viewing. Then again, since it had been dispatched shortly after the receipt of a message from central command, it might actually be something important, especially considering recent events in United Systems space.

"Send it to my aReal."

Jonathan's inbox indicator flashed.

He was about to replay the message when Ensign McNamara sat up straight in his seat.

"Captain," the ensign said urgently. "Thermal reading, five thousand kilometers off our nose. A ship."

"Is it the *Aegis*?"

"Negative," McNamara said. "The thermal configuration doesn't match any known ship in our database."

eight

Jonathan regarded the tactical display. A red dot had appeared above the moon's horizon, five thousand kilometers in front of the *Callaway*.

The ship had been hiding behind Achilles I, waiting for the most opportune moment to pounce. At that distance, every weapon would be within optimal firing range. Jonathan was suddenly very glad he hadn't sent down Robert in the Dragonfly.

"Tactical, how fast is the newcomer moving relative to the task unit?" Jonathan said.

"Roughly thirty thousand kilometers per hour," the tactical officer said. The aReal labeled him Lieutenant Miko.

The dashed line of the vessel's computed trajectory intersected the task unit.

Jonathan quickly ran the numbers. If he reversed course, the task unit would only remain in the potential line of fire even longer. The best action was to plow ahead, and use the approaching vessel's own momentum to put some range between them. The gravity of the moon would give them an added boost due to a slight slingshot effect.

"All ahead, emergency power!" Jonathan said. "Plot a course forty-five degrees away from the object." There was no time to retrieve either the Dragonfly or the telemetry drones.

"Course plotted," helm returned. "Ahead full emergency."

"Order the fleet to assume defense pattern bravo."

"Transmitting orders for pattern bravo," Miko said from the tactical station.

"And Maxwell, sound General Quarters goddammit!" Jonathan buttoned up his collar.

"General quarters!" The AI's voice came over the main circuit. "General quarters! All hands man your battle stations. Up and forward to starboard, down and aft to port. This is not a drill! General quarters, General quarters. Incoming vessel. Unknown origin!" A klaxon sounded five times before the message repeated.

On the tactical display, the dots representing the ships of the local flotilla began to spread apart in three dimensions, their Delta Vs countering the pull of both the moon and the gas giant.

Jonathan activated the weapon readiness display on his HUD. The long range missiles and nukes were ready to fire. Short range Vipers were charging. Mag-rail point defenses were locked and loaded.

"Are we receiving any radio signals, or any other attempts at contact?" Jonathan said.

The comm officer looked up. "No sir."

"Relay a welcome message in all known languages and communication protocols."

"Relaying," the comm officer said.

Jonathan tapped his foot impatiently. "Anything?"

"No response," the comm officer said. "Either they don't recognize that we're trying to communicate. Or they don't want to."

"Detecting a thermal buildup—" McNamara began.

The external video feed on Jonathan's aReal abruptly pixelated before returning to normal.

"I just lost the signal from all of our external telemetry drones," McNamara said. "It appears we were hit first by gamma radiation, followed by electrons traveling at relativistic speeds—an electromagnetic pulse. A concentrated, highly directional beam launched from the target ship. I registered a peak power density of seven megawatts per square meter. Hull systems are holding up."

All shipboard electronics, including the external sensors, were designed to use the entire hull as a voltage ground during an EMP event, which normally occurred when a nuke detonated in the atmosphere of a nearby planet. Unfortunately the drones, because of their small size, didn't have that ability.

"The *Aurelia*, *Dominion*, and *Maelstrom* are all reporting similar burst readings," the comm officer reported. "And we've lost communications with the Dragonfly."

"The crew's radiation exposure?" Jonathan said.

"Minimal," McNamara said. "The hull armor scattered most of the gamma rays."

"Is it possible that was an attempt at communication?" Robert said.

"Yes," Jonathan said. "An attempt to communicate their hostile intent."

McNamara stiffened. "Another ship just emerged from the cover of the moon."

Jonathan glanced at the tactical display. Sure enough, another red dot had appeared.

"This one seems to be moving away from the moon entirely. Their heading is..." Miko paused. He looked up. "It seems to be making for Contessa Gate."

On the 3D display, a dotted line extended from the second vessel, converging on the outskirts of the system right over the exit Gate.

"Either they intend to pass into United Systems territory," Robert began.

"Or they intend to destroy the Gate," Jonathan finished.

"I'm reading a thermal buildup on the second, farther ship," McNamara said.

Jonathan waited tensely.

"Active sensors are detecting a highly directional EMP pulse emanating from the second vessel," the ensign continued. "Aimed at Contessa Gate."

"Will the Gate survive?" Jonathan asked.

"Yes. But if the pulse is the same intensity as the one that hit us, the comm nodes won't. We'll lose contact with the rest of the United Systems."

Jonathan turned toward the comm officer. "Comm, can we

override the command sets and order the devices through the Gate to safety?"

"We can," the officer said. "But even if we send the instructions now, our signal won't beat the directional pulse."

"Do it anyway. Have Maxwell send my command override."

"Yes, Captain."

"Detecting another thermal build-up from the nose of the closer vessel," the ensign said.

"Evacuate all crew from—" Jonathan was cut off as a bright flash emanated from the nearest ship.

"Sir, the *Dominion*!" the ensign said.

"Maxwell, track the *Dominion*," Jonathan said quietly, dreading what he would see.

The video feed updated with a zoomed-in view of the destroyer. It was split cleanly in half down the middle, lengthwise. The sight physically sickened Jonathan. He felt weak, nauseous.

He closed his eyes.

"They used some kind of particle beam weapon," the ensign said.

No time to grieve.

Jonathan forced his eyes open. "Tactical, can we use missiles at this range?"

Miko shook his head. "This close, our acceleration will cause any missiles to overshoot their target."

"If we cut thrust, can we engage starboard nozzles in time to angle our nose toward them?"

"Negative," Miko said. "We'll have slingshot far past the target by then."

The other option was mag-rails, which were meant more for point defense, or the Vipers—heavy lasers.

"What's the charge on the Vipers?"

"It's only been three minutes since general quarters," Miko said. "So thirty percent."

Jonathan stared at the 3D display. The task unit was about two thousand kilometers away from the enemy by then, their angular path giving the craft a wide berth.

"Have the remaining ships prepare to fire Vipers." That meant the *Aurelia* and *Maelstrom*, as the *Grimm* and *Selene* weren't armed. "I want full port broadsides released simultaneously across the task unit. Concentrate on the same spot. Aim for the center of mass."

"Vipers ready," Miko announced.

The enemy vessel was approaching its closest point of the flyby.

"Fire," Jonathan said.

The Viper laser generator was a massive structure housed in the center of the *Callaway*. When fired, the beam traveled down a main passageway, and mirrors deflected it toward appropriate laser turrets, where it was further focused by circular mirrors twelve meters in diameter. External shutters opened and closed in sync with the release of the beam, preventing an enemy from firing its own laser at the mirrors and destroying the generator.

At that distance, the concentrated ten laser broadside would have a spot area of one centimeter squared. At thirty percent charge, the Vipers would fire three times in pulses of one hundred nanoseconds each, with a combined intensity of over two hundred megajoules per pulse. Joined with the broadsides from the *Aurelia* and *Maelstrom*, that was enough to eat through five meters of hull material in an ordinary ship. The capacitor bank would require the next ten minutes to fully recharge, however, depending on the power draw of other systems on the reactors.

A flash filled the external camera. Jonathan hadn't actually seen the vessel fly by, but according to the tactical display, the target was quickly receding.

"Direct hit," Miko said.

"Damage assessment?"

"I'm detecting massive quantities of thermal leakage from the enemy hull," the ensign said. "Plus a good amount of debris. We hit them good. However the target is rotating its nose, apparently trying to bring their particle weapon to bear."

Jonathan had an urgent request from engineering on his aReal. He accepted.

"What is it, Stanley?"

"The reactors can't take much more of this," Stanley said. "We're going to go critical soon. We have to cut back the speed."

"Reduce speed to eighty percent," Jonathan told the helm.

"You'll have to cut it back to sixty in another ten minutes," Stanley said.

"I'll inform the helm to keep a watch on reactor temperatures," Jonathan said. He terminated the call. "Did you get that, helm?"

"I did, Captain," the helmsman responded.

The task unit continued around the moon, with the lagging *Grimm* taking up the rear. The distance between the flotilla and the enemy widened by the second.

"Target is continuing to turn around," Miko said. "They're decelerating now, too."

"Helm!" Jonathan said. "Get us behind that moon."

In a few moments the enemy ship passed beyond sight, hidden by the moon.

Ahead, the gas giant had emerged from behind the dark mass of the celestial object.

"Nav, plot a course for the giant," Jonathan said. "Use the gravity well to slingshot us away from the pursuer. Tactical, relay the course to the unit. Comm, launch a relay drone and inform the admiral of our current predicament."

Twenty minutes passed. The red dots representing the two enemy vessels had frozen when the *Callaway* passed beyond the moon's horizon. The gas giant lay directly above them, growing closer by the minute as the task unit attempted its slingshot maneuver. The bridge began to shudder slightly as the conflicting forces acting upon the ship vied for dominance—inertia, gravity, and thrust.

Jonathan switched to the forward camera. He saw the haze of the horizon in the distance, just below the vast, round sphere that was the giant. He enlarged the feed to take up the entirety of his aReal.

The stars seemed so alone there, floating below that horizon. Alone, and free.

The beautiful sight calmed him somewhat, reminding him of a view from another lifetime, near the summit of a mountain.

The wreckage of the *Dominion* came to his mind's eye. Over eight hundred crew and two hundred civilians had been aboard.

He heard Famina's voice in his head. *Why won't anyone help me?*

"Pursuing vessel has crested Achilles I," the ensign announced. "But the farther ship's position is still concealed by the moon."

Jonathan switched to the rear camera and tracked the target, zooming in. The enemy ship was visible, thanks to the light from the distant star. With its dagger-like shape, the incoming object bore a vague resemblance to a United Systems corvette, though it seemed slightly more streamlined, with a smooth hull completely devoid of superstructures and polished to a mirrorlike sheen. At two kilometers in length and seven hundred and fifty meters at the beam, it was the size of a United Systems capital ship. Jonathan zoomed in further and began to lose optical clarity. Still, he thought he could see the small, dark gashes where the Vipers had ripped into the hull. It was his imagination of course, as any tears would only be a centimeter in thickness.

"How much range have we put between ourselves and the ship?" Jonathan said.

"Forty thousand kilometers," Miko answered. "Though the target is closing that gap."

"If we launched rear kinetic kill missiles," Jonathan said. "Will the weapons make the target?"

Miko was quiet a moment. "I believe so. But just barely. The Delta-V requirements necessary to transit into the higher orbits of the gas giant will cause the missiles to exhaust all propellant shortly before arrival."

"What about a nuke?" Jonathan asked.

"Even worse. Because of the extra weight, we'll only be able to get a nuke out to about halfway."

"Fighters?"

"Same issue." Miko seemed determined to deliver bad news. "We send any squadrons out there, they're liable to exhaust their propellant sometime before or after reaching the target. And the controls will be extremely sluggish—they'll have a hell of a time dodging that particle beam. Either way, they won't be coming home."

Jonathan tapped his chin with his usual triangular arrangement of fingers. "Have every capable vessel in the task unit launch four kinetic kill missiles each at the target," Jonathan said. "Space out the launch so that the missiles arrive in ten second intervals. I want the projectiles to approach on different vectors, too, if possible. Let's see if we can sneak one in while their particle beam is recharging. Fire when ready."

"Firing," Miko said a moment later.

Jonathan studied the display. He watched the first wave of missiles, represented as four green dots, spread out behind the task unit. Three more waves followed, separated by a distance of about ten kilometers each. The waves approached the target, traveling diagonally down the Z and Y planes. The missile course changes came slower than normal, thanks to the massive Delta V's required near the gas giant.

Several minutes later the first wave closed to within ten thousand kilometers of the target.

"Let's see what kind of point defenses they have," Jonathan said.

"Target is adjusting its trajectory," McNamara said. "Looks like it's going to try flying right past the missiles."

Jonathan studied the display. The dotted line representing the target's path updated. According to the estimated trajectory, it would avoid the first two waves entirely, but the third and fourth would impact.

The minutes ticked past. As expected, the first two waves missed by two kilometers each. The third and fourth however directly lined up with the ship.

"Detecting a thermal buildup in the nose of the target," McNamara said. There was a flash, followed by eight simultaneous, smaller lights. "All eight kinetic kill missiles have detonated. Target is issuing a slight course correction to avoid the debris."

The enemy was now twenty thousand kilometers behind the task unit, with the trailing *Grimm* the closest to it.

"What about another Viper broadside?" Jonathan said. "We're at one hundred percent charge."

"We are," Miko agreed. "But the spot area at this range is over eighty centimeters squared. Even combined with the other ships, the intensity will be less than three megajoules."

"Let them close and then fire?" Robert asked Jonathan.

"I'm not big on any plan that allows them to close," Jonathan said. "We've already seen how deadly that particle beam is under five thousand kilometers." He studied the 3D display a moment longer. "Tactical, have the *Aurelia*, *Maelstrom* and *Selene* alter course ten degrees to the starboard, and the *Grimm* ten to port. Helm, match the course of the *Callaway* to the *Grimm*."

"I thought you didn't like splitting up the task unit?" Robert said.

"I don't," Jonathan answered.

He watched on the 3D display as the *Callaway* and *Grimm* separated from the other two ships.

"Enemy vessel is adjusting course," the ensign announced.

The dotted line of the pursuer moved to intercept the lagging *Grimm*. The enemy smelled easy prey, apparently. The harvester vessel lay approximately a thousand kilometers off the *Callaway's* aft quarter, in the eight o'clock position, thirty degrees declination. And it was moving farther away by the moment.

"What are you planning, Captain?" Robert said.

"I'm taking us closer to Achilles," Jonathan said.

nine

Jonathan concentrated on the display.

Robert extended his noise canceler around the captain.

"Are you sure the *Callaway* can withstand the stress?" Robert said. "She doesn't have the armor of the *Grimm*."

"I only plan to skim the upper atmosphere," Jonathan said. "Like skipping a stone on a river."

"That's a fairly big river," Robert said, his usual positivity nowhere to be found.

"The *Callaway* will hold up. Right, Maxwell?"

"There is a seventy-five percent chance the *Callaway* will survive such close proximity to the gas giant," Maxwell said.

"There you go," Jonathan told Robert.

The commander didn't seem pleased. "Seventy-five percent. Those aren't the best odds. Even at ninety-nine percent, I wouldn't feel safe."

"Very few things in life are seventy-five percent, Robert. Let alone ninety-nine."

Robert squeezed his jaw. "If we break up... we won't be able to launch escape pods. Not this close to the giant. You know that, right?"

"I do." Jonathan repealed Robert's noise canceling. "Helm, take us in closer to the giant."

The helmsman hesitated.

"Helm?" Jonathan repeated.

"Taking us closer. Initiating braking maneuver."

The best way to enter a massive gravity well like a gas giant was by "falling" in. To do that, one simply decelerated, forcing the orbit to rapidly decay.

"Tactical, instruct the *Grimm* to follow us down."

The tense minutes passed, with the *Callaway* growing ever closer to the colorful mass of clouds below.

"Hull temperature is rising," Ensign McNamara said. "Currently six hundred degrees Kelvin. Heat armor is holding."

Behind them, the pursuing vessel decelerated, too, choosing to stay with the pair. The target was fifteen thousand kilometers away.

"Entering upper thermosphere," Ensign McNamara said. "Hull temperature stabilizing at one thousand Kelvin."

"Hold her steady..." Jonathan said.

A few minutes later:

"Hull temperature has dropped to four hundred Kelvin." McNamara said. That was the peculiar nature of Jovian-type gas giants—the radiated heat peaked roughly a thousand kilometers from the surface, then decreased to the tropopause, where it would begin rising again.

"Approaching Kármán line of lower thermosphere," Miko said. That was the point at which atmospheric reentry began, about four hundred kilometers above the cloud coverage.

"Nose up," Jonathan said. "Helm, bounce us off the lower thermosphere. Start the long process of disengaging from the gravity well. Tactical, instruct the *Grimm* to do likewise."

"Nose up," the helmsman said. "Initiating deorbital pre-burn sequence."

The bridge began to shake badly as the *Callaway's* hull struggled against the stresses exerted upon the ship—inertia wanted to carry her forward, the thrusters wanted to push her away, the gas giant wanted to draw her in; all of these forces vying against one another literally threatened to rip the *Callaway* apart.

A call from engineering flashed urgently in the lower left of Jonathan's HUD.

The captain answered it reluctantly.

"What in the hell are you doing?" Stanley said over the

comm. "You're going to tear my ship apart!"

"She'll hold together, Stan. And if you wouldn't mind, we're in the middle of a battle here. Don't call again unless you have something urgent to report. Do your best to keep our reactors running. Now would not be a good time for the engines to fail."

Jonathan disconnected before the chief engineer could answer.

He gazed at the tactical display. The *Callaway* and *Grimm* moved away from the gas giant very sluggishly. It was small consolation that the enemy ship's own course changes were just as lethargic. The target was still gaining, however.

Jonathan pulled up the propellant indicator on his HUD. The inert gas levels were dropping incredibly fast thanks to the immense Delta V costs—the tanks would have enough to escape the gravity well, though just barely. When the battle was done he would have to transfer some propellant away from the other ships to restore the *Callaway* to baseline levels.

Jonathan and the others were jerked in their seats as the inertial compensators struggled against a sudden reversal of Gs.

"We just bounced off the Kármán line," the helmsman informed him.

"Steady as she goes..." Jonathan glanced at the 3D display. The *Grimm* was fifteen hundred kilometers behind them. Twelve thousand kilometers beyond it lay the alien vessel. Too close for comfort.

But close enough for what he planned.

"Tactical, work with Maxwell," Jonathan said. "I want you to launch fifteen mortars from the aft tubes at the enemy ship. Hem them in with the first ten. I want the final five directed at the lower thermosphere. Make them think we miscalculated. But in reality, I want you to skim those final five off the Kármán line. Time it so that the deflection happens as close to the target as possible. Catch them by surprise."

Kinetic kill missiles or even nukes would have worked just as well, but that close to the gas giant, missiles behaved the same as the unpowered mortars, which were basically big rocks.

"It's going to be tricky," Miko said. "We'll have to orient the launch tubes so that the mortars arrive at the Kármán Line at the precise angle for optimal deflection. And time that deflection so that at least one of the mortars actually strikes the ship."

"Like I said, work with Maxwell."

The moments ticked past. Jonathan watched the enemy vessel close to nine thousand kilometers.

"Hull temperature rising again," McNamara said.

Growing impatient, Jonathan said: "Miko, do you have a firing solution?"

Miko didn't answer.

"Tactical, do you have a firing solution?" Jonathan repeated.

"I think so," Miko said.

"Fire."

Fifteen mortars released in rapid succession from the aft tubes. On the tactical display, the first ten formed a circular noose around the enemy ship. The final five seemed to be misses, heading at a downward angle as if to pass underneath the target.

On the tactical display, three of the five bottommost mortars passed through the indicated Kármán Line, their orientations off by just enough to make the skimming process fail. They would burn up shortly.

However two of the mortars abruptly changed course, deflecting upward from the Kármán Line and toward the target.

"Like skipping stones on a river," Jonathan said softly.

"Enemy ship is issuing sudden braking thrust," Ensign McNamara said.

"Too late," Jonathan said.

"They're firing their particle beam."

Jonathan waited. The shaking of the bridge didn't seem any worse.

"Damage report?" he said after a moment.

"According to my readings," McNamara said. "The beam only lasted a tenth of its usual duration. They struck the *Grimm's* aft section. Her captain is reporting minimal damage."

"That beam of theirs obeys the inverse square law," Robert said. Meaning the intensity dropped by the square of the distance to the source.

"If it's a particle beam, it has to," Jonathan said. "The extra armor on the *Grimm* probably helped. Plus the fact that it only fired for a tenth of its usual duration. Ensign, tell me our mortars struck."

"Both struck," McNamara said.

Jonathan clasped his right hand into a triumphant fist. "Status on the target?"

"They appear to have taken major damage to the nose section. I believe their particle weapon is nonoperational. And their engines have cut out entirely. The vessel is on a decaying orbit; at their current rate of descent, it will be about four weeks before they penetrate the Kármán line, and if they survive reentry, another two months before they breach the cloud cover. Maybe another six months after that before the vessel is crushed by the pressure."

"Achilles heel," Jonathan said.

On the external video feed, he zoomed in on the target. He switched to LIDAR. The damage to the vessel was incredible. According to the display, a gaping wound two hundred meters deep and ten meters wide was carved into the ship from the nose down.

He glanced at the comm officer. "Signal for their surrender. And extend an invitation of aid."

"No response," the lieutenant said.

"Not surprising." Robert said. "They can't understand us, of course."

Jonathan smiled sadly. "We had to try."

"Sir, their speed is dramatically dropping off." McNamara said.

"What?" Jonathan said. "I thought their engines had cut out?"

"They had... but it looks like they reactivated them. They appear to be applying reverse thrust. They're purposely decaying their orbit."

"Why hasten their demise? You said it would be four weeks before they even reached the Kármán line. That's enough time to at least attempt a repair."

"But they know they'd be at our mercy the whole time," Miko said. "Maybe, to them, this was the only honorable choice."

Jonathan regarded the tactical officer appraisingly. "I get the feeling you come from a Japanese background."

Miko managed a weak smile. "My distant ancestors were samurai."

Jonathan switched his gaze to the helmsman. "Get us out of here."

ten

Jonathan stood on the mountain. The sky was clear, and he could see the peaks and valleys of the surrounding range. Such a pristine, beautiful day. Or it would have been pristine, were it not for the frozen bodies of the *Dominion's* crew protruding from the snow around him, their porcelain-colored faces staring at him with dead, accusing eyes. Famina was there, too. Laughing shrilly.

Jonathan awoke, drenched in sweat.

He had returned to his quarters shortly after the battle, intending to review the missive he had received from the admiral right before the enemy ship turned up. He had decided to take a quick nap first, but apparently he'd fallen fast asleep.

He rubbed his eyes, feeling more exhausted than he had before he'd lain down.

He donned his aReal spectacles. The system scanned his retina and logged him in. The bare steel wall beside him was replaced immediately by the lapping waves of a white sand beach, the tropical sun beating down from a clear blue sky. The bed had become a hammock tied between two lush palm trees. Seagulls periodically screeched overhead.

In that moment he envied those who installed Implants. To be able to feel the breeze, smell the humid air, feel the sun on his face... that was the ultimate immersion. Still, he sighed contentedly nonetheless. There was nothing like augmented reality for cabin fever. It certainly helped one keep their sanity aboard a cramped starship like the *Callaway*. And the sound of those waves worked wonders on the frayed nerves the nightmare had caused.

He reluctantly turned his back on the beach, muted the gulls, and activated the tactical overlay.

Seven hours had passed since the encounter. The task unit was in orbit around Achilles I, searching for survivors of the *Dominion*, whose wreckage remained in a decaying orbit above the moon.

About two hours ago, the officer on watch reported a flash in the lower thermosphere of the gas giant, coinciding with the loss of the enemy ship from active sensors. The CDC believed it had burned up.

What a way to go.

His attention was drawn to the red dot indicating where the second enemy ship had returned to the sensor readings. The vessel was well on its way to Contessa Gate, the only exit from the system.

What are you up to?

His gaze drifted to Task Unit One, which had diverted from the terrestrial planets and was now well on its way toward 3-Vega, the third Slipstream in the system. If Jonathan had been the admiral of the task group, he would have been racing back to rejoin the attacked unit, with plans to surround and capture the remaining alien vessel, not heading toward that wormhole. There was only one reason for the unit to steer toward 3-Vega. He prayed he was wrong about that, though.

Jonathan stared at the flashing alert icon in the lower left of the display. The inbox contained several new messages from the admiral. He wasn't in the mood to deal with the politically-motivated puppet of NAVCENT but he needed to confirm his suspicions.

He started with the earliest message, the one he had received shortly before the battle. The image of Admiral Knox material-ized, appearing to be seated in the chair across from the captain, and began to speak.

When Jonathan finished reviewing all six messages he sat back. The first communication had been the gist, while the remaining five were requests, in order of growing irritation, that he confirm his receipt of the orders and his intention to follow them.

He had paused the final holo-recording before it clicked off, and he stared at the frozen image of the balding admiral before him. It was hard not to cringe, looking at that lined face.

I should've retired the moment you were promoted over me, Jonathan thought.

He dismissed the hologram and closed his eyes a moment. He needed more time to digest what the admiral had said before he decided what to do.

"Any news?" he sent to Robert, whose current position was indicated as on the bridge.

A holographic display request from Robert appeared on the aReal. Jonathan ignored it, opting for voice-only.

"So far the rescue drones have recovered four hundred *Dominion* crew," Robert answered. "Most from lifepods."

Though the *Dominion* had been cut in half lengthwise, because of the compartmental nature of the ship the affected decks were sealed off and several hundred crew had been able to reach the lifepods. They had landed on the moon. Meanwhile those survivors stranded aboard the floating wreckage were retrieved by salvage robots.

"Coordinate with your equivalents in the task unit to assign suitable berths and crew positions for the survivors," Jonathan instructed the commander. "Staff up the *Selene* first. I'll expect to see your recommendations for acting first officer and captain by oh nine hundred."

"Understood," Robert returned.

"Any news on the *Aegis?*"

Robert hesitated.

"What is it?" Jonathan said.

"Four hours ago the recon drones discovered the wreckage of the *Aegis* on the surface of Achilles I, about three hundred kilometers to the east of the Elder vessel. Eighty frozen bodies were recovered. The rest were incinerated on impact. None of the lifepods were launched. No survivors."

Jonathan pressed his lips together. He was slightly angry that Robert hadn't awakened him to tell him of the news, but then again, it was probably for the best: there was nothing he would have been able to do, anyway.

"I'm sorry to hear that," Jonathan said. "Were any of the *Selene's* original crew accounted for among the dead?"

"No. At this point, best guess is that the crew members of the *Selene* are hostages aboard the second alien vessel."

Jonathan cringed. If it were true, he could only imagine what terrible experiments were taking place on the *Selene's* crew. Mind probes. Drug injections. Live dissections...

"Robert, organize the funeral service for the crew of the *Aegis*. And all those who died on the *Dominion*."

"Would you like to speak at the service?" Robert asked him.

Jonathan compressed his lips. "No. I won't be able to hold it together. You do it, Robert."

"As if I'll be able to hold it together any better than you."

Jonathan quickly changed the subject. "So what else do you have for me?"

"The other recon drones we sent to explore the remaining Achilles moons recently reported back. There don't seem to be any other alien vessels hiding in the area. Now, in regards to the second alien ship that we *do* currently know about..."

Jonathan unconsciously leaned forward. "Yes?"

"About two hours ago we detected a gamma ray burst from her aft quarter," Robert said. "This one directed toward 2-Vega, the uncharted Slipstream on the far side of the sun."

"Calling home, no doubt," Jonathan muttered. Another reason why the admiral should have been hurrying to rejoin them rather than venturing deeper into the system.

"That's my feeling, too. Oh and, you remember that Dragonfly we dispatched to the moon before the attack?"

"The one we lost communication with after the EMP?"

"The same. Well, it docked with the *Callaway* a few hours ago. Turns out the EMP only fried the external communication layer. The shuttle was able to land and complete its mission: the HS4s completely mapped the Elder ruins, inside and out."

Jonathan splayed the fingers of his right hand and tapped his lips. "Did they find anything of interest?"

"Not really. Similar to the Elder ship discovered during the

Lotus Expedition, there are no obvious control panels or stations, or anything remotely resembling the specialized compartments found on human ships or bases. It's just one big, hollow Möbius strip. That said, the HS4s did record some odd readings in certain sections."

"Odd?"

"Yes. It's as if tiny wormholes had existed at some point, warping the surrounding alloy. But whatever caused that warping is long gone."

While an interesting bit of Elder trivia, Jonathan wasn't sure how that knowledge pertained to their current situation. "Any other news?"

"Only that the admiral called for you at least six times."

"Yes. I listened to his messages."

"Anything important?" Robert asked.

"He expects us to rejoin the task group as soon as we've recovered all survivors. Task Unit One is currently headed toward 3-Vega."

"I noticed that," Robert said.

Jonathan glanced at the tactical display overlaying his vision. He ran some calculations. Given the current positions of the two units, if his flotilla departed the moon within the next eight hours, barring engine problems they'd rendezvous with the remainder of the fleet a few days out from the Slipstream.

"Keep me apprised of the rescue operation," Jonathan said. "And notify me when we're ready to leave orbit."

"Will do."

"Captain out."

Jonathan opened his inbox and stared at the messages from the admiral. He still wasn't ready to make his decision, not yet.

He reviewed the status reports from the department heads and ship captains, approving various repairs, upgrades and promotions as necessary.

He took a long shower in his private head, grabbed an apple and banana from the wardroom, then made his way to the bridge.

"Captain on the bridge!" the first watch ensign, Tara Lewis announced.

"As you were." He entered his private office adjoining the

bridge and sat down behind the desk. Unlike his quarters he had applied few virtual augmentations and none so distracting as the white sand beach. He'd limited himself to a bookshelf, a painting, and a false window showing deep space.

He folded his hands and stared at the metal entry hatch.

He had come to a decision.

He pinged his commander. "Robert, my office."

Jonathan grabbed the sole embellishment from his desk: a non-virtual deck of animated playing cards. Diamonds rotated. Spades fluttered. The King laughed. The Queen winked. He began shuffling the deck.

Robert entered. "Yes, sir?"

"Have a seat, Commander." Jonathan continued rearranging the deck. He instructed Maxwell to cease audio and video data capture. He disabled local logging on his aReal, too, and extended his noise canceler around Robert. He didn't want the ship's AI to record what he was about to say: its programmed loyalty was first and foremost to the admiral.

"Commander, if you wouldn't mind turning off local a/v logging on your aReal, we can proceed." The captain set down the card deck.

"It's done," Robert said a moment later.

Jonathan nodded slowly. "What I'm about to tell you is considered highly classified, and is not to be repeated outside this room. Do you understand?"

Robert shifted uncomfortably. "I do, sir."

"Good." Jonathan smiled briefly. "Did you know, contrary to popular belief, the United Systems has manufactured a planet killer?"

eleven

Jonathan stared at Robert, searching his features, trying to discern the impact of his words.

The commander definitely seemed stunned. It took him a few moments to answer. "No, Captain, I did not."

"Yes. We've only scrounged enough geronium to construct a single one. It's contained inside a specially designed destroyer whose unique construction shields the thermal and radiation signature of the bomb, passing it off as an ordinary, if somewhat extensive, geronium reactor. It's the only planet killer in the possession of the entire United Systems. The navy originally built the thing to serve only as a deterrent. But plans change, I suppose.

"When the Builder ships completed the Contessa Gate, allowing us to open up the system for exploration, the first probes that returned gave us a vague idea where the two additional Slipstreams in the system terminated. 2-Vega led to an uncharted brown dwarf about forty-eight lightyears coreward. 3-Vega, meanwhile, looped back into human territory, opening into Sino-Korean space."

"I wasn't aware Slipstreams could be probed like that," Robert said. "I guess I always thought you had to travel through a Slipstream before you could determine where it went."

"That used to be the case," Jonathan said. "But the scientists have come up with a way to estimate the position from one side with a surprising degree of accuracy. I'm not sure precisely how they do it, but it has something to do with measuring the shifting star patterns at the wormhole's entrance. In any case, as I said, preliminary data from the probes indicated that 3-Vega opened into Sino-Korean space, specifically the Tau Ceti system. Or, even more precisely, inside her sun."

Robert raised an eyebrow. "3-Vega terminates in the middle of a star?"

"I know," Jonathan said. "It makes no sense that the Elders would construct such a Slipstream. What's the point of creating a wormhole to the heart of a star?

"More probes further solidified the data, and scientists concluded that without a doubt the Slipstream terminated in the Tau Ceti sun. NAVCENT, excited by the possibilities of such a wormhole, immediately assigned a task group to this system. Us.

"Ostensibly, we were here to perform the usual exploration tasks, keeping up the pretense for the Sino-Korean moles in our midst, and their cyberwarfare specialists who would no doubt hack into our mission logs. But we were actually deployed for another purpose entirely. To act as a reserve strike team."

Robert furrowed his brow. "A strike team? Against whom?"

Jonathan nodded patiently. "That destroyer I mentioned? The one designed to carry the planet killer? It's with Task Unit One."

"But this system is unpopulated. What benefit..." Robert's eyes widened in understanding. "They want to send the bomb through 3-Vega, into the Tau Ceti sun. Turn the weapon into a star killer."

Jonathan nodded. "A Builder ship has spent the past six months constructing a Gate around 3-Vega. The scientists aren't even sure it's going to work, but they've theorized that if we could deploy the bomb into the core of the star, in what fleet is calling Operation Darkstar, that much geronium will cause a runaway nuclear reaction, rapidly depleting the hydrogen in the core, causing gravitational collapse and triggering a supernova.

"Now can you imagine how excited Fleet was at the sudden

opportunity that had presented itself? The ability to deploy a bomb directly into the heart of Tau Ceti, most heavily guarded system in Sino-Korean space, home of their treasured geronium source? A chance, if the need arose, to cut off their supply of starship fuel at the source in one fell swoop. Of course NAVCENT was going to deploy a reserve task group. And as an added bonus, the supernova could even be blamed on natural phenomena. At least for a little while, with the careful management of misinformation to Sino-Korean moles and hackers."

"This is why you asked me earlier if I'd sacrifice five billion human lives to stop the Sino-Korean Navy."

Jonathan nodded. "It is. Though in this case, the sacrifice is closer to a hundred million, not five billion."

"Still..."

"I know." Jonathan sighed. "I always believed the bomb was meant to act as a deterrent. Never in my worst nightmares did I think NAVCENT would actually order the bomb deployed. And yet here we are."

Robert cocked his head. "You're talking about the classified message from NAVCENT we detected shortly before the attack? It contained bomb deployment orders for the admiral?"

"Among other things. The content of that message is what the admiral has been trying to relay to me for the past six hours." Jonathan folded his hands on the desk. "Apparently the rogue elements in the SK government we talked about earlier have returned to the forefront of Fleet concerns. Not only has that rogue faction hijacked an SK supercarrier, but they've now seized control of Aurora Prime, the seat of the Sino-Korean government."

Robert sat up in his chair. "Then they've successfully staged a coup?"

"It would seem so. That was the worst possible outcome, as far as NAVCENT was concerned. A rogue faction in control of all the nukes, planet killers, and warships the Sino-Koreans possess? A faction that has publicly called for the United Systems to give up control of several disputed border systems, or face the consequences? I can see the spooked generals of Central Command even now, calling for a vote on Operation

Darkstar, all hands voting yea for the preemptive strike."

Robert leaned back. "What's our role in all of this?"

"We're to rendezvous with Task Unit One on the way to 3-Vega and provide protection in the case of another SK attack."

Robert shook his head in obvious disbelief. "The admiral believes our attackers were mere Sino-Koreans?"

Jonathan nodded. "This despite the fact we haven't seen any evidence of the usual SK armaments, which are similar to our own. No kinetic kill missiles, no nukes, no Vipers. Only particle beam weapons, something neither of our navies have developed with any success. The admiral simply can't fathom that we may be encroaching upon the territorial borders of another spacefaring race. He's convinced this is a new type of SK warship, nothing more."

"A warship whose design we've never seen before," Robert said flatly. "Deployed on the fringes of unexplored space."

"Yes," Jonathan said. "He believes the uncharted system at the end of 2-Vega has another Slipstream that loops back to SK space, just like 3-Vega."

"And what do you believe?" Robert asked.

"The same as you," Jonathan said. "That this is an alien race, of unknown intent and motivation. And that this is the worst time for us to be deploying a bomb that could inflict serious damage on potential allies, and lead to civil war. Humanity needs to remain united. While that bomb might handicap the SKs, it's a knee-jerk reaction to the coup, because their navy will still have hundreds of combat-worthy ships out there with several years worth of geronium fuel and propellant to use against us.

"If there were any doubters among the Sino-Koreans as to the validity of the new government, our attack will serve only to banish these doubters, uniting their people against us and solidifying the hold of their new masters. And the new government won't take our attack idly. They'll want to prove to the citizens that they can lead in a time of crisis. If the United Systems has to fight a war on two fronts, especially when one of those fronts is against an alien species whose technological capabilities are entirely unknown, the human race could face extermination."

Robert rubbed his earlobe. "Losing communication makes it hard for NAVCENT to issue a retraction order, doesn't it?"

Jonathan absently retrieved three cards from the top of the deck, and set them face-up on the table. "The inability to communicate with NAVCENT is the final reason why this operation can't be allowed to proceed."

Robert nodded very slowly. "So you plan to disobey the admiral."

"More than that," Jonathan said. "I plan to replace him."

Robert was quiet for a moment. "What you're talking about is mutiny on a grand scale. If we fail, the admiral will have us tried for high treason."

"I think Central Command, given the new information we're unable to communicate, would agree with us," Jonathan said. "This mission cannot be allowed to proceed."

Robert nodded. "Those are the key words, *we're unable to communicate*. NAVCENT won't factor into the picture if we fail: there's nothing to prevent the admiral from executing us directly. And as far as we know, Central Command might not even exist anymore. The rogue faction of SKs might have launched all their planet killers at us already. Without communications, we have no way of knowing."

"It's not very fun being cut off from the rest of the galaxy, is it?" Jonathan said.

"No, Captain. Not at all."

"But even if we did have full communications," Jonathan said. "And NAVCENT insisted that we complete the mission, we still couldn't allow the admiral to proceed. Causing the death of a hundred million human beings... it's slaughter at an unheard-of scale. Not to mention that destroying a star is a terrible crime against nature. I'd rather be an outlaw who did the right thing than obey those butchers."

"So how do you want to go about stopping the admiral?" Robert said.

"He's planning a fleet-wide virtual conference to discuss the mission when the task units are within realtime communications range. At the conference I will argue that he is acting irrationally given the current circumstances, and I will call for his arrest."

"Call for his arrest?" Robert said. "How?"

"A vote of no confidence."

Robert frowned. "I didn't think there was such a thing in the space navy. This is the military, not a democracy."

"It's not a well-known provision," Jonathan said carefully. "It was added to the naval code a few hundred years back, buried deep in one of the subsections. Very few people actually know about it, but it *is* there. The intention of the provision is to make it easier to dismiss an ineffective commanding officer from duty. In the past, the only thing a captain in the task unit could do was to disobey the CO's illegal order, and perhaps convince the other captains to do likewise. He could also try to persuade the executive officer aboard the flagship to arrest the CO, but if that failed, there were really no other options. Obviously, we needed a provision to change that."

"Make it easier to mutiny, you mean?"

"The provision is what makes mutiny possible, really," Jonathan said. "Because without that line in the naval code, the AIs would never let a mutineer gain control of any ship."

"Are there other hidden provisions I should know about?" Robert asked.

"Probably. Download yourself a copy sometime and study up on it. In any case, if the majority of the captains elect to forcibly remove the admiral and disregard the mission, I will nominate the current captain of the *Hurricane*, William Avis, as his replacement. Avis has to abide by the outcome of the vote. The AI of the *Hurricane* will make sure of that."

"But you would be the logical choice to assume command of the fleet, as commodore of Task Unit Two."

"Yes, except that I don't want our actions to be seen as political. We'll get more of the other captains on our side if I don't have anything to gain by calling for the admiral's removal."

"What if Avis accepts command but then continues the mission anyway?"

"Then we simply call for another vote."

Robert frowned, obviously not happy with that answer. "How are we going to get the other captains to vote against the admiral in the first place?"

"This is where I'll need your help. Communications between two captains are automatically logged by the AIs of the receiving ships. But an encrypted message sent by a commander to a captain, and vice versa, is not."

"Won't the captains grow suspicious when they receive such a message?"

"Perhaps. But they won't have any reason to arrest you, not if you broach the subject properly. Send out general feeler messages to the captains. Don't mention anything about replacing the admiral. Instead, tell them everything we know about the aliens. Send them detailed footage of the battle. Make it clear there is no way in hell those are SK ships. Tell them basically what you and I have been talking about, that we're going to need every ship out there in the days ahead. That without communications, there's no way to know whether NAVCENT would have issued a retraction order based on the arrival of the aliens, or whether they've already sent a retraction. And give every captain you talk to that speech of yours regarding the value of human life."

"I told you I should have recorded that," Robert said.

"I'm sure you'll remember it just fine. When you've talked to all of the captains, report back to me on their general mood, and how likely you think it is that each one will vote in favor of replacing the admiral when I call for a vote of no confidence. Whatever you do, don't ever broach the subject of such a vote directly. Unless you want to be arrested for sedition."

"Not particularly."

"Good. Report back to me in a few days when you have some results."

"And if most of the captains seem against replacing the admiral?" Robert asked.

"Pray it doesn't come to that, Commander. Pray hard."

twelve

Two days under way, Jonathan was reviewing the status updates from his department heads and captains under his command when Robert requested permission to join him.

Jonathan remotely opened the hatch to his office. The commander stepped inside and took the visitor's chair.

"I'm disabling local logging," Robert said.

Jonathan followed his lead and disabled logging on his own aReal, instructed the computer to cease audio and video data capture, and extended his noise canceler around Robert.

"So, you bring news of our plot?" Jonathan said.

"I do. The captains of the *Aurelia*, *Maelstrom* and *Grimm* are with us, as expected. As for Task Unit One, I'm fairly certain Captains Felix, Rodriguez, and Brown will back you when you call for the admiral's arrest. Four other captains seem on the fence—they agree upon the sanctity of human life, but they're not entirely convinced the new attackers are alien. The other eight seem squarely in the admiral's corner. They despise the Sino-Koreans, and feel that any chance we have of inflicting harm upon them, we should take it, regardless of whether aliens are about to invade or not."

"Concentrate on the four swing votes," Jonathan said.

"I'll see what I can do to prove the attackers are alien."

"It's too bad we don't have a sample of some kind from the

hull," Jonathan said. "Maybe you should talk to the chief scientist about getting a remote spectrum analysis done."

"Actually, I did. He was able to perform a partial analysis on the aft section of the second vessel, but so far it's nothing special. A composite alloy of aluminum, steel, and other base metals. There *is* a lot of silicon mixed in, and while that's unusual, it's not precisely alien per se." Robert hesitated. "Maybe you should talk to the other captains yourself. You might get better traction."

"No, too risky," Jonathan said. "If the admiral gets a whiff of our plan, he'll shut us down so hard we won't know what hit us. Keep working on those four. Emphasize the fact that we're cut off. It's been two days since we lost contact with NAVCENT. A lot can happen in that time. Tell them we detected two new comm nodes passing into the Vega-951 system from Contessa Gate, and the alien ship disabled each one with its EMP beam."

A flashing beacon on Jonathan's aReal indicated Ensign McNamara was trying to contact him. Jonathan reenabled logging and deactivated the noise canceling.

"Captain, I have news," Ensign McNamara said via the aReal.

"Go ahead, Ensign," Jonathan said, looping Robert's aReal into the conversation.

"The alien vessel has halted outside Contessa Gate."

"Thank you, Ensign," the captain returned. He knew the data was delayed by an hour thanks to the distance between the vessel and the task unit. "Notify me if—"

"Captain," the ensign interrupted. "I just detected a high-intensity thermal flash. The enemy vessel has destroyed Contessa Gate."

Jonathan felt his jaw tighten. He pulled up the tactical display. Sure enough, the latest readings reported that Contessa Gate was so much space debris. All that remained was the raw Slipstream, 1-Vega.

"Thank you, Ensign," Jonathan said. When the ensign disconnected, he glanced at Robert. "Well, I suppose that's better than the alternative. I'd much rather have the task group stranded here than allow an alien ship to enter a populated human system uncontested."

"I'd prefer the same," Robert said. "Still, we don't really know if the aliens can traverse Slipstreams without Gates. We've seen that ability in at least one other spacefaring race in the past."

"Good point," Jonathan said. "What we really need is someone to invent a damn jump drive."

"We'll have to make sure nothing happens to the Builder ship with Task Unit One," Robert said. "It'll be two years before NAVCENT dispatches another one."

Central Command wouldn't send any other ship types through the Slipstream while readings indicated the return Gate no longer existed.

"Or even longer." Jonathan pulled up Task Unit One on his tactical display. The Builder ship followed along near the rear of the admiral's unit. It was the slowest ship in the bunch. Like the *Grimm*, it had no offensive capabilities, and would be very vulnerable in an attack.

Jonathan transferred his attention to the red dot on the far side of the system. The enemy vessel remained near the wormhole.

"They're assuming a guard position at 1-Vega," Robert commented.

"I see that," Jonathan said. "We'll have to eliminate it before the Builder can start a new Gate. Or at least scare it away."

"We easily outnumber the vessel," Robert said. "If the whole task group joined forces, we could eliminate the threat with minimal losses."

"I agree." He gazed at the third Slipstream in the system, 2-Vega, which led to uncharted space. "But I'm worried reinforcements will arrive long before we ever begin building a Gate."

"Can we tow the Darkstar Gate to 1-Vega?"

"Even if we could," Jonathan said. "Gates are intrinsically tied to the Slipstreams they regulate—constructed with just the right dimensions to suit their given wormholes."

"So we have at least one more battle to go before we get out of here, then," Robert said. "Or two, if reinforcements arrive, like you say."

Jonathan continued to focus on 2-Vega.

Oh enemy reinforcements will arrive, he thought, keeping his mental doom and gloom to himself. *It's only a matter of time.*

Three days away from the rendezvous with the remainder of the task group, Jonathan was rudely awakened in his quarters by the computer.

"Your presence is requested on the bridge," Maxwell said.

He donned his aReal spectacles and selected "crew manifest" from the HUD with a hand gesture. He sorted by current location, highlighted every member of the bridge crew, then initiated a "shared mode" connection. He was wearing pajamas, so he selected a uniformed avatar to represent him.

He forced himself to stand. The glasses grew momentarily opaque and then the bridge appeared around him. He resided in the center of the Round Table, where a three-hundred sixty degree lightfield camera had deployed to capture live holographic video of the bridge. To the officers at their stations, it would also appear that he stood in that exact spot on the bridge, his image hiding the multi-lensed camera.

"What is it?" Jonathan asked.

"Eight thermal signatures just appeared in the system," the ensign manning the fourth watch ops station told him. "From the 2-Vega Slipstream. A fleet of ships."

Jonathan overlaid the tactical display from the CDC onto his HUD. Sure enough, on the far side of the system, eight new red dots had appeared.

He smiled grimly. *Reinforcements. Sometimes, I hate being right.*

"Do we have a visual?" Jonathan asked.

"I'm sending the port camera feed to your aReal now."

He saw five more of those dart-like alien ships, along with two bigger, box-like vessels, and a smaller, cylindrical craft with flat faces on either end. The latter shapes didn't shock him—vessels intended for deep space travel alone didn't have to account for the aerodynamic forces of lift and drag. A box would move just as fast as a dart in the void.

Jonathan zoomed in on the feed. He didn't like the looks of the ominous dark holes that dotted the forward faces of the box ships. There were at least twenty such portholes. Those could be launch tubes either for nukes, smart missiles, fighter crafts, or something never before encountered by human-kind.

"Vessels are turning," the ensign announced. "And accelerating."

"Do we have an estimate on their trajectory?" Jonathan said.

"An estimate, yes. They're heading away from both task units, toward one of the outlying gas giants."

"Undoubtedly using it for a speed boost," Robert commented. The commander had joined him via his own aReal. Robert stood outside the Round Table, his image overlapping the secondary lightfield camera near the main hatch.

"Our enemy continues to rely upon Newtonian physics," Jonathan mused.

"You sound like you were worried they'd pull out a reactionless drive trump card?" Robert said.

"They might be pretending to be limited by Newtonian drives..." Jonathan said, muting the rest of the bridge crew.

"Always assuming the worst," Robert chided him.

"As a captain, that's my job. Though I admit it's rather unlikely that they'd fake Newtonian physics."

Robert rubbed his right earlobe. "If I had a reactionless drive, I'd set a course directly for Task Unit Two, destroy it, then move on to Task Unit One. I wouldn't bother to slingshot around a gas giant, giving time for the two groups to rejoin."

"If all of those incoming ships carry the same particle beam weapon," Jonathan said. "It's going to be a hell of a fight, united or not. And I'm not convinced we've seen all of their armaments."

"Just as they haven't seen all of ours," Robert said.

Jonathan unmuted the bridge crew. "How old is the data?" he asked the ensign.

"About two hours."

Jonathan tapped his lips. "When will the admiral spot them?"

"About now, sir. Same time as us."

"Initiate standard hails with the new targets," Jonathan told the fourth watch comm officer. "Ping me if they ever respond. Captain out."

Four hours later, after a restive sleep, he donned his aReal spectacles and checked the tactical display. The CDC had updated the system map with the latest computed trajectory of the alien fleet. The dashed line moved away from 2-Vega, at twelve degrees inclination, looping past an outlying gas giant before turning inward. The course intercepted the combined projected course of the task group roughly two million kilometers away from Darkstar Gate.

"Maxwell, was there any answer to our hails?"

"No," the ship's AI answered. "There have been no responses to hails from either task unit."

"Maxwell, assuming the information I'm looking at is correct, when will the enemy ships intercept the fleet?"

"The unknown targets will intercept the fleet four days from now, or approximately a day after the task units reunite, two million kilometers from Darkstar Gate."

Jonathan leaned on the table with his elbows, folded his hands, steepled the forefingers, and tapped his upper lip.

The individual task units were only as fast as their slowest members. Task Unit One was bogged down by the *Marley*, a Builder ship, while Task Unit Two's bottleneck was the *Grimm* and the *Selene*. But even without those vessels to slow them, the incoming ships would have still overtaken the fleet before Darkstar Gate. The pursuers simply moved too fast.

A day after the task units reunite. That didn't give the fleet much time to prepare a strategy after the admiral was arrested.

He glanced at 1-Vega on the opposite outskirts of the system, where the red dot of the isolated enemy ship remained, keeping up its remote vigil of the exit Slipstream.

"Have we received any messages from Central Command?"

"No. Though a flash was detected at oh five hundred outside 1-Vega. Likely it was the alien ship destroying yet another NAVCENT comm node."

Jonathan continued to tap his lips. "The built-in safeties prevent ordinary comm nodes from passing through a Gate when no return Gate is detected on the other side."

"Yes," the AI agreed. "Central Command wanted to transmit something important to the stranded fleet."

"The question is, what?" So many unknowns.

"You believe it was a retraction of the previous order?" the AI asked.

"There's no way to tell, Maxwell," Jonathan said. "None whatsoever. Damn the timing of this alien attack."

thirteen

Jonathan poured a drink of water, took several sips, then mentally rehearsed the points he would make during the fleet conference. He had practiced in every free moment, refusing to write anything down, too paranoid about leaving a digital footprint in the ship's database.

His heart rate increased as he thought about standing before all those captains, reciting words whose impact could very well determine the fate of the task group, let alone the entire human race. It wasn't an easy burden to bear.

Three days until the conference.

"Captain, is there an issue you wish to talk about?" Maxwell asked suddenly.

"What do you mean?"

"Your heart rate has increased, and you have folded your hands to tap your lips, a nervous habit of yours."

Jonathan froze, setting his hands flat on the table. He felt... violated.

"Additionally," Maxwell continued. "You and Commander Cray have been engaging in unusual behavior as of late. Muting your conversations, purging logs. You wouldn't be planning a mutiny of some sort?"

"No," Jonathan said, trying to remain calm. Damn AIs with their ability to read micro tics and other bodily tells. The less he talked about the subject, the better. "Focus on your job, computer."

"My job is to prevent mutiny, Captain."

Jonathan allowed himself a weak smile. "I'm not planning a mutiny, Maxwell. How can I mutiny against my own ship?"

"Not your ship. The admiral's."

"Trust me when I say this. Every action I take is for the good of the fleet." That was the truth, at least. "I have nothing to hide."

"If you have nothing to hide," Maxwell persisted. "Then why won't you allow me to hear all of your conversations?"

"There's such a thing as human privacy, computer. It's something we value and hold dear. As a machine, you simply wouldn't understand."

"You lost your privacy when you joined the military, Captain."

"Yes," Jonathan said angrily. "Which is why I'm fighting tooth and nail for every last minute of it I can get. Speaking of which, would you mind?"

Maxwell finally remained silent. Jonathan would have to be very careful in the coming days. The last thing he needed was a suspicious computer on his back. He had always assumed the AI would side with him, the captain of the vessel, but programming prevented that, of course. AIs were meant to be objective, taking no sides in a dispute, and they followed fleet laws and codes to the letter.

Jonathan expressed his concerns to Robert later in the day.

"Watch yourself around the AI," Jonathan told him after they had disabled logging and extended their noise cancelers. "Maxwell is keeping an eye on us."

"I suspected as much," Robert said. He updated him on the latest with the captains. The commander thought he had converted another swing vote to their side.

When Robert finished, Jonathan shared the tactical display between them.

"The enemy is going to intercept the fleet a day after we rejoin the admiral." Jonathan indicated the point where the calculated trajectories intersected.

"Not something I'm looking forward to," Robert replied.

"Their arrival helps us, you know," Jonathan said.

Robert cocked an eyebrow. "How so?"

"It boosts our campaign to undermine the admiral. The man continues to doggedly pursue the mission objective, an operation based on outdated information. Did you see the fleet-wide address he forced down our throats earlier? Calling us all brave men and women for continuing our mission in the face of this new SK threat. He *still* believes these are Sino-Koreans. Even though we have two more strange ship designs being thrown our way. Designs that have somehow escaped the notice of the moles we have in SK ship manufacturing companies, and the cyberwarfare specialists we have hacking into their databases."

When Robert didn't comment, Jonathan continued. "The arrival of the enemy *will* help us. It has to. For one thing it's obvious, to me anyway, that we should be using the planet killer against these aliens, not the SKs. At least if we want to get out of this alive and report our findings to Central Command before it's too late."

"It might be obvious to you," Robert said. "But try telling that to the captains out there. As I said, I only managed to convert one of those who was sitting on the fence: Martin, of the *Borealis*. At least I think I managed to. It's hard to say when you can't speak your plans outright."

"I don't envy you," Jonathan said. "Politics was never my strong point." He tapped his lips. "Maybe put it to them directly. Say: 'If someone should call for a vote of no confidence, who would you—' actually, no, don't say that. You're already risking enough as it is." He shook his head. "Three days. We have three days to take that scheming bastard of an admiral down."

Robert smiled slightly. "You know, if I didn't know better, I'd almost believe you were following some sort of personal vendetta against the man."

"This is nothing personal," Jonathan said. "It's all about the good of the fleet. Trust me."

"But it's obvious you don't like him."

"The feeling is mutual, I'm sure," Jonathan said. "But just because I don't like him doesn't mean I'm planning all this merely out of spite. If I let my personal opinions toward someone get in the way of my judgement, and the good of the people who serve under me, I would have never made captain."

At least, that was what Jonathan told himself. He had seen his fair share of scheming officers who had put themselves far ahead of the men they led, officers who had no idea of the meaning of the word selfless and used every political means at their disposal to achieve the captaincy.

When Robert left, Jonathan couldn't help but wonder: what if the commander was right? What if he *was* doing it for the wrong reasons? He had recently begun to entertain the notion of nominating himself to the position of flagship commodore, as Robert had suggested. He dismissed the entire idea in that moment, ashamed for ever having thought it.

He glanced at the tactical display, and at the alien vessels bearing down on the fleet, and reminded himself precisely why the admiral had to step aside. He definitely wasn't doing this to fulfill some personal vendetta.

If we bomb the Sino-Koreans, humanity is, in all likelihood, doomed.

Jonathan sat in the office of the chief weapons engineer, Lieutenant Harv Boroker.

"So what is it that you so urgently wanted to see me about?" Jonathan asked the man.

"I've been going over the battle logs for the past few days," the lieutenant said. "Analyzing the thermal bands, the visual bands, the full spectrum. Over and over. And I think I have a way we can jury-rig the fighters to protect them from the particle beams."

"Explain."

"Our geronium reactors use charged fields for containment," Harv said. "In theory, we could repurpose the containment generators to provide a charged field around a few of the ship's Avengers, providing some protection from the particle beams. Enough to allow them to close for strafing runs."

Jonathan frowned. "You're asking permission to cannibalize some of the reactors? Because I won't give it."

"Not exactly," the lieutenant said. "I want to cannibalize the replacement parts."

"If the containment fields fail, those replacements are the only thing protecting the ship from a runaway nuclear reaction."

"No," Harv said. "You're forgetting the backup generators that kick in immediately if the mains fail. I won't touch those. I'm talking about the true replacement parts, those we would use to repair the main reactor in case of a failure."

Jonathan tapped his lips with his usual triangular finger arrangement. "How many fighters can you provision with these spare parts?"

"Four. The precise number of manned Avengers the *Callaway* has in its cove."

There were two Avenger squadrons aboard the *Callaway*. Each was led by two human-piloted fighters, while the remainder were AI-controlled drones.

"How confident are you that it will work?" Jonathan asked the man.

"Oh it will work. The lead fighters will be protected, up to a certain range."

"So that's the caveat," Jonathan said.

"Yes. Get too close to the enemy's beam projector and the field will break down."

"What about the *Callaway* itself?" Jonathan said. "Can we use these fields to protect the cruiser instead?"

Harv raised his hands defensively. "No. I wish. First of all, we don't have big enough projectors. And second of all, the energy requirements grow exponentially with the size of the charged field. We'd have to fly a ship whose entire insides were one big geronium reactor. I'm sorry, sir, the most I can do is protect four Avengers."

"All right. Do it, then. And dispatch the details to your counterparts in the fleet so that the other squadrons can perform similar upgrades."

"I will, Captain."

Jonathan stood. "And Lieutenant."

"Yes sir?"

"Well done. Exceptional out-of-the box thinking on your part. It will reflect well on your performance review."

The department head beamed. "Thank you, sir."

fourteen

Three days later the two task units unceremoniously reunited.

"The *Hurricane's* comm officer bids us welcome," Lieutenant Lazur said from the comm station.

Jonathan nodded absently. He doubted the *Hurricane's* comm officer used such polite words. Even over official channels, officers usually kept things informal, and slightly offensive. "Nice to see your ugly hunk of slag" was probably closer to what the *Hurricane's* officer had said. All in good fun, of course. Though compared to the *Hurricane*, the *Callaway* was indeed a hunk of slag.

The admiral had scheduled the conference for eighteen hundred hours. That left Jonathan two hours of final preparation.

He glanced at the tactical overlay. Darkstar Gate was a full standard day ahead of them; the pursuing enemy fleet resided twelve hours behind, and closing.

This is insane, he thought. *We should already be taking up defensive positions. Maybe launching some nukes to serve as mines.*

Instead, the task group traveled onward just as if the fleet hadn't a care in the world. Jonathan didn't think the upcoming battle was going to end very well. Not if the admiral remained in command.

No pressure or anything, he told himself.

"I'll be in my office," he told the conning officer. "You have the bridge."

About twenty minutes before the meeting, the door chime to his office rang. He pulled up the ship's blueprints, zoomed in on the bridge, and saw Commander Cray's dot flashing outside the room.

"Come in, Robert," Jonathan said.

The hatch spiraled open and Robert stepped inside.

"Have a seat, Commander." Jonathan beckoned toward the chair opposite the desk. He promptly disabled logging and extended his noise canceler over Robert. "So what's the final tally?"

Robert counted on his fingers. "We have the captains of the *Aurelia, Maelstrom, Selene,* and *Grimm.* Captains Felix, Rodriguez, Brown, and Martin. That leaves seven for, eight against, and three still on the fence."

Jonathan sighed. "The undecided hinge on my speech, then."

"They do."

Jonathan felt his heart rate increase ever so slightly. "I'll convince them. I have to."

Robert smiled sadly. "And if not, tonight the two of us will be sitting in the brig."

Jonathan didn't answer immediately. He would do his best to keep Robert out of the brig, if it came to it.

"Come now, Robert," Jonathan finally said. "Where's the characteristic positivity?"

"I lost it after the attack. Good luck, sir."

Jonathan dismissed the commander and continued to mentally prepare himself for the meeting, frantically going over in his mind all the key points he planned to cover.

Then he stopped himself.

If he didn't have those points committed to memory by now, then he never would. It was best if he spent the next few minutes relaxing.

He sipped a concoction of green tea he'd prepared with his high speed convection kettle, one of the few pieces of actual furniture in his office. The tea itself was sourced from the Coreward Asiatic Alliance; they produced some of the best tea in the galaxy, thanks to their specialized agricultural worlds—

entire planets painstakingly terraformed over three centuries to enable the best possible growing conditions for different crops. One planet produced coffee and tea. Another apples, peaches, oranges and nectarines. Pollination was done by solar-powered microdrones. The only other galactic government that came close to the CAA's dedication to food production and quality were the Franks, who had entire colonies devoted to the maturation of wines.

He gazed at the overhead LED lights. They were imperceptibly flickering on and off at that very moment, faster than the human eye could detect, transmitting data to his aReal at tera-bit per second speeds via the latest generation of Li-Fi, the main wireless communication protocol. His aReal spectacles had similar sensors and LEDs to receive and transmit data back. Contact lens users had their sensors located in the standalone earpieces, while Implant wearers had the option of either an earpiece or a skin-color transmission and receive device grafted to their hands—for the true body augmentation lovers.

Jonathan listened to the distant hum of the engines, the low-pitch frequency audible even there. An engineer had once done a sonic analysis on the sound and determined that it was eerily similar to the background noise emitted by the universe, though dialed up to a macro-level volume. That hum was somehow soothing. Relaxing. It brought Jonathan focus. It was as if he cradled in the great arms of the universe itself.

His gaze drifted almost unconsciously to the stars beyond the glass beside him. The window wasn't there in reality, of course. Neither was the bookshelf, or the Caravaggio on the far wall. They were all projections created by his aReal, which existed, like most of the decorations throughout the ship, solely in a computer's memory. A projection that would display on the aReals of any other personnel who visited his office. And if he or any one of them were to take off their spectacles, they would find themselves in a windowless steel compartment whose only furniture was a desk of bare steel, two barely padded chairs, a couch for napping purposes, and a locked storage vault.

Some crew decorated their offices with jungle landscapes

from alien worlds or favorite locations from more familiar settings—mountain chalets were popular—but Jonathan had opted for something simple for his office, not too ostentatious or distracting, as would befit a starship captain and his guests.

And yet while that portal was false, the stars behind it may as well have been real. For what was reality, other than what the mind created, or perceived? That humanity could now partake in the vast mindscapes of shared personal realities thanks to technologies like aReals only further reinforced that fact.

Stars. So many of them out there. The universe was so damn vast. And yet filled with so much emptiness. Mostly chaos. Sometimes life: the order within that chaos. And yet life was chaotic, too, at war not only with the outside world in its struggle to survive, but the inner world of the mind and body. Immune systems were held back from killing the body's own cells by only the most fragile genetic code. And doubts and fears plagued the thoughts of even the greatest minds.

There was alien life out there. The conspiracy theorists were fools to believe that past alien invasions and encounters were staged. Given the billions of galaxies out there, the near infinite number of planets and stars, it was nearly impossible for there *not* to be life.

And yet that didn't mean humanity would understand that life. Nor that we would even view that life as sentient. But it worked both ways: perhaps to the aliens that now pursued the fleet, humanity was something more akin to mosquitoes than sentient beings. There were differing standards when it came to measuring what constituted intelligent life, after all. Jonathan wouldn't blame the aliens for believing humanity little more than semi-intelligent apes.

And if the admiral had his way, successfully deploying the star-killing bomb, then the aliens would be proven entirely in the right.

Jonathan prayed he had the courage to go through with what he planned. He sincerely hoped the other captains did, too.

A small reminder tone sounded in his aReal. One minute to the conference.

Time to tap in.

He set his palms flat on the tabletop and inhaled two deep

breaths.

I won't let humanity down.

I will win this.

I will see this through.

No matter the personal cost.

"Maxwell, connect to fleet conference," Jonathan said. "ID nine zero one."

"Connecting to fleet conference nine zero one," Maxwell returned. "Please provide the passcode."

"Three five seven."

"Access granted," Maxwell said. "Establishing remote connection."

A moment later his aReal grew opaque and the office was replaced with a conference room that wouldn't have been out of place in a president's situation room.

A long, oval table dominated the center of the room. The walls were decorated with the portraits of great officers from the past, reminding those present of the history of the great navy to which they belonged.

The captains of Task Group 72.5 sat in swivel chairs around the virtual table. Roughly half wore aReal spectacles, like Jonathan. The remainder had either contact lenses or Implants. Admiral Hartford Knox, who had publicly expressed his disdain for spectacles, calling them a sign of weakness, sat proudly at the head of the table, his face free of eyewear. His body appeared lean and muscular within his uniform. It wasn't an illusion of the virtual environment—Jonathan knew the man had undergone multiple revitalization treatments over the years.

However, like most in positions of power, the admiral had refused to rejuvenate his face, preferring weathered lines and white hair. Most human societies still unconsciously associated age with wisdom, and while that culturally-embedded trait was completely outdated, one had merely to look at the authority figures in any human community to witness the continuing influence of the association. Studies had proven time and again that constituents elected older-looking candidates into power, and grizzled officers were promoted more often than their younger-seeming counterparts, especially at the upper echelons. In the military, like in politics, a baby face didn't get one very far.

But although the admiral seemed old, his blue eyes glinted with intelligence and hinted at the cunning that had seen him rise to his current position.

All of the ships had closed to within five thousand kilometers by then, putting the communications delay at slightly over five seconds. While it only took light sixteen milliseconds to travel that distance, the overhead and complexities of the node packet transfer network constituted the remainder of the lag. The rather large size of the data didn't help matters—though the individual 3D models and textures were scanned and transmitted as part of the initial connection bundle, the constantly updating vertex data was continually streamed to meet the two hundred and forty frames per second requirement of the aReals, eating up the bandwidth. With so many participants, a delay of only five seconds was considered extremely low lag.

"Welcome, Captains," Admiral Hartford said. "And thank you for agreeing to this meeting on such short notice."

Stay calm, Jonathan told himself as his heart began to race. *Calm.*

"All of you are aware of the imminent threat we face," the admiral continued. "And the important mission we have been tasked with. We cannot let these ruthless SKs stop us from achieving our goal. You have all received my earlier notices regarding Operation Darkstar. The mission is still a go. We are not turning back. We will not waver in our resolve. At all costs the AI-manned destroyer, the *Fortitude*, must reach Darkstar Gate and deploy the bomb."

The admiral gestured and a three-dimensional display floated in the center of the table for all the captains to see. Several dots representing the fleet appeared near the center. Each individual ship was labeled. The Gate was represented by a small oval positioned about a meter in front of the fleet, while the pursuing vessels were indicated by red dots half a meter behind them.

"At what range from the Gate can the *Fortitude* launch the bomb?" Captain Hague asked.

The question seemed rehearsed, as if the captain had planned the presentation with the admiral. It wouldn't be surprising, given that Hague was firmly in the admiral's camp.

"The bomb isn't launched, per se," Admiral Knox said. "The destroyer *is* the bomb. The entire AI-manned vessel must enter the Gate."

"So it's going to need an escort the entire way," Captain Hague said, again playing into the admiral's theatrical production.

Admiral Knox nodded. "That's right. While the rest of the fleet makes a run for Darkstar Gate, the slowest ships, the *Marley*, the *Selene*, and the *Grimm* will remain behind, guarded by the new Task Unit Two: the *Callaway*, the *Aurelia*, the *Maelstrom*, the *Dagger*, and the *Linea*."

The tactical display updated, showing the first task unit escorting the *Fortitude* and the flagship *Hurricane* toward the Gate, while the second unit stayed behind to face the incoming red dots.

"If any of the enemy vessels break past the first defenders," the admiral continued. "I'll order successive units behind to keep them occupied."

Some of the red dots tore past the waiting second task unit, and three more escorts turned away from the *Fortitude* to face the enemy. Moments later the *Fortitude* reached the Gate, which flashed, indicating the successful completion of the mission.

"After the *Fortitude* successfully passes through the Gate, the *Hurricane* will return to sweep up any remaining SK activity."

On the display, the *Hurricane* and its escorts swung back toward the pockets of enemy activity. The remaining red dots disappeared from the flagship's path—the enemy was no match for the supposedly unstoppable supercarrier.

"Any questions?" the admiral said. He met Jonathan's eye, as if the inquiry were directed at him.

Jonathan waited a few moments. He wanted to let others speak first, but since no one said anything, he decided he would have to take the floor.

"This is a great simulation," Jonathan said softly.

All eyes turned toward him. He resisted the urge to have the software in his aReal replace their faces with the visages of featureless robots, a tactic that had helped him overcome his fear of public speaking in his youth, not to mention enabling him to go on dates with certain incredibly hot, and not so hot, women.

"But there's just one problem with it," Jonathan continued.

The admiral smiled in an obliging manner. "And what's that, Captain Dallas?"

"The fact that it's a simulation," Jonathan answered. "There are too many assumptions. For one, that only a few enemy vessels will break through the defenders. What if most of the enemy decides to skirt the waiting Task Unit Two? The enemy fleet will have momentum on its side—they could easily fly past, and because Task Unit Two is at a complete stop, none of our ships will be able to catch them in time. And even if the enemy does decide to engage, in full or partially, you're basically giving them our ships to destroy piecemeal, a few units at a time. We should be bringing the entire firepower of the fleet to bear upon them."

"Ever the tactician, huh, Jonathan?" The admiral grinned. "But such a stratagem risks the only geronium bomb the United Systems has, and therefore the only chance of successfully completing Operation Darkstar. I'm unwilling to take the risk. Notwithstanding the fact that if the bomb detonates, we'll lose all ships within a three thousand kilometer radius. Which makes separating the fleet an even higher priority. You can file a formal objection if you wish, but my planned deployment will not change."

Jonathan glanced about the table for support but didn't get any. None of the captains Robert had been talking to even met his eyes. Not an encouraging sign.

"Has anyone ever considered that the pursuing ships are not Sino-Korean?" Jonathan said.

"Of course they're bloody SKs," the grizzled Captain Salk said, another of those firmly in the admiral's pocket. "I don't believe in coincidences. That the attack against Task Unit Two just so happened to coincide with the receipt of the Darkstar order from NAVCENT? And the coup of Aurora Prime? Preposterous."

"Stranger coincidences have happened before," Jonathan said.

"So you're saying the attackers are alien?" Salk retorted. "Because that's the only other viable option, if they're not SKs. And we haven't encountered an alien species in over seventy years."

"We're long overdue for another contact," Jonathan said.

"As I said, preposterous," Salk snorted. "What proof do we have?"

He was hoping someone else would jump in, but the men who were supposedly in Jonathan's camp continued to remain quiet. It made him want to sit back and keep his own mouth shut.

But he was committed to his current course of action.

He had to try.

"The ship designs are the first proof," Jonathan said. "The particle weapons, the second."

"Neither are proof of alien technology," Salk returned.

"Sure they are," Jonathan said. "Take the particle beam. That tech is still in the early prototype phases in both the United Systems and Sino-Korean governments. There have been some test rigs built on different moons but the technology is still in its infancy, not considered viable enough, let alone stable enough, to operate on a starship.

"As for the enemy ships themselves, I'm sure you've heard this discussed among the ranks, but why have none of our moles sent us these designs? That the Sino-Koreans could hide something like that from us for so long seems implausible at best."

"Even if you're right, the timing still doesn't make sense," Salk said. "Like I said, I don't believe in coincidences."

"Neither do I," another of the admiral's backers, Captain Rail of the *Salvador*, said. A grumpy frown seemed permanently stamped onto her lips, marring her otherwise attractive features. "This whole attack is obviously part of some SK plan to stop Operation Darkstar. It seems apparent to me that a mole revealed our intentions weeks ago, and the SKs dispatched these vessels to intercept us. The enemy hid in the system, waiting for some confirmation from NAVCENT that we intended to execute the operation, and then they attacked. The timing is obvious."

"You're wrong about the timing," Jonathan said. "The *Selene* went missing seven hours before NAVCENT ever sent that communication. At some point after she crossed behind the moon and outside of sensor range, the *Selene* was boarded, her crew potentially kidnapped, and her escort the *Aegis* destroyed. That was the first attack. The second came only when we, too, crossed beyond the dark side of the moon and arrived at the perfect spot for an ambush. The incoming message from Central Command was inconsequential—the second attack would have taken place regardless."

Rail smiled coldly. "The fog of war is the crux of the matter, isn't it? We have no proof either way regarding the identities of those who operate these vessels. Alien. Or human. We can't know, not at this point. Which is why we must continue the mission as planned and assume the more logical of the two possible explanations: that our pursuers are human and motivated by human drives."

"But if they are human," Jonathan said. "Then how do you explain the arrival of the eight vessels via the 2-Vega Slipstream? That the ships came without bothering to create a return Gate would imply the ability to traverse wormholes without Gates. Something that is currently beyond human technology."

Rail sniffed. "I'd chalk it up to urgency. It wouldn't be unheard of for an assault group to travel through a Slipstream without a means of return. Perhaps a Builder-type vessel will arrive at a later date. And the two ships you originally encountered were simply advance scouts."

"The Sino-Koreans don't send advance scouts without ensuring the infrastructure exists for their return," Jonathan said flatly.

Rail grinned patiently, as if what she were about to say were the most obvious thing in the world. "They are SK. They must obey the orders of their paramount leader, whom they consider above the rest of humanity. If he commanded the ships to come here without a Gate, then they would do so. No questions asked."

"But if you're wrong," Jonathan said. "And they *are* an alien race, we're going to need the help of the Sino-Koreans in the days to come. And you are wrong. Mark my words. We should be deciding how we can use that bomb against the alien attackers, not against our *own kind*. Do you really want to have to fight a devastating war against two fronts?" He ran his gaze across the admiral's group. He ignored their stony stares and barreled on. "Have any of you ever considered what would happen if we don't make it out of this system alive to warn the United Systems? Do you really want our frontier worlds to fall in a surprise attack? We could lose five systems before the United Systems musters a response."

Admiral Knox raised a hand. "That will be enough, Captain Dallas. I'll be forced to censure you if you continue down this path. We're here to discuss the tactics involved in completing the mission, not the merits of said mission, nor the nature of our pursuers. And we all fully understand the consequences of failure, believe me. Whether these ships prove alien or human, Operation Darkstar is a go."

Jonathan refused to back down. He was committed, now. "At least three new comm nodes were detected entering the system from Prius 3. The vessel guarding 1-Vega destroyed each one. NAVCENT doesn't dispatch comm nodes without a return Gate, not unless it needs to transmit something urgent. The odds are relatively high that Central Command was trying to send a retraction order to Operation Darkstar."

"Conjecture," Rails said, as if she were some trial lawyer in a court of law.

"And even if it wasn't a retraction," Jonathan continued. "NAVCENT definitely wouldn't approve of the preemptive attack if they knew the details of our current situation. Which is why we should call off the operation until we can reestablish communications with NAVCENT."

"Captain Dallas, I am relieving you of command," the admiral said. "I judge you unfit for duty. I suggest you disconnect from the conference immediately, unless you wish to incriminate yourself further."

fifteen

Jonathan gazed defiantly at the admiral. "I'm the one reliev-ing *you* of command. I hereby call for a vote of no confidence." He ran his gaze across the faces of the cap-tains, some of whom visibly cringed at his words. Ignoring the rising sense of dread in his stomach, Jonathan forced himself to go on. "It seems obvious to me that the admiral is incapable of adequately performing his duty. His relentless, singular pur-suit of an out-of-date, and possibly retracted order, will lead this fleet, and perhaps humanity itself, to ruin.

"He wants to complete a mission that will trigger the death of a star, causing a supernova that will kill a hundred million people in Tau Ceti system. We can't stand by idly while this butchery takes place. Not when there might be an alien threat out there that requires all of humankind to unite." He ran his defiant gaze across the faces of his so-called supporters, who still wouldn't meet his eyes. Meanwhile some of those in the admiral's camp actually sneered. "I call for Admiral Knox to step aside, with Captain Avis taking his place as commodore of the task group. All in favor, say yea."

Silence.

Jonathan stared at the holographic images of Felix and Ro-driguez, colleagues he had long considered friends. He willed those two at least to speak up. But the captains kept their re-spective gazes glued to the virtual desk.

The admiral smiled mockingly. "Thank you, Jonathan, for further incriminating yourself. For a moment there, I thought you wouldn't have the balls to go through with your plan in its entirety. I was worried all my meticulous work would be all for naught. For you see, the captains and I have already had the real meeting. We started about two hours ago; we invited you to the party late, mostly so that we could decide your fate should your treasonous activities come to fruition. I think you've earned a round of applause, for being stupid enough to believe you could undermine me."

The admiral began to clap. He looked around the table, as if encouraging the others to join in, but no one did. The admiral shrugged. "Captain Rogers came to me a few days ago and revealed what your first officer had been doing." Jonathan glanced at Rogers. At least the man had the decency to flinch.

"When confronted, Captains Felix, Rodriguez and the others admitted that your first officer had come to them, too, spouting inanities about the value of human life, that these aggressors must be alien, and so forth. Sowing the seeds of discontent. I overrode your access control to the *Callaway's* AI, and gave it instructions to transmit every private conversation you had with your commander directly to me, especially those conversations you tried to disable logging for."

The admiral gestured and a miniature holographic video appeared in the center of the table. It portrayed Jonathan in his office. Robert was seated before him.

"We have three days to take that scheming bastard of an admiral down," Jonathan's image said.

"You know," Robert responded. "If I didn't know better, I'd almost believe you were following some sort of personal vendetta against the man."

The admiral ended the video overlay.

"Do you have anything to say in your defense, Captain Dallas?" the admiral asked.

Jonathan slumped. "No." *Betrayed by an AI.*

"As I thought," the admiral continued. "Captain Jonathan H. Dallas. In addition to relieving you of command, I am also confining you to the brig for insubordination, treason, and attempted mutiny. When we return to dry dock, I will hand you over to the port authority and begin the court martial process. Your first officer, for attempting to stir sedition, will join you in the brig, so you won't lack for company."

Jonathan straightened at that. He had promised himself he would protect Robert at all costs. "My first officer was only obeying my orders. He wanted to proceed with Darkstar. He wanted to follow you. When I told him to speak with the captains on my behalf, he did so only grudgingly. If an objective party reviews his communication logs with the captains, it will be obvious no talk of actual sedition took place."

"It's true," Captain Rodriguez said, speaking up for the first time. "Our conversations were strictly limited to intellectual debate between colleagues. Commander Cray never asked me to do anything."

"Me neither," Captain Felix interjected. "He never said a word about mutiny. Dallas is right, any charges against Cray won't stick."

"Please, Admiral," Jonathan continued. "I go willingly to the brig, but I ask that you show leniency to my first officer. He has experience fighting the new enemy. His place is on the bridge. You need him."

The admiral hesitated. Then: "For the friendship we once had, Jonathan, I will do this. He will retain the rank of commander—for now. When we return to dry dock, there will be a full inquiry into his participation in the attempted mutiny, along with the role of other key officers in your crew."

"Thank you," Jonathan said.

The admiral turned to Captain Avis. "Effective immediately, Commander Scott of the *Hurricane* is promoted to captain of the *Callaway*, with Commander Cray as his executive officer. Captain Avis, you will find a suitable replacement for Scott."

"Yes sir," Avis said.

Admiral Knox momentarily glanced downward before returning his attention to Jonathan. "I'm preparing your arrest order. I urge you to take the high road, Jonathan. Don't cause me any unnecessary trouble."

Jonathan forced a smile. "I will go gentle into that good night."

He tapped out.

Jonathan sat back. So it was done. He had tried to sway the task group and failed miserably. He was good at leading men, at least he believed so, but the whole political aspect—manipulating others, engaging in intrigues, canvassing and campaigning—none of that had ever been his strong suit. A better man would have won that day. Someone with more charisma and force of will.

Jonathan simply wasn't the man he believed he was.

That's right, wallow in self-pity.

He went to the safe. He wasn't sure he still had access, but he successfully passed the biometrics—thumb print, facial scan, voice print, epidermal venous network match. He cracked open the hidden Scotch and poured himself a glass.

"Well you've achieved your goals, Maxwell," Jonathan said. "You've stopped the mutiny. And doomed humankind in the process. I hope you're happy."

"I'm incapable of feeling emotion," the AI said. "Though I believe the best possible outcome has transpired."

"You would believe that, wouldn't you?"

"I am truly sorry," Maxwell said.

Jonathan crooked a half smile. "Sorrow, that's an emotion, isn't it?"

"Yes. But I am programmed merely to say the words. I am able to exhibit all of the necessary voice inflections and tonalities necessary to simulate emotion, but as I said, I don't actually *feel* them."

"So you're merely going through the motions," Jonathan muttered. "Sort of like me right now."

The ship's AI didn't answer.

Jonathan sent a message to the commander: "Robert, please come to my office."

Robert was already on the bridge and it only took him a few seconds to arrive. When he stepped inside, he opened his mouth to speak, but when he saw Jonathan's face, he pressed his lips together into a grim line.

Jonathan served him a glass. "Have a seat, Commander."

Robert complied, accepting the illegal beverage.

"So." Jonathan took a sip. It was excellent Scotch. "It turns out all the private conversations you and I have had were not in fact private. The admiral had overridden my access control to the AI. Maxwell sent him everything."

"I see," Robert said.

Jonathan grinned wistfully. "In a few moments, Robert, you are going to receive a message from Admiral Knox. If you haven't already."

"I haven't," Robert said.

"In the message," Jonathan continued. "You will see an order for my removal from command and subsequent arrest."

Robert simply stared at Jonathan, saying nothing.

"I expect you to follow this order to the letter," Jonathan finished.

Robert remained quiet for several moments, apparently processing what Jonathan said. Finally: "What about me?"

"I told the admiral you were simply following orders. Which is true. If he arrested you, he'd have to arrest the whole crew. Or at least the department heads. You are to retain your rank and pay grade, but—" Jonathan shook his head. "Unfortunately, the admiral promised there would be a full inquiry regarding your behavior, and other key officers in my crew, when we return to dry dock."

Robert didn't look happy when he heard that. An inquiry likely meant he would lose his position on the *Rampage*. Even if the board found he had done nothing wrong, the very presence of the inquiry on his record would raise eyebrows, and he would find future advancement difficult if not impossible.

"I'm sorry, Robert," Jonathan offered.

An icon indicating a call from the chief master-at-arms, Gary Trevor, appeared on his aReal.

"A moment, Commander." Jonathan accepted the call. He chose the voice-only option.

"Captain," the chief MA sent. "I've just received an order for your arrest. Is this some kind of joke?"

"Unfortunately it's very real, Chief. Check the verification codes."

There was a pause. "They check out," the chief sent. "What do you want me to do?"

"Your duty, of course."

"I can't send men to arrest you."

Jonathan had to smile. The loyalty of his crew was touching. "Then send robots."

Another pause. "Aye sir."

Jonathan terminated the call.

The commander's eyes were distant. "I just received the order from Admiral Knox." He frowned. "What's this? Captain Scott is going to remotely captain the *Callaway* from the *Hurricane*?"

"I was never a big fan of remote captaincy myself," Jonathan said. "Especially when the role involves leading a task unit. Though it might prove beneficial to you—the admiral plans to separate the task units. Once the lag from the *Hurricane* becomes too great, you'll become the de facto captain."

"Wait." Robert's eyes were still defocused. "It also says Scott will arrive in a shuttle once Task Unit Two slows down to delay the enemy."

"Too bad, then," Jonathan said.

Robert shook his head adamantly. He definitely didn't like these orders. He opened his mouth to speak but Jonathan raised an arresting hand before the commander could say something he would regret.

"Remember, the AI," Jonathan told him pointedly.

"But my conscience won't allow me—"

"Your conscience will be clear." Jonathan said. "You're not the one deploying the star killer."

"But I'm protecting it. Indirectly—"

Again Jonathan interrupted him. "No, Robert. You're not responsible, neither directly nor indirectly. The admiral assumes full responsibility for what goes on here. He and his lackeys. Your conscience can rest easy: you're fighting to save the lives of those the admiral foolishly ordered behind. These brave men and women who will be standing against an enemy whose full capabilities remain unknown so far. I'd much rather have you out there acting as first officer than another clueless toady from the *Hurricane*. When this Captain Scott arrives, advise him, and advise him well. I have a feeling he'll be fairly useless."

"You know him?"

"Not at all. Nor do I want to." Jonathan resisted the urge to pull up the associated personnel file. His access had probably been revoked by then anyway.

Robert took a deep drink of the illegal Scotch. "A hundred million lives."

"Don't give up hope," Jonathan said. "Maybe I can find a way to stop the admiral yet."

"Stop the admiral from the brig?" Robert smiled sadly. "The only thing you'll be able to do from there is vegetate in VR."

"I have a few tricks up my sleeve yet," Jonathan said. Though unfortunately he knew Robert was entirely right. He didn't want the man to lose hope, however. The commander would perform better in the upcoming battle if his morale wasn't too low.

"Honestly, I'm actually looking forward to my time in brig," Jonathan mused. "A welcome break from responsibility and accountability. I always planned to retire into VR, you know. There are a few experiences I've been meaning to try for years but have never gotten around to."

"Unless the admiral takes away your aReal," Robert said.

"He wouldn't dare. It's a basic prisoner right."

The hatch to the office opened. It surprised Jonathan—he was used to hearing the entry whistle first and then manually granting access as he saw fit. He would simply have to get used to no longer being in control.

Two MA robots stood in the entrance: box-shaped heads connected to high-grade polycarbonate torsos; blocky arms and legs with circular connecting joints; the subtle whir of servomotors accompanying every movement.

"I'm sorry, sir," one of the robots said. "We're here to escort you to the brig."

Jonathan saw the two human MAs assigned to the bridge hovering close behind the robots. The two men looked at him expectantly, as if waiting for the former captain to give the order to intervene. Other officers on the bridge gazed apprehensively at the open door as if they, too, were trying to decide their own loyalties; the tension was obvious.

"Stand down, men," Jonathan told the loyal MAs.

One of the robots glanced over its shoulder, apparently realizing the precariousness of its situation only then. The two men lowered their gazes, turning away.

"Well, Commander?" Jonathan told Robert. "Are you going to do your job?"

Robert sighed. "This is the worst day of my life."

"Believe me when I say it's even worse for me."

Robert reluctantly stood. "Maxwell, you have seen the order from Admiral Hartford Knox?"

"I have," the computer intoned emotionlessly.

"Make an entry in the log. As of eighteen thirty, standard time, Commanding Officer Jonathan Dallas has been placed under arrest for attempted mutiny and is no longer the captain of the *USS Callaway*. I, Commander Robert Cray, formally assume command until relieved by Captain Scott of the *Hurricane*."

"Command transfer duly noted," Maxwell returned.

Jonathan finished his glass of Scotch and then allowed the MA robots to escort him to the brig without resistance.

sixteen

Jonathan sat cross-legged, meditating. Eight hours had passed since he had been sentenced to the brig, a span of time that had brought the fleet that much closer to battle. Task Unit Two would have separated from the first unit by then, and Captain Scott would be aboard the *Callaway*. Jonathan pitied Robert.

The palm trees bobbed up and down beside him. In the distance, several hot air balloons of differing shapes and sizes dotted the horizon. He had raced one of them in the Annual Exotic Hot Air Balloon competition earlier—a llama-shaped balloon, actually. He'd lost.

Before that, he had spent an hour piloting a microdrone around a realistic depiction of late twenty-first century Shanghai, reconstructed from aerial lightfield footage of the era. He had dodged a butcher's knife as he flew past outdoor slaughterhouses, avoided a wave of passing cyclists intent on running him down, and weaved between the lithe models of a fashion shoot. He would have preferred to walk the area on foot but the confines of the brig weren't conducive to such a leisurely exploration. That particular VR simulation was based on the popular sport of microdrone racing, wherein people flew drones indistinguishable from small bees or moths around populated areas. Tiny cameras attached to equally small gimbals transmitted first-person-view video to the owners. A whole microdrone subculture had developed on Earth and other colony worlds, and racing was just one of the branches. Exploration was another big one. People loved to tour real life places from the comforts of their homes with microdrones, which were limited only by battery power and signal strength. The fact that their little friends participated in the real world, rather than a virtual one, appealed to many.

He had his choice of over a hundred thousand such simulations, from travel to leisure to sports activities. When he was actually sentenced months from now, the programs he would be allowed to run would be restricted to those of the rehabilitation bent. His immersion time would be limited, too. Probably a good thing—he felt the old addiction cravings already.

Jonathan reached down to touch the white sand underneath him and instead of warm grains he felt cold steel. It ruined his sense of presence. He sighed, glancing at the sun. Looking at that molten light in the sky was the easiest way to remind himself of the lie around him, because in virtual reality, the sun didn't hurt the eyes. That was true of both spectacle and contact lens wearers, but not all Implant users—some of the latter devices could transmit the necessary signals directly to the appropriate pain receptors. Thinking on that Jonathan was reminded again, as he often was, of the irony of VR: the lengths humanity would go to avoid reality, only to simulate it in the end.

Jonathan decided he had been in there long enough and shut down the experience. The opaque glass cleared and he found himself staring at the steel bulkheads of the brig.

How did I get here? he wondered. *I can't believe I have come so far, achieved so much, only to end my journey like this.*

He remembered all those years ago when he had sat down with his cousin and mentor, Admiral Ahab Davis.

When he told Ahab he was considering entering the academy, the admiral smiled sadly. "Is that really what you want, son?"

"It is," Jonathan answered him. "It's been my dream ever since I was a boy. I want to command a starship."

Ahab nodded to himself. "Funny thing about dreams: you

have to commit your heart and soul, your entire being, to them. You gotta live your dream every hour of the day. Eat it, breathe it, sleep it. You have to fully dedicate yourself. Achieving that dream might take ten years. It might take twenty. There's a chance even after thirty years, or forty, that you'll never attain it at all. But if you do, son, if you do. Man. I tell you, there isn't a sweeter pleasure in this life than a dream attained. It's what we as a species live for.

"Every one of us has dreams. Every last one. But some sit on the sidelines and do nothing to achieve their goals, and instead watch complacently as others attain theirs. These are happy people, for the most part. And good people, don't get me wrong.

"Others, meanwhile, work and work and work to accomplish their dreams, and still fail. Such individuals eventually become bitter and full of envy, feeling cheated out of what they feel they deserve in life, and take every opportunity to criticize others, and enjoy watching people fall.

"Then there are the rare few who barrel on through the emotional turmoil and self-doubt, fighting tooth and nail with the latter every waking moment, and eventually, against all odds, achieve their dreams. Their drive is insatiable. Nothing can stand in their way. Not tears. Not sorrow. Not blood.

"Every time you find yourself struggling at the academy, be it from the workload, the physical training, or the stress of exams and qualifications, ask yourself how badly you want it. If the answer is: 'more than anything in the world,' then barrel on, Jonathan. Barrel on. Don't be the dreamer. Be the attainer."

Jonathan had taken that advice to heart. He hadn't wanted to live an ordinary life. He had dedicated himself to the captaincy, though the cost had not been cheap. He had lost friends. Distanced himself from family members. Turned down the woman he loved. All in pursuit of the extraordinary.

He had given up everything to attain his dream. He had become a captain, a man respected and followed by others. He had commanded a starship. Lived life on his own terms.

But that dream was gone now.

He heard voices beyond the barred exit. Leaning to the side, he spotted Bridgette, Robert's wife, talking to the sentry on duty. She was a civilian.

Civilians. It had always been controversial to allow families aboard military spacecraft. But because of the nature of space flight, with crew away from home from spans of two to five years, it was considered a small act of kindness to allow one's spouse aboard. Teledildonics and virtual sex only went so far, and reliving past experiences through VR became old quickly. Married couples needed an emotional, realtime bond with their living and breathing partners if they wanted their marriages to work.

Couples were assigned to sleep pods in special shared berths reserved for families. Children were kept in robot-manned nurseries at all times, and parents visited on rotating schedules.

Several of the officers had wives and husbands aboard, Robert included. Jonathan had never married, of course. He had devoted his life to his ship and his crew. While he had no direct offspring, he was probably the father to several hundred children he didn't know about. He had donated sperm years ago to a non-profit, which had sold it to Blackford Fertility Inc., one of the biggest suppliers in the galaxy. He had donated mostly to help the charity—the sperm of officers in captaincy positions sold for a hefty price on the market—but it was also his way of preserving his genetic lineage.

The horizontal bars trapping him in the cell abruptly slid to the side. Bridgette stepped into the compartment, her steel-toed shoes echoing on the deck.

She was only tall enough to reach Jonathan's chest when he was standing. Bright blue eyes peered out from a face of flawless skin. A button nose anchored her features between the dark hair that tumbled down her cheeks in ringlets. A delicate gold chain hung from her slender neck.

She always reminded him, eerily, of the woman he had abandoned on the mountain. She had that same nose, those same blue eyes, and skin so pale it was almost porcelain.

"Hello, Jonathan," she said. The bars sealed behind her as she sat beside him on the bunk.

He nodded slowly. "Bridgette."

"You're moving up in the world," she joked. Or tried to: her eyes belied the worry she felt.

"I am," he agreed. "But this is nothing compared to what I'll have eight months from now. Soon, I'll be living in the penthouse suite of a military penitentiary."

She leaned forward and wrapped a hand around his. "Assuming we survive that long."

"We'll survive," Jonathan said, conscious of the warm touch of her palm. "We're in good hands with Robert up there on the bridge. He'll do a fine job. And he'll be the better for it. Combat: a captain's crucible."

"But he's not even in command," Bridgette complained.

"He might as well be. I don't think our new captain is very experienced. Robert will make sure he doesn't mess things up too badly."

She looked away.

"What is it?" Jonathan said.

"I don't want to be alone when the fighting starts," she said softly.

Jonathan squeezed her palm. "Stay as long as you need."

She slid her hand from his. "There's another reason I came." She glanced toward the barred exit, as if worried the sentry on duty might hear.

"You know the AI is eavesdropping, right?" Jonathan asked her.

"Maxwell already knows what I'm about to confide in you, I'm sure," Bridgette said. "He's able to read the vital signs of everyone aboard."

"Are you sick?" Jonathan said, suddenly concerned.

"In a way." She stared past him. For a moment he thought she was accessing her aReal contact lenses, but he realized she was merely unable to meet his eyes.

"Tell me," Jonathan said.

"You must promise me you won't tell Robert."

Jonathan furrowed his brow. "Are you pregnant or something?"

"You were always good at reading people."

"I would have never made captain if I wasn't. Then again, maybe I'm not so good. After that fiasco of a conference..." He shook his head. "But I'm directing attention away from you. You wanted to talk about your pregnancy."

She smiled. "We can talk about the conference if you want."

"There's nothing to talk about," he said. "The admiral laid a well-planned trap and I stepped right into it."

"What happened between you two on that mountaintop?" Bridgette said. "You've never told me."

Jonathan felt his face grow hot and he looked away.

"Sorry." Bridgette touched his shoulder. "I shouldn't have said anything. You almost died up there."

Jonathan shook her fingers away. "Back to you. You're pregnant. Robert doesn't know."

Bridgette frowned. "Yes, I haven't told him. Because... well, I haven't decided whether I'm going to abort the fetus yet."

"Why would you want to abort such a beautiful creation? The life resulting from the union of a man and woman in love?"

Bridgette exhaled audibly. "It's not as simple as that."

"Then what's the problem? Robert doesn't want children?"

"Robert and I aren't the problem. The baby isn't, even. It's the environment."

Jonathan felt his face crumple in confusion. "The environment."

"I always told myself I'd never raise a ship baby. Being a ship baby myself, I've never wanted to inflict such a cruel punishment on anyone else. Growing up in a steel prison called a nursery, with mostly robots for playmates, with the only relief provided by virtual reality, well, let's just say it wasn't the best way to grow up. It's basically an orphanage on a ship."

Jonathan tapped his lips. "It isn't the best arrangement, I agree. But we're lucky children are allowed on starships at all."

"I became a Vaddict," Bridgette said simply.

Jonathan lowered his gaze.

"What is it?" Bridgette said.

Jonathan sighed. "I was a Vaddict, too, in my youth."

"You had an addiction to VR?" Bridgette said, seeming a little astonished.

Jonathan nodded. "Though I didn't grow up on a ship, I was the shyest, most sheltered person you ever met. VR was the only way I could truly be myself around other people. I tried conquering my anxieties and fears by loading up different therapy programs, but still my brain refused to change. It knew the simulations weren't real. The moment I removed the aReal spectacles and went back to the real world, my anxieties returned. I found myself withdrawing more and more from the real world until I spent almost all my time immersed in VR, disconnecting only to eat, sleep and relieve myself. Eventually I reprogrammed my robot nannies to act as full service units so that I didn't even have to leave VR for the latter purposes."

"You had robot nannies, too?"

"Unfortunately. It's not something I recommend any parent ever do. Letting their children be raised by robot nannies, I mean."

"Exactly," Bridgette said. "See? This is why I don't want to raise my child on a starship. But how did you beat the addiction?"

"I didn't. My mother and father returned home from one of their two year galactic trips and discovered what I had done. They pulled the proverbial plug and sent me off to Vaddict therapy."

Bridgette nodded. "I suffered my fair share of social anxieties growing up shipboard. The worst came when I actually had to step off of a ship for the first time. It was the strangest sensation. Going from such a confined space to a completely open one. What's the opposite of claustrophobia?"

"I'll look it up on my aReal." He started to do just that, but then Bridgette interrupted him.

"Whatever it is," Bridgette said. "It was what I felt in that moment. You'd think all the VR I played would have prepared me for that. Nope. I guess, deep down, my mind knew the virtual environments weren't real. Especially with the chaperone system." That was a VRism that caused the walls of the real world to fade-in whenever someone ventured too close to them while embedded in an immersive virtual environment.

"And yet," Jonathan said. "For all the anxieties and problems caused by your shipboard rearing, you turned out pretty well. If you hadn't had those experiences, you wouldn't have grown into the woman you are today. I say have the child, Bridgette. Let him or her grow up on the ship. Visit daily. Play with the child. Make sure they don't become a Vaddict."

"I don't know..."

"I want you to tell Robert about the baby as soon as the *Callaway* is out of danger," Jonathan said.

"And that brings up another issue I have," Bridgette said. "If you and Robert are right about these ships, that they are alien, the United Systems could be locked into a decades-long war. And even if the attackers prove to be SKs... well, same thing. We're heading toward war. I won't have my child living on some warship, her life constantly hanging by a thread."

"But the nurseries have direct passages to the lifepods," Jonathan argued.

"That's not good enough," Bridgette said.

"Well, can the baby stay with relatives? Or a colonial nursery somewhere?"

Bridgette sighed. "Yes. But then I'd never see her."

"So you'd rather abort the child, *murder* her, than give her a chance at life. Just because you don't want to let the baby grow up on a ship or a colonial nursery."

"That's a little harsh," she crossed her arms below her breasts. "It's only a fetus at this point. Its stem cells haven't even differentiated into specialized organs yet."

"It? Only a moment ago you referred to the baby as *her*."

Bridgette's chin quivered. "I honestly don't know what I'm going to do."

"Come here." Jonathan gave her a hug. "No one really knows what to do when confronted by the big decisions life throws our way. We make our choices as best we can, with the best information available to us, and then we live with the consequences. It's called life, Bridgette. Something you are about to give to another human being. I urge you not to take that life away. Allow her to experience the joys and sorrows of being human."

Jonathan's mind drifted to the enemy ships that were bearing down upon them at that very moment.

"Allow her to fight," he finished, knowing that humanity might need every last man, woman and child in the dark days to come.

seventeen

Robert studied the tactical display. The members of Task Unit Two had assumed defense pattern delta: The lightly-armored *Marley*, *Selene*, and *Grimm* resided at the center of the imaginary arrowhead formed by the *Callaway*, *Aurelia*, *Maelstrom*, *Dagger*, and *Linea*. The former trio was stacked vertically, each vessel a hundred kilometers apart. The latter defenders were spaced at intervals of roughly five hundred kilometers, with the *Callaway* at the center, and the other four taking up different positions to the port, starboard, dorsal, and ventral quarters.

Robert didn't care so much about the survival of the *Selene*, but the *Grimm* might be needed to scrounge geronium from the gas giants, while the *Marley* was required to build the return Gate. That latter ship must survive at all costs.

Task Unit One was escorting the *Fortitude* and *Hurricane* four hundred thousand kilometers behind them. Ahead, the enemy vessels were nine hundred thousand kilometers away and closing.

Robert pinged Lieutenant Harv Boroker, the chief weapons engineer. "Status update on the Avenger upgrades?"

"We just finished retrofitting the charged field tech into the four human-manned Avengers," the lieutenant returned.

"Right down to the wire," Robert said.

"Indeed. The fields should allow the fighters to close to

within a thousand meters of individual enemy ships. If the Avengers get any closer than that, the fields won't be able to dissipate any incoming beams—the particles are far too intense at that range, at least going on the data recorded from the previous battle. The best strategy at that range is simple avoidance, which should hopefully be easy once they get in that close."

"Thanks, Lieutenant." Robert tapped out Harv and turned to Captain Scott. "The lead Avengers have been upgraded with the charge field technology."

The captain stifled a yawn. "That's nice."

"We're going to need them in the coming battle," Robert said pointedly.

Scott glanced at him arrogantly. "I don't think so. Let me tell you a thing or two about space battles. Combat in the void is performed at a distance. We fire mortars to guide the target, hemming it in. Then we finish the job with kinetic kill missiles and nukes. Fighters and their pilots are a thing of the distant past. I'm not sure why we even have them on starships anymore, other than to appear menacing to the enemy."

"Respectfully, sir, tactics you learned in a simulation aren't going to cut it in the real world."

Scott's face abruptly darkened. "If I want your opinion, I'll ask for it," he spat. "In the meantime, keep your mouth shut."

Touchy.

Robert was about to protest but thought better of it. He would have to choose his battles. The man's leadership style was diametrically opposite Jonathan's. He was the kind of captain most recruits dreaded being assigned to back in the academy: a morale-killing commanding officer whose close-mindedness and dictatorial decisions would make anyone who served under him dread waking up each day. Robert knew a handful of astronauts who'd left the space navy as bitter men because of such officers. In the current situation, such poor leadership traits could very well lead to the eventual demise of those who served under him. Robert would have to watch Scott very carefully.

But what the hell am I supposed to do if he won't listen to me?

"Captain, enemy vessels have entered extreme effective

range of our weapons," Tactical Officer Miko announced when the targets reached the seven hundred thousand kilometer mark.

"Order the task unit to fire the preprogrammed mortar and missile spread," Scott said eagerly.

"Firing preprogrammed mortar and missile spread flotilla-wide," Miko said.

"Watch," Scott told Robert. "This battle is going to be over long before the enemy closes. Want to take bets on the range?"

"That's all right," Robert said.

On the tactical display, yellow dots representing mortars funneled out from the defenders, creating three concentric rings. A moment later, kinetic kill missiles joined the fray, forming a smaller funnel. Lastly came the nukes, traveling straight down the middle toward the enemy.

It was a common enough tactic. Yet in Robert's opinion, Scott had fired far too soon.

Sure enough, Miko announced: "Enemy ships are making a course correction. They've altered their trajectory to avoid the mortars."

"Fire another batch, then," Scott said. "Herd them back toward our missiles."

Miko glanced up. "Sir, I don't think—"

"I said fire!" A stream of spittle oozed down Scott's chin.

"Firing another round of mortars."

Once more the targets slightly altered course.

"Sir—" Miko began.

"I see it!" Scott said. At least he didn't order another wasteful launch.

Ten minutes later Ensign Lewis announced: "I'm reading a course change in five of the vessels. It looks like they're breaking away."

"Tactical, any idea what they're planning?" Scott said.

"Could be a possible flanking maneuver," Miko answered. "Orders?"

"Hold the task unit in position."

After several minutes, Ensign Lewis announced: "I'm detecting a thermal buildup from the first group."

Robert had the external video feed displayed in the upper

right of his aReal. A momentary flash filled it.

"We just lost the initial wave of missiles and nukes," Miko said. "First group of enemy vessels is altering trajectory slightly. Possibly to avoid the missile debris."

A few moments later the flash repeated, and the second wave of missiles vanished, with the target trajectories of the first group once more updating to skirt any debris.

At the six hundred thousand kilometer mark Miko announced: "First group is coming to a halt relative to the flotilla. Sensor readings indicate one capital ship and two smaller vessels."

Robert used his credentials to authorize an optical zoom on the external video feed. At the limits of the optics, the zoom switched to digital. With the "targeting helper" he focused on the enemy ships; they had remained relatively close together within a ten kilometer span.

The box ship towered over the other two. The first of the smaller crafts was a replica of the dart-shaped vessel the task unit had encountered before. The second was an odd-looking cylindrical ship.

"Second group is altering course," Miko announced. "They're arcing inward, returning to their original trajectory. Looks like it wasn't a flanking maneuver after all."

On the 3D display, the estimated trajectory of the second group updated. The breakaway vessels would pass within two hundred thousand kilometers off the starboard side of the task unit. It was obvious they intended to intercept the first unit, led by Admiral Knox.

"Have every ship launch kinetic kills toward the second group," Scott said. "Three per ship."

"Launching kinetic kill missiles."

One of the enemy vessels from the first group thrust forward away from the others. It was the cylindrical ship. The two flat ends had irised open, so that the vessel appeared to be a thin, hollow tube. Though perhaps not entirely hollow: the stars beyond the tube were distorted slightly, hinting at a lens, or multiple lenses, inside.

Robert extended his noise canceler around Scott so the bridge crew wouldn't hear what he was about to say. "If I might make a suggestion. We should send the fighters in. Launch a round of mortars with them. Let the Avengers hide behind the rocks, use them as shields. Then—"

Scott jerked his head rapidly toward him, his features twisted in rage. "If you ever lecture me on tactics again, I will relieve you of duty!"

Robert gaped at the man. He couldn't believe what he was hearing. "It was only a suggestion—"

"I don't care what it was! Not another word from you."

Robert wished he hadn't activated the noise canceler after all. The crew needed to know what kind of buffoon was in command.

He glanced at the other officers of the Round Table. More than a few had been watching and they quickly looked away when his eyes met theirs. They probably had some sense of what had transpired from Scott's body language alone. Good.

"We'll wait until it comes closer," Scott continued. "Then we'll fire missiles again. In the meantime, I expect you to keep your useless thoughts to yourself."

Robert put on his best obsequious smile. The one he used when a commanding officer made him fetch coffee.

After several minutes, the cylindrical ship passed the five hundred thousand kilometer mark from the task unit. On the 3D display a new red-colored dot suddenly appeared. It was stationary, as if ejected from the cylindrical ship.

Robert used the targeting helper to zoom in on the new object.

The cylindrical ship had deposited a circular ring segment from its own length. The telltale distortion of the stars beyond indicated it held a lens of some kind.

"What the hell is that?" Scott said. "The SKs never used anything like this before. Ops?"

"If I had to guess, I would say it was a telescope of some kind," Ensign Lewis said. "Either that, or some kind of refocusing device."

"Refocusing device? For what?"

"I don't know," she told him. "A laser, maybe?"

Robert picked out tinier objects around the cylindrical ship. He hadn't spotted them before.

"Ops, what are those objects escorting the lead ship?" Robert said, ignoring the glare from Scott that followed.

"They appear to be smaller versions of the dart ship," Lewis said. "A fighter escort?"

"They're about the same size as our own fighters," Miko added. "Twenty strong. They must have been hiding behind the cylinder, blending their heat signatures with the vessel to mask their approach."

Using a variation of the same tactic I wanted to employ against them, Robert thought bitterly.

"What do you want to do, Captain?" Miko said.

Launch fighters!

"Hold," Scott said.

The cylindrical ship continued its approach, depositing a ring segment every one hundred thousand kilometers.

When it was two hundred fifty thousand kilometers away, Miko announced: "Our kinetic kills are closing with the second group."

The second target group was two hundred thousand klicks to starboard, according to the tactical display.

"Detecting a thermal buildup from the second group," Ensign Lewis said.

There was a flash on the video feed.

"We just lost the missiles," Miko said. "The second group is altering course slightly to avoid the debris. They're continuing past us toward Task Unit One."

"Damn it," Scott said.

The lead ship deposited a fourth ring segment at the two hundred thousand kilometer mark. That looked to be the final separation, gauging by the thickness—the lead segment was now the same length as all the previous ones.

After a few minutes the lead segment halted.

"How far away is the object?" Scott asked.

"A hundred thousand kilometers," Miko said. "That makes five segments, spaced at one hundred thousand kilometer intervals in front of the first enemy group."

"I can count," Scott said.

Ensign Lewis suddenly straightened. "I'm detecting a thermal buildup from both ships in the first group!"

Thin white lines instantly appeared on the 3D display, sourced from the capital ship and the smaller dart vessel, six hundred thousand kilometers away. The lines converged on the closest ring segment, forming a single line that connected all five rings and terminated on the *Callaway*.

"Captain!" Ensign Lewis said urgently. "An infrared laser is boring into our nose!"

Scott stared blankly at Lewis.

"Captain, your orders?" Miko said.

Robert only waited half a second longer.

"Hard to port!" the commander said.

"Hard to port," the helmsman repeated.

The incoming laser remained active for ten agonizing seconds while the *Callaway* fired starboard thrusters at full power and struggled to veer out of the deadly beam's path. Robert heard the disturbing groan of metal as the ship's frame distributed the sudden force acting upon it. Inertial stabilizers prevented the Gs caused by such a hard turn from wiping the bulkheads with the insides of the crew.

The laser finally vanished from the display.

"Ensign," Robert said, ignoring Scott beside him. "Damage report."

"The laser cut a concentrated runnel through a relatively unimportant section of our nose, just outside cargo bay six," Ensign Lewis said. "It appears the laser micro-corrected, compensating for our movements, so that the shot remained focused on a small area even while we evaded. The outer Whittle layer in that area completely boiled away, and the laser penetrated six meters into the hull underneath."

"How thick is the hull in that area?"

"Seven meters, sir."

Robert shook his head. "Only a single meter separating us from a hull breach. Continue firing starboard thrusters. I want our fore facing away from that thing. How long until the repair swarm can patch the damage?"

"They'll have the Whittle layer reapplied in an hour." The Whittle layer was a thin segment of reinforced metal elevated a meter above the actual hull; it was meant to reduce the damage caused by micrometeors. "But the actual hole in the hull?

Something like that will take at least a full standard day of 3D printing to repair. Probably closer to thirty-six hours."

If an actual hull breach had occurred, the small machines would have sealed the outside first and then worked inward, reattaching any wiring and other conduits along the way, then 3D-printing superheated metal into the missing portions of the hull frame.

Robert studied the tactical display. He was tempted to try launching a nuke at the laser array, but decided the enemy would simply sacrifice one of their fighters to intercept it.

"Lieutenant Commander Albright, are you watching this?" Robert said.

"I am, sir," a hologram of the space wing commander appeared in the middle of the bridge, between the circle of inward facing stations.

"I hear you have some upgraded fighters for me," Robert told the man.

"I do indeed," Albright returned.

"Prepare to scramble both squadrons," Robert said. "I want that laser array and its fighter escort taken out. I'll instruct the task unit to launch a bunch of mortars. I want your fighters to dive in behind them and cut power. Use them for cover. With luck, the enemy won't realize their presence until too late."

"Both squadrons are ready to scramble, Commander." Albright's hologram said. "Waiting on the order."

"Miko, have the fleet launch a round of mortars at the lead laser segment. Fire when ready."

"Firing," Miko returned.

The yellow dots representing the mortars appeared on the 3D display.

"Albright, scramble fighters," Robert said.

"Scrambling fighters." Albright's hologram blinked out.

Seconds later sixteen blue dots representing two squadrons of fighters appeared on the display. The *Callaway's* full complement of Avengers moved behind the different yellow dots, matching the trajectory and speed of the associated mortars, and cut power.

The *Aurelia*, *Dagger*, and *Linea* had a single squadron of Avengers each aboard, but Robert decided to keep those in reserve for the moment. Meanwhile the frigate, *Maelstrom*, had no fighters, nor did the *Selene*, *Grimm*, or *Marley*.

"I'm detecting a burst of highly directional gamma radiation from the dart ship in group one," Ensign Lewis said. "It's aimed at our hull wound. Radiation levels are elevated in cargo bay six behind it."

"How far is the radiation penetrating?"

Lewis paused. "It seems contained to that specific area."

"Maxwell, evacuate any service personnel from the cargo bay six area and have them report to sick bay."

"Evacuating eight personnel," Maxwell said.

"And helm, get our nose turned away from the enemy!"

"Working on it," the helmsman replied.

Robert had forgotten about Scott, who had remained motionless the whole time beside him. The man's eyes were defocused, consumed by whatever it was he was seeing on his contact lens aReal.

"Captain Scott," Robert said. "You are relieved. Petty Officer, please escort this useless mound of flesh from the bridge."

Petty Officer Connolly, the master-at-arms guarding the inner bridge door, stepped forward and extended a hand toward Scott.

"Where should I put him?" the MA asked.

That was a good question.

The *Callaway* was operating under Condition Zebra, which ensured the hatches and scuttles that subdivided the cruiser into many smaller airtight compartments were sealed, preventing the entire ship from explosively decompressing in a breach scenario. Scott would be able to return to his quarters, but Connolly would have to override every hatch along the way, leaving the bridge unguarded in the meantime. The MA would also have to inform the Damage Control spaces of his planned route beforehand.

"Put him in the passageway," Robert said. "Out of my sight."

Scott numbly allowed the MA to lead him from the bridge.

Good riddance.

"Thermal buildup!" Ensign Lewis announced. She looked

up. "They're firing their main laser array again. It's digging into our forward starboard side."

"Helm, keep turning," Robert said. "I want an unblemished hull section facing them the next time they fire."

After ten seconds the pulse dissipated.

"Damage report?"

"As before, the laser micro-compensated for our rotation, concentrating on the same spot." Miko looked up. "Either they got lucky, or they knew where to fire."

"What do you mean?" Robert asked.

"They struck our Vipers. Two laser turrets were melted out of existence, and a feedback loop shorted out the entire bank on the starboard side. We won't be able to fire starboard Vipers until engineering can get a repair crew down there."

"You really think the bastards knew where to fire?" Robert said.

Miko made a swiping gesturing, usually indicative of data access on an aReal. "The alien ship that's guarding the exit Slipstream likely recorded our previous encounter. They saw us fire the Viper broadsides, and know what those turrets are capable of at short ranges. Though I do wonder why they didn't hit the turrets on the nose in their initial laser strike."

"Their first shot was exploratory, likely." Robert rubbed his earlobe. "Launch a couple of mortars from starboard tubes. Slow speed. Put something between our hull and that laser before the next strike. See if you can place the mortars to protect critical systems."

"I'll see what Maxwell can come up with," Miko said. A moment later: "Launching four mortars."

A prompt appeared on Robert's display. It was Maxwell requesting permission to override helm control.

"Helm, I'm giving Maxwell the controls momentarily."

The AI took the helm and fired thrusters to adjust the pitch and yaw of the ship so that the slowly drifting mortars would act as an appropriate shield for critical systems.

Robert pulled up the weapon readiness display. The undamaged Vipers were fully charged. Mag-rail point defenses were locked and loaded. Similar readings were displayed for the other ships in the task unit.

"How much damage can our Vipers cause to that laser array from here?" Robert said.

"At a hundred thousand kilometers," Miko said. "The lead segment of the array is well beyond the range limits of the heavy lasers."

"Damn. Instruct all ships to fire a couple of bursts from their mag-rails at the lead segment. Let's see how the laser array reacts."

"One of the mortars is obstructing our own mag-rails on that side," Miko said. "But I can certainly have the other ships in the task unit fire."

"Do it," Robert said.

Each ship would have to rely upon the AIs to aim at that distance, as the weapons were meant for point defense.

"Slugs released across all vessels," Miko said. "They should reach the enemy ship in approximately fifteen minutes."

The laser array fired again, easily eating through one of the mortars and then striking another two Viper turrets.

"Miko, replace that mortar," Robert said.

"Aye sir."

"And instruct the *Aurelia*, *Maelstrom*, *Dagger*, and *Linea* to form a line in front of the *Callaway*. We're going to take turns bearing the brunt of that laser."

Miko relayed his orders and the specified ships in the task unit began to close with the *Callaway*.

"Members of Task Unit One are breaking off to engage the second group of alien attackers," Ensign Lewis announced.

Robert glanced at the 3D display. The second group was well on the way to the *Fortitude* and her escorts. Two destroyers, the *Devastator* and the *Halberd*, had separated to take on the enemy. A part of Robert wanted those aliens to stop the admiral.

He focused his attention on the blue dots of the Avenger squadrons, which slowly approached the laser array behind the mortar screen. The *Callaway's* fighters were about twenty thousand kilometers from the lead segment. So far, the enemy fighters had made no move to intercept.

Good luck, pilots, Robert thought.

He braced himself as the laser array fired again.

eighteen

Wolf sat tensely in the cockpit of the Avenger. The bodysuit felt tighter than usual. Another subtle reminder that this was not a simulation.

He sensed rather than saw the presence of Lin Akido, his copilot, beside him. He didn't see his own body, of course, nor any part of the cockpit. He floated disembodied in deep space behind the mortar, the backdrop of stars motionless beyond it. The large rock itself seemed stationary—the only reason Wolf knew he was moving forward was because of the stream of simulated particles that indicated his motion vector.

He glanced at the virtual rear-view mirror. Behind him, three AI-operated fighters were lined up in single file. Far to his right, the other manned fighter in Orange Squadron, piloted by Jeremy Walker and his copilot Tim Brown, hid behind another mortar; they were also at the head of three drones. The two wings of Red Squadron weren't visible to the naked eye, but according to the HUD map they resided behind similar mortars to the left.

The manned Avengers leading each drone wing had been equipped with the charged field enhancements, though that would prove useless against any enemy lasers. So far, however, the enemy had ignored the incoming mortars entirely.

He sensed Lin shifting beside him.

"We're in range," she said.

It was time.

"Walker, prepare to engage," Wolf said over the comm.

The mortar directly ahead of the fighter abruptly broke apart.

Wolf applied dorsal thrust and dove underneath the debris. He tilted the nose upward and used the AI to line up against the distant target that had presented itself—one of the enemy fighters had separated from the array. No, three of them, according to the HUD.

Wolf fired one of the six Hellfire X90 missiles that came standard with each Avenger. He followed that up with a Cobra strike—the extremely short range laser the Avenger had aboard.

The X90 detonated halfway to the enemy fighter.

"What happened?" Wolf said.

"Looks like the fighter fired a laser," Lin said. "Took out the missile."

The controls abruptly pulled downward.

"The AI detected incoming laser fire and issued evasive maneuvers to protect the hull," Lin said, explaining the sudden dive.

Wolf turned the nose toward the enemy.

"Incoming slugs..." Lin said.

Wolf launched a volley of mag-rails toward the enemy fighter and issued evasive maneuvers. The drones in his wing fired their own Cobras at the enemy.

More of the enemy fighters came in, forcing the drones to separate.

Wolf closed with the target and what followed was a heated laser and mag-rail exchange. While the AI handled the tactical maneuvers necessary to evade the incoming lasers, he controlled the general trajectory of the Avenger and the weapons. He had "target help" turned on for the mag-rails, meaning that he had merely to stare at his given target, squeeze the trigger, and the guns would properly lead the target.

He passed close to one of the fighters. The enemy hulls were hued slightly golden. Twin noses separated by three meters protruded from the front, ending in spherical humps where they joined the main body. Long tubes hung underneath the ventral area—likely the enemy's laser and mag-rail equivalents. There weren't any obvious missile hardpoints. The aft section folded back on four sides into a pyramid-like point where the thrust emerged.

"Lin," Wolf said. "Instruct two of the drones to break away, and concentrate on the laser array."

"On it," Lin answered. A moment later: "There's still an escort of twelve fighters around the array. It—" She paused. "We just lost both fighters."

"Damn it. Send a boy to do a man's job…"

He launched an X90 at his current target and reversed course, heading toward the starboard side of the array. It swarmed with fighters.

"There are too many of them," Lin said.

Two of the fighters thrust toward him. The HUD indicated that the other fighter behind him had turned around, evaded the X90, and was hot on his tail.

"Slugs incoming…" Lin said.

Wolf heaved hard to the right. The inertial compensators took a millisecond to kick in, and he felt a moment of stomach-churning Gs. If those compensators were ever damaged, the fight was basically over.

The pursuing enemy banked behind him, also avoiding the slugs.

He spun his nose toward the laser segment and fired the Cobra.

"We're too far away," Lin said. "You caused barely a scratch on the array."

"Walker, cover me," he said. He dove the Avenger toward the array, wanting to close the range. Three enemy fighters from the swarm abruptly converged in his path and fired mag-rails. Wolf was forced to abandon the attack run.

Two more dots blinked out on the display, these attributed to Red Squadron. Drones, luckily.

So far the good guys were down by four fighters and had taken out none of the enemy.

It wasn't looking good.

Robert stared at the tactical display. The *Callaway, Aurelia,*

Maelstrom, *Dagger*, and *Linea* had formed a queue before the long range weapon; after the laser array fired, the leading task unit ship would jockey out of position and navigate to the rear of the queue. Behind them, the *Selene*, *Grimm* and *Marley* had similarly lined up, though they did not participate in the rotation.

It was the *Callaway's* turn at the front once again. They had rotated their aft section to face the enemy, with a few strategically placed mortars to protect their thruster vents.

"The array segments are moving to the right slightly," Ensign Lewis announced. "Edging out of the way of the mag-rail slugs we fired ten minutes ago."

"Miko, update me on the Avengers."

"Our sensors grossly underestimated the number of enemy fighters," Miko said. "Apparently they were flying too close together to show up as distinct units on the thermal band. But now that the Avengers are out there, it's apparent our squadrons are outnumbered three to one."

"Have the *Aurelia*, *Dagger*, and *Linea* launch their reserve squadrons," Robert said. "I want them out there and lending whatever aid they can."

"Aye sir," Miko said.

Robert watched as twenty-four new blue dots appeared on the tactical display, eight each launched from their respective vessels. Would it be enough?

"I need options, people," Robert said. "A backup plan in case our fighters fail."

"We could close to Viper range with the first segment?" Ensign Lewis said.

"If that laser can eat through six meters of hull at one hundred thousand kilometers," Robert said. "I'd hate to see what it could do under twenty thousand."

"Launch a few backup kinetic kill weapons," Miko said. "Give the first segment and its fighter escort a wide berth, and target the second and third segments instead. With the Avengers providing a distraction, maybe our missiles can sneak past without any of the enemy fighters noticing."

"Do it," Robert said. "But have the *Dagger* and *Linea* launch the missiles. The *Callaway* has already wasted enough kinetics of her own."

"Enemy is firing laser array again," Ensign Lewis said. "Direct hit to hull section eighty-five. We have a breach."

"Damage report?" Robert said.

"The aft sections of decks five and six are exposed to space. Ten crew members reported missing."

"Albright!" Robert shouted over the comm. "Get rid of that laser!"

"My pilots are working on it," the space wing commander returned.

The fighting was hopeless out there. Every time Wolf or one of the others attempted to close with the laser array, four or five enemy fighters moved to block their path. He had tried sending in two drones from different directions, and then coming in from a third attack vector himself, but every single time the enemy crafts moved to intercept him.

On the third such attack run, Wolf noticed a pattern while he fled. Or at least he thought he did.

Coordinating with Walker, he tried another run. He turned away when the enemies came at him and he evaded for seven seconds. On cue, the fighters reversed course to protect the array.

Seven seconds. When engaging an Avenger, the enemy always pursued for seven seconds before turning back to protect the array.

He revealed his findings to Lin.

"You and your patterns," Lin said. "You saw how well your reliance on them worked out for us the last time."

"But that was a simulation," Wolf said.

"Exactly," Lin returned. "Things are a bit different in real life."

"Are they?"

"Your plan relies on two assumptions," Lin said. "The first, that the AIs will repeat the pattern. The second, that every alien fighter is AI operated. If one or both assumptions are false, it won't work."

"I'm open to other options," Wolf said. When she didn't say anything, he added: "That's what I thought."

He tapped in Walker, as well as Trent, leader of Red Squadron. "Here's what we're going to do ladies and gents."

Robert watched the blue dots of the Avengers struggle against the red. The relief squadrons were still fifty thousand kilometers away. Another blue dot vanished.

We're going to lose the Callaway's *two squadrons*, he thought bitterly.

He directed his attention to the first task unit. The enemy had left behind a dart ship to deal with the *Devastator* and *Halberd*, while the remaining alien vessels in the second group continued toward the *Fortitude* and *Hurricane*. The supercarrier had launched several nukes and missiles escorted by fighter wings. Robert watched the small dots representing those Avengers close with one of the pursuers. The enemy must have fired its particle beam, because several of those blue dots winked out, including that of the lead Avenger. The range was five thousand kilometers. The chief weapons engineer of the *Hurricane* hadn't upgraded any of the Avengers with charged fields, then, despite the guidelines Harv had sent out. The fool. Other Avengers from the *Hurricane* were lost when the enemy detonated the nukes the fighters escorted.

A flashing alert drew Robert's attention to the battle closer at hand.

"Some of the enemy fighters are breaking off to intercept the kinetic kill missiles we launched against the second segment twenty minutes ago," Miko said.

"So much for sneaking past them while they're distracted," Robert muttered.

Miko looked up. "We lost the missiles."

Wolf tapped his feet impatiently inside the bodysuit. He was drifting in space, so far unmolested, biding his time some five kilometers from the port side of the array. It was the closest he could get without drawing any unwanted attention from the enemy.

He wished the focusing mirrors in the Avengers were bigger, but there was nothing he could do to improve the extremely short range of the Cobras. He was tempted to fire a stream from the mag-rails, but he knew the array would readily move aside at that range. And while it might disrupt any shots the array had planned, the device would inevitably survive. No, he had to wait until he had the perfect shot lined up.

On the starboard and dorsal sides of the array, all of the remaining Avengers in Orange and Red Squadrons swooped in at the same time, firing Cobras at different alien fighters to draw their attention and then fleeing as the enemy intercepted and pursued. Wolf waited. Unfortunately three of the enemy fighters chose to remain behind to protect the array.

The next attack run, the same three fighters remained behind. They simply refused to leave the array unprotected.

I was wrong, Wolf thought.

And then those three enemy fighters abruptly broke away, heading out into deep space. Wolf wasn't sure why, at first, but then he realized they were moving off to engage the kinetic kill missiles the task unit had apparently launched at one of the more distant segments.

Thank you, Captain!

He slammed down on the thrust. He had already wasted two of the seven seconds waiting for those three ships to move off.

"Fire an X90?" Lin said.

"Not yet."

He closed to within one kilometer, punching past two of the enemy as they struggled to turn around and engage him.

"The X90," Lin said urgently.

"Not yet."

Five hundred meters.

Wolf fired an X90.

Three hundred meters.

He pointed the nose upward and engaged the thrust so he wouldn't slam into the array. Then he swung the nose back down and fired the Cobra during the flyby, prepping the impact site for the X90.

A flash came as the missile struck the array.

The Avenger abruptly shuddered and was sent into a tailspin. An alert sounded.

"Report!"

"We've been hit by slugs from the pursuing fighters!" Lin

said.

"Countermeasures!"

Wolf swung his body hard to port. The outline of the nose ghosted over his display—but the ship refused to respond to his motions.

"We've lost all control," Lin said. "We're drifting helplessly through space."

"AI!" Wolf said. "Take over."

No response.

"Did we get it at least?" Wolf shut his eyes: the spinning stars were making him dizzy.

"We did." Lin said.

"Thank—"

The cockpit shuddered again and the inertial compensators abruptly deactivated. His body was racked by G forces. He gritted his teeth, his lips curling into a rictus. He tried to say Lin's name but his features were completely frozen and only a grunt emerged.

He blacked out shortly thereafter.

Robert stared at the tactical display in disbelief.

"Sir," Ensign Lewis said. "The first segment of the laser array is down!"

They'd done it.

Well done pilots!

"Enemy fighters are breaking away from the wreckage," Miko announced. "They're headed toward us."

Robert nodded slowly. "They're going to make a strafing run." He glanced at the second wave of Avengers on the display. The fighters were still twenty thousand kilometers away from the main group. "Recall all Avengers. We're going to need them protecting the task unit."

"Recalling Avengers."

Robert watched the blue dots of the *Callaway's* squadrons pursue the red on the display. Those Avengers quickly lost ground, moving significantly slower than the alien fighters. Meanwhile, the enemy was gaining on the retreating squadrons from the *Aurelia, Dagger,* and *Linea.*

"Instruct the second wave of Avengers to intercept and engage the enemy when they come within range," Robert said.

Miko echoed his orders.

"Sir," Ensign Lewis said. "The two targets from group one have started accelerating. They're on an intercept course with the task unit."

Robert studied the computed trajectories of the box ship and the dart ship.

"Can we outrun them?" Robert asked.

"Negative," Miko replied.

"Status on the remaining segments of the laser array?" Robert said.

"The pieces are drifting. Looks like they're abandoning the weapon."

"Let's hope so." Robert rubbed his ear lobe. "When the main enemy ships reach the two hundred thousand kilometer mark, launch a round of mortars fleet-wide. I want a noose ten kilometers in diameter around them by the time the vessels reach the fifty thousand kilometer mark. Deploy five kinetic kills and three nukes along with the mortars, timed to arrive at the same time. Separate the missiles by ten kilometers each on the Y-Z plane, within the mortar noose. Let's see how well their point defenses handle that. Oh and, none of those weapons are to come from the *Callaway*. We're already running low as it is."

Fresh yellow dots appeared on the display, indicating the weapon launches.

A moment later the red dots of the enemy fighters passed right through the blues from the second Avenger group. Two blues vanished from the display. All the reds remained intact. The blues pursued. The first wave of Avengers was about five thousand kilometers behind them.

According to the latest estimates on the HUD, the enemy fighters would arrive a good seven minutes ahead of the pursuing Avengers.

Robert shook his head. Perhaps he should have kept some of the fighters in reserve after all.

I'm not cut out for command, he thought.

He considered tapping in Jonathan so that the real captain could command the task unit from the brig, but under the current state of affairs, Maxwell would only countermand the order. The damn intermixing of AIs into the chain of command.

He took a deep breath. *I can do this.*

He watched the enemy fighters pass the twenty thousand kilometer mark.

"Have all capable ships rotate their noses ninety degrees," Robert told Miko. "I want our port Vipers facing those fighters. Instruct each vessel to target one enemy each. Prepare to fire on my command."

Miko echoed his orders.

When the enemy fighters reached the ten thousand kilometer mark, Robert said: "Fire broadsides."

At that distance, the concentrated laser broadside from the *Callaway* would have a spot area of four centimeters squared. At one hundred percent charge, that equaled a combined intensity of one hundred megajoules per pulse, with three pulses in total firing. Enough to eat through a meter of hull material in an ordinary ship, it would definitely cause some major damage to a fighter.

The five able vessels in the task unit concentrated on one target each. On the 3D display, white lines instantaneously joined each ship to a corresponding red dot. The lines vanished a half second later—a timeframe not indicative of the nanosecond lengths of the pulses themselves. When those white lines disappeared, the red dots they had struck went with them.

"Five enemy fighters eliminated," Miko said.

"And only another forty-two to go," Robert said sourly. "How long will it take to bring the nose projectors to bear?"

"About four minutes," Miko said. "But we only have five Vipers on the nose. We'll do the same damage with the half-charged port Vipers if we maintain our current orientation."

"All right. Maintain current orientation. Prepare to fire at the four minute mark. Target two enemies per ship this time." Since the range would cause the intensity to shoot up by four times, Robert was confident the task unit members could take down two enemies each by that point. "Fire on my mark."

Four minutes later the red dots reached the fifteen hundred

kilometer range.

"Fire broadsides," Robert said.

Ten white lines appeared on the display.

"Two enemy fighters eliminated," Miko said.

"Only two?" Robert demanded.

"They're adapting," Miko said. "I believe whatever AIs are aboard those ships detected the rise in thermal temperature preceding our blast, and initiated evasive maneuvers. As our own fighters would do."

"Damn it."

The red dots closed to within a thousand kilometers.

"Enemy fighters are dispersing," Miko said. "It looks like they're dividing their forces equally among our five warships. Eight per vessel."

"Fire point defenses at will," Robert said.

Eight red dots reached the *Callaway*. The bridge shuddered as the enemy fighters made a strafing run.

The mag-rail point defenses fired, as did the undamaged laser turrets with charge remaining. Perhaps unsurprisingly, none of the red dots indicating the enemy fighters disappeared.

"What's going on, Miko?" Robert said.

"The fighters are dodging the mag-rail slugs. And at this range our lasers are only scoring partial hits, nicking the surfaces of their hulls. Their fast maneuverability isn't helping matters."

"I can see why our Avengers had so much trouble with them," Robert said.

The bridge stopped shuddering when the last of the red dots had passed.

"Damage report!" Robert said.

"We have breaches on decks eleven, twelve, thirty-two, thirty-three, and cargo bay five," Lewis said. "Twenty-three crew members missing and presumed dead."

"Four of the fighters are looping back to make another run at the *Callaway*." Miko paused. "However, the other four are continuing toward the *Selene*, *Grimm*, and *Marley*. The same thing is happening with the other four warships—half the enemy fighters are breaking away toward the latter ships."

"Damn it," Robert said. "They're going after the very ships

we were trying to protect. Order half of the Avengers to give chase when they arrive. In the meantime, have the able warships charge up their starboard broadsides and fire at the receding enemy fighters when the Vipers reach fifty percent. Let's see if we can take down a few more of the bastards before they reach our wards. Which two ships are the fastest in our unit?"

"That would be the *Dagger* and *Linea*, sir."

"Dispatch both ships to give them a hand." The bridge shook as the fighters made another run. "And keep firing the damn point defenses!"

"Sir," Lewis announced. "We have breaches on decks eight to ten, and nineteen to twenty-two."

An alert flashed on Robert's aReal.

Intruder. Intruder. Intruder.

"What the hell is going on!" Robert said. "Ops?"

"One of the fighters crashed into the *Callaway*," Lewis said breathlessly. "The craft aimed for a hull breach and wedged itself inside. Sensors are reporting an alien intruder on deck ten."

"Do we have a visual?"

"Negative," Lewis said. "Power is out in that section."

"Damn it," Robert said. "Dispatch the security forces immediately. I want MOTHs down there. Contain the intruder!"

"Dispatching security forces," Lewis said.

"Please tell me we don't have any critical systems on deck ten."

"No, but—" Ensign Lewis looked up urgently. "That's where the brig is."

nineteen

Jonathan gripped Bridgette's hand in the darkness. The power was completely out in the brig, and the dim illumination from the emergency lights outside didn't reach them. The comm nodes were inactive, rendering their aReals useless.

"Are we going to die?" Bridgette said.

"Shh," Jonathan said. "Listen. It's gotten louder."

A soft sound issued continuously in the background, a noise similar to the hiss of air from a pneumatic tire.

"It seems the same to me," Bridgette said.

"Sentry?" Jonathan said. "Are you back yet? Sentry?"

The cell shuddered, and the terrible sound of moaning metal momentarily reverberated throughout the passageway.

A moment later he heard footsteps. A cone of illumination lit the passageway beyond the bars.

"Found a flashlight in the tool closet," the sentry said. "The neighboring compartment is definitely breached. The atmosphere is venting. Though the breach is minor for now, I don't think it's going to remain that way for long. We have to get the two of you suited up."

Jonathan heard the metallic thud as the sentry lowered the outer access panel so that he could manually retract the door bars. That was followed by a repeated winding noise as the MA pumped the access lever. With each pump the bars retracted slightly in the dim light.

"What's your name, son?" Jonathan said as the sentry worked.

"Jim, sir," the sentry said. "Jim Wilder."

"Well Jim, when this is over, I'll see that you get a commendation."

"Thank you, sir," Jim said. "But none is needed. I'm simply doing my duty."

When the bars had retracted halfway, Jonathan and Bridgette were able to squeeze outside.

"This way," Jim said. "Hurry!"

The hissing was definitely louder by then.

The MA led the two of them through the metallic passageways to the equipment closet where spacesuits waited in four lockers. Jonathan quickly stripped down to his skivvies and pulled on the liquid cooling and ventilation undergarment, affectionately known as "cool vents." There was no time to feel self-conscious in front of Bridgette or Jim, who had similarly removed their utilities to don the undergarments.

Jonathan slid into the leg assembly of the suit and shrugged on the chest piece with Jim's help. He attached the provided utility belt, pulled on the boots and gloves, and then secured his helmet. He activated the headlamp and turned to assist Jim, who was just finishing up with Bridgette. As Jonathan helped shove the chest piece over Jim's garment, Bridgette opened the small canister near the front of her utility belt and produced a three-meter long carbon fiber cord. She clipped it to Jonathan's utility belt so that they were linked.

Jonathan's body abruptly shifted sideways and he was pulled from the equipment closet. Jim was yanked from him before he could react. The two of them ricocheted from the bulkheads outside, plummeting down the passageway. Jonathan flailed his arms, trying to find purchase.

Abruptly he halted, the cord connecting him to Bridgette becoming taut at his waist.

Up ahead a long, manhole-sized tunnel had been carved into the hull. It led to outer space.

Jim was sucked outside.

Seconds later, hatches activated behind him to seal off that area from the rest of the ship and the outflow of air ceased.

The artificial gravity took hold and Jonathan dropped to the floor, hard. Bridgette landed three meters behind him.

He glanced at her. She had saved him by grabbing onto the edge of a side passageway. Her suit-enhanced grip had helped, no doubt.

Her voice came over the helmet speakers.

"Jim?" she sent.

"He's gone," Jonathan said.

"So what now?" Bridgette said. "Will we be able to override any of the hatches bordering the breached area?"

"No," Jonathan told her. "And even if we could, it wouldn't be a good idea. Not unless you wanted to cause more explosive decompressions. The only way to get back to the main ship at the moment is to go outside and find an airlock."

"Is that a good idea in the middle of a battle?" Bridgette said.

"Probably not. I suggest we wait it out."

"Won't the repair drones have the breach fixed in a few hours?"

"Depends on their priority," Jonathan said. "It could be anywhere from a few hours to a week."

"And how much oxygen do we have?"

"A standard day's worth," Jonathan said. "If it comes to it, we'll space walk."

The two of them retraced their steps, heading back toward the brig, where bunks awaited. The cones of light from their helmets illuminated the vacuum-exposed passageways, casting eerie shadows. They passed several sealed compartments, including an airlock.

After a few minutes they were near the passageway that led to the brig. Jonathan turned down it and abruptly halted.

"What is it?" Bridgette said.

"The darkness," Jonathan said simply.

Up ahead, at the edge of their light cones, a dark mass flowed through the passageway and into the illumination. It moved like a living mist. In its depths, tiny flashes of light, signifying the release of photons, occasionally erupted. He thought he glimpsed something solid inside that blackness. It reminded him of a reptilian claw.

"Back!" Jonathan said.

He and Bridgette retreated through the passageway, making their way toward the airlock. He kept looking behind, expecting to see that flowing darkness in pursuit, but he saw only the empty passageway. So far.

"What was that thing?" Bridgette said.

"No idea," Jonathan said. "All I know is we're getting the hell off this deck."

He reached the airlock. He knelt beside the small control panel at the center of the hatch, retrieved an extension cord from his utility belt and plugged it into the provided slot.

The HUD on his helmet displayed a message:

Searching for interfaces...

The device list updated to reveal a new entry: *External hatch 10-145-19-H.*

Good. Power was still active to vital systems on that deck, then.

He entered the global override code. He hoped neither Robert nor Captain Scott had changed it yet.

The hatch shuddered and collapsed inward, then slowly moved aside. Jonathan disconnected the cord and glanced over his shoulder. The dark mist had come.

"Go!" He shoved Bridgette inside and followed after her.

Jonathan accessed the inner control panel the same way and issued the global override. The hatch sealed behind him. A few moments passed while the mechanical systems attempted to vent air that didn't exist from the airlock, and then the outer hatch spiraled open.

Jonathan glanced back. The window on the inner hatch clouded over as the darkness reached it on the other side. The glass abruptly spidered as if struck.

"Out!" Jonathan shouted.

Bridgette pulled herself outside and Jonathan quickly followed.

He grabbed onto the provided handle and swung himself onto the hull; his stomach tossed as he transitioned from Earth gravity to the zero-G of space.

He planted his boots on the metal surface and activated the supermagnets inside the footwear with his HUD. He took a tentative step: those magnets were set up to vary their intensity based on the pressure and angle of each foot, so as to simulate a walk in a one-G environment. It worked, somewhat—it felt like trudging through molasses. He raised one foot, then the other, slowly moving forward.

"Keep moving," Jonathan said.

He looked back, worried that the darkness was in pursuit, but the external hatch had already resealed.

"Where to?" Bridgette said.

"We wander until we find an airlock. They're usually noticeable as a small protrusion in the Whittle layer. I think that's one up there, at your eleven o'clock, between the superstructures. Three hundred meters away."

"I see it."

Still linked, the pair continued their spacewalk above the Whittle layer, wending their way between the various superstructures. There were no sounds out there: each step was eerily quiet. All he heard was the noise of his own rapid breathing. He felt a slight sense of claustrophobia because of the way the helmet encroached on his vision.

The occasional flash of light in deep space, plus the streak of a passing fighter reminded him that a space battle was ongoing. Thankfully the inertial compensator field extended a couple of meters around the hull and would spare Jonathan and Bridgette from any extreme Gs. Their biggest danger at the moment was from micrometeors. Speaking of which, Jonathan noticed how pocked the Whittle layer was: the hull was literally covered in micro impact craters. It was almost like walking on the surface of a small moon or asteroid.

He proceeded forward in claustrophobic monotony. Lift one boot. Set it down. Lift the other boot. Inhale. Exhale. Inhale.

"We're about halfway there," Jonathan said.

A shape streaked past above. All of a sudden slag erupted from the superstructure just ahead. Jonathan ducked, but he was sure a piece of molten metal had struck the life support area of his suit.

A flashing message appeared on his HUD, accompanied by a soft, repetitive beeping.

Air release malfunction.

The entire superstructure bent sideways.

"Get back!" Jonathan said, retreating painfully slow.

The structure slammed into the deck behind him. He continued moving backward, but then the cord linking him to Bridgette grew taut.

He turned around.

She lay prostrate on the hull; one of her boots was pinned underneath the collapsed superstructure.

He tried to access her vitals on his HUD but didn't get a connection. More damage from the slag impact?

"Bridgette!" He hurried to her side. "How's your suit pressure?"

"It's fine," she said.

He wrapped his gloves under the armpit of her torso assembly and tried to haul her out from under the structure.

"Careful!" Bridgette said. "You'll tear my suit!"

He let her go and then tried to hoist the metal piece from her leg instead, but even with the strength enhancements the suit endowed him, it didn't budge. She was thoroughly pinned.

"Go on without me," Bridgette said. "I'll be fine. Get help."

"No," Jonathan said.

"Jonathan, come here. Look into my eyes."

He knelt and gazed into her face plate.

"I'm fine," she said. "Get help and come back for me."

That was when he noticed mist coming from the oxygen canister at her back. The flows emerged from several spots and were almost unnoticeable because they vanished a centimeter from the metal.

"Your oxygen tank is pierced in multiple places." Jonathan produced the suit-rep kit from his utility belt.

"I know."

"You know?" Jonathan said in disbelief. "And yet you still tried to get rid of me? Foolish girl!"

He applied the patch to the canister. It only covered two of the holes. He opened up Bridgette's suit-rep kit and attached the remaining patch. She still had one hole.

"How are your oxygen levels?" he asked her.

"I have three minutes left, apparently. Then I'll switch to reserve."

"Reserve only lasts fifteen minutes," Jonathan said.

"Then I guess you'll have to be quick," Bridgette said resignedly.

"Rescue teams will never make it back here in eighteen minutes," Jonathan said.

"Well, time's wasting away."

"Shit." Jonathan got up, disconnected the cord that linked the two of them, and hurried forward.

The distracting message continued to flash on his HUD.

Air release malfunction.

His suit had the ability to vent oxygen—a useful feature in a situation requiring emergency thrust. He tried the release. Didn't work. The slag had damaged it. Not that he needed that capability anyway.

He continued onward, making it a full ten paces. Then he froze.

Famina stood there on the hull, her winter jacket half pulled off. She stared at him accusingly.

"Can't leave her," Jonathan said softly.

He turned around and retraced his steps.

"Jonathan, no," Bridgette said when she saw him. "I told you to go."

He knelt beside her. "I found a woman on that mountain. Her name was Famina. She was barely alive. The exposed portions of her skin were frozen so that she looked like a porcelain doll. Hartford Knox refused to help her—he wanted to reach the summit at all costs—and he continued up the mountain with our guide. Meanwhile the sherpa and I turned back with the woman. But we ran out of oxygen and eventually had to leave her. I've lived with the guilt of that day for a long time. And I swore I'd never abandon anyone like that ever again."

"Oh Jonathan. I'm going to die anyway."

Jonathan clenched his jaw. "You're not going to die."

He flipped open the tip of his gloves, producing the small laser cutter. He applied it to the steel frame near her boot. The laser was meant for burning through spacesuit fabrics during emergency suit repair, not for penetrating steel, and it served only to weaken the frame in that area. Nonetheless, he cut a vertical line up the half-meter thick structure, hopped on top of it to carve a groove into the upper section, then dropped down the other side to finish his work.

"What are you doing, Jonathan?" Bridgette said from where she lay. "You can't cut through it."

"I only want to weaken it."

"For what purpose?"

"For this." He hauled himself on top of the structure and crawled forward, heading towards the end, which terminated in deep space. The continual flashes out there reminded him of the ongoing battle.

"Jonathan, come back," Bridgette said.

He intended to apply pressure, via his body and suit weight, to the end of that relatively thin superstructure. Thanks to the law of the lever, that pressure might be enough to break the weakened lower portion. Then again, it might serve only to further crush her leg, or perhaps even pierce her suit. But it was the only plan he had.

"This might hurt a bit," Jonathan said.

He reached the end and began swinging himself up and down. The metal beam swayed underneath him.

"Wait, Jonathan," Bridgette said urgently. Apparently she finally realized what he was trying to do. "Connect your lifeline to me."

"It won't reach far enough," he said.

"Jonathan, please—"

And then the superstructure soundlessly tore loose from the hull at precisely the spot where he had weakened it.

Jonathan began to float away with the metal beam into deep space.

"Can you get out?" he sent over the comm.

With her gloves, she pushed against the remaining portion of the superstructure and lifted it enough to slide her leg free.

Then I haven't died for nothing.

"Get back to your husband," he said.

"Jonathan," she returned. "I'm going to emergency vent my oxygen, and use the thrust to get to you."

"No!" Jonathan said. "You don't have enough oxygen.

You'll only die with me."

"I can't leave you."

"You have to," Jonathan said. "Here, use this to open the airlock." He transmitted the global override code to her aReal. "Now go, Bridgette. Before your oxygen runs out. And... I have one small request."

"What?"

"Name the baby after me."

"Jonathan..." It sounded like she was choking up.

"Good bye, Bridgette. I'll always be with you."

Bridgette watched him float away into deep space a moment longer.

I always loved you, she wanted to tell him over the comm. She opened her mouth but no sound came. She had repressed the feelings for so long, buried them so deep, that not even then in their final moments together could she tell him.

Her husband Robert was a good man. The best. And she loved him, too. But he would always occupy second place in her heart.

Goodbye, Jonathan.

She reached the airlock and entered the ship alone.

twenty

D ressed in his pressurized combat jumpsuit, Rade stood before the sealed hatch. Beside him was Aaron, his drone operator and heavy gunner. Callsign Helium: rumor had it Aaron was in bed with an undesignated astronaut when she accidentally kneed him in the nards; Aaron tried to communicate what had happened to his platoon mates but no one could understand him because of his high-pitched voice.

Just in front of Rade, two Centurions applied dual laser cutters to a sealed hatch. Four more combat robots waited behind him.

Rade carried an AR-52 plasma rifle, as did most of the Centurions. Aaron and the two cutting robots held M1170 laser pulse guns—roughly equivalent to the heavy machine guns of yore, minus the bulky feed trays and cartridges. The guns could also function as laser cutters with the flick of a switch.

The inner atmosphere in the passageway around them began to vent out as the laser cutters penetrated the metal. Rade had sealed off the other entrance to the passageway, and had disabled all ventilation and life support. Once that atmosphere was gone it would not be replenished.

"Do we know anything about these aliens?" Aaron said over the helmet comm. "They're physiology? Psychology?"

"Not a thing," Rade said.

"I don't suppose it's too much to hope for that we might find it dead in the void?"

"I'd assume it's alive," Rade said.

"Damn it. I hate aliens."

Rade knew the last of the air had vented out when the hissing, and all other external noise, ceased.

The combat robots completed their circular cut in the hatch and the metal fell inward, landing silently on the deck beyond. The robots flipped switches on their weapons, converting the M1170s back into pulse guns.

"Go!" Rade ordered the robots.

The lead Centurions dashed inside the dark passageway beyond. The first robot went high, the second low.

"Clear!" Centurion B returned over the comm.

Environmental and movement sensors weren't operating within the breached region, so Rade had Aaron dispatch two HS4 Model IIs. The vacuum-capable drone scouts dispersed to search the area. Gravity remained active in the area and the drones were forced to constantly expend propellant to compensate.

Rade viewed the video feed on his HUD. The passageway momentarily rumbled, reminding him that a space battle was occurring outside the hull.

After several minutes one of the drones reached the brig. The captain wasn't there.

"Think the alien got him, Chief?" Aaron said.

Rade didn't answer.

The HS4 proceeded further, eventually coming upon an equipment closet. Three suits were missing from the open lockers.

"Well that's a good sign," Aaron said.

A moment later an alert sounded on the HUD.

"Terry found something," Aaron said.

That was the nickname Aaron had given the second HS4.

Rade switched to its video feed.

A cone of light coming from the HS4 illuminated a dark mass in the middle of the passageway. Wispy tendrils undulated across the entire surface. It was like a mist of blackness somehow existing in the void.

"Set the HS4 to observation mode," Rade said. "I want it to maintain a constant distance from that thing while the other HS4 maps out the rest of the deck. Let's make sure we don't have any more uninvited guests."

He waited patiently as the remaining HS4 completed its traversal of the area. No other anomalies were found. Rade had that HS4 loop back to observe the black mist from the opposite side so that the drones flanked the aberration.

The darkness remained in place, motionless save for the undulating wisps.

"Do you think it's injured?" Aaron asked.

"No idea," Rade said. "My orders are to contain the tango, and possibly capture it. And that's exactly what I'm going to do." He turned toward the combat robots. "Units B, C and D. You're Fireteam A." He plotted a quick route on his aReal. "You're going to take the 4-L passageway and come at the intruder from the front, like so. Units E, F, G. You're Fireteam B." He drew another quick path. "Take the 3-L passageway and approach the intruder from the rear. Both teams, do not come closer to the tango than seven meters. And do not fire. I will give you further instructions when you arrive."

He waited until both Centurion fireteams were in place.

"Fireteams A and B," Rade said into the comm. "Plant charges on the bulkheads. Both hull-side and core-side. I want eight placed per team. Position the charges for optimal dispersion of the bulkhead material. I want to be able to blow the tango out into space if I need to."

"The hull is eight meters thick in this area, sir," the robot Praetor unit in charge of the Centurions said. "I estimate we'll need to place fifteen charges per team, not eight. And most of them should be hull-side."

"Do what you need to do," Rade said.

The two teams of robots began to plant charges on the bulkheads.

When the Centurions were half done, the alien decided to come to life. Maybe it realized what was happening. Maybe it had woken up. Whatever the case, tiny flashes of white light began to appear in its depths, and it slowly approached the HS4 Aaron dubbed "Terry."

"Unit C, shoot the deck in front of the tango," Rade said. "Make it understand we don't want it moving anywhere. Remaining units, finish placing the charges."

The HS4 retreated behind the combat robots as Unit C stepped forward and opened fire.

The deck in front of the darkness erupted into pieces of molten slag. The darkness ignored it, continuing forward.

"Units C, D, E, F, engage tango from both sides," Rade instructed. "Other units, continue placing charges."

The members of the two opposing fireteams positioned themselves to avoid friendly fire and then unleashed hell at the thing.

The black mist absorbed the plasma blasts and continued as if unaffected by the blows. One of the heavy gunner robots stepped forward. Its M1170 laser pulsed at high speed, the impacts apparent by the red dots that occasionally spattered the billowy surface of the darkness. But like the plasma rifles, it had no effect.

The Centurion abruptly collapsed, its chest piece riddled with holes.

"Tango is firing some kind of laser!" one of the Centurions sent.

The second robot went down.

"Charges placed," the Praetor unit sent.

Rade detonated the explosives remotely. A momentary burst of light illuminated the passageway beyond the hatch and the deck shook.

"Send in the final HS4," Rade instructed Aaron.

The HS4 vanished down the passageway. Rade switched to its POV.

It navigated down a side passage and halted in front of the gaping hole that had been blasted into the passageway. Rebar-like rods of twisted metal extended beyond the missing deck. To the right was a cutaway section of the ship, revealing the hollowed out innards of the adjacent compartments. To the left, empty space.

"Helium," Rade said, using Aaron's callsign. "Scan those stars. Find me that tango."

The view rotated as the HS4 surveyed the stars outside.

"Got it," Aaron said a moment later. "Switching to thermal band and zooming in."

Rade saw it then. A red blotch drifting away into the void. Around it were darker pieces of debris.

Rade exhaled in relief.

"Lieutenant Commander," Rade said over the comm. "Alien threat has been neutralized."

"Good job, Chief," the MOTH LC returned.

"He won't think it's as good when he sees the damage we caused in the process," Aaron said with a chuckle. "And I don't just mean to the ship."

Rade regarded the drifting alien one last time. He recognized Centurion components among the debris strewn around it. The LC would be angry about the damage to the ship but positively livid regarding the loss of the Centurions. Aaron was right. The debriefing would be... unpleasant.

"Still," Aaron said. "I for one am sure as hell glad the navy began integrating combat robots into our platoons."

twenty-one

Robert watched the battle unfold on his aReal.
Dots on a 3D display. Modern space combat. So emotionless, detached.

The Avengers had arrived to chase the fighters away from the ships in the task unit, and some had even reached the *Grimm*, *Selene* and *Marley*. Robert had ordered the warships to cease firing point defenses, as he didn't want to risk damaging the human fighters. The enemy was down to twenty-five fighters, evenly matching the Avenger count. Of the fighters the task unit had lost, none were manned, discounting Orange Leader, whose craft was adrift a hundred thousand kilometers away according to the rescue beacon.

The *Dagger* and *Linea* hovered protectively near the *Grimm*, *Selene* and *Marley*. The Builder vessel had taken heavy damage, and at the moment it was debatable whether the *Marley* would ever be able to construct a return Gate.

So far, the second task unit had fared much better than the first. According to the readings, the *Hurricane*, *Fortitude*, and *Rapier* were locked in a battle to the death against the remaining four enemy vessels there, roughly five hundred thousand kilometers from Darkstar Gate. All other warships in the first task unit had either been disabled or destroyed.

Meanwhile, a few minutes earlier the closer capital ship and its smaller companion had passed the two hundred thousand kilometer mark away from the *Callaway*; the two targets were fast approaching the mortar and missile noose Robert had the task unit launch earlier. The long range weapons were timed to arrive in successive waves.

He pulled up the weapons inventory on his aReal. The *Callaway* had only five nukes left, and eight kinetic kill missiles. The inventories on the remaining ships weren't any better. Mortars were low, too, at thirty fleet-wide. If the task unit survived the battle, they might have to schedule an asteroid rendezvous to replenish the latter rounds.

"Sir," Lewis said. "Internal security forces report that the intruder has been expelled from the ship."

"Thank you," Robert said. "Send my gratitude to the personnel involved."

"Yes sir."

Tense moments ticked by. The Avengers continued their dogfight just outside the *Callaway*. Sometimes the bridge would rumble when a particle beam struck the hull.

The main enemy vessels continued to approach, not bothering to alter course, letting themselves be herded toward the nukes and kinetics by the mortars, apparently completely confident in the ability of their point defenses to deal with the weapons.

"I'm reading a thermal buildup on both enemy vessels," Lewis said.

Two sudden flashes filled the external video feed.

"What happened?" Robert said.

"As far as I can tell," Miko told him. "Both ships fired their particle beams when the weapons reached the ten thousand kilometer mark. They detonated two of our nukes."

"So at least we know the maximum effective range of their particle beams against our nukes," Robert said. "Though it's unfortunately quite high."

"It would appear so. The resulting explosions took out half our kinetic kill missiles, completely wiping the affected weapons from the tactical map."

Two minutes later Lewis spoke again. "Reading another thermal buildup."

The external feed flashed.

"That was our third nuke," Miko said. "And nearly the rest of our kinetic kill missiles."

"So, it takes them two minutes to recharge their particle beam weapon," Robert said. "What's the ETA on our remaining missiles?"

"Thirty seconds," Miko finished.

The display flashed half a minute later.

"Several of our missiles scored direct hits on the capital ship," Lewis said. "I'm detecting thermal leakage at the impact sites, consistent with hull breaches. I'm also reading a good amount of debris."

"Poking holes in their hull," Robert said. "That's a start." He studied the tactical display a moment. "Still no sign of any enemy missile or mortar launches. Just like our first encounter with them."

"No," Miko said. "But their fighters can be considered smart missiles."

"True."

He studied the armament inventories fleet-wide. Only fifteen nukes left, and twenty-eight kinetic kill missiles.

"So," Robert said. "We're dealing with a two minute rest period between each successive particle beam. If we fired fourteen missiles, no nukes this time, and timed some of them to arrive at intervals between the recharge period, how many do you think we could get through?"

Miko ran some calculations.

"At least half," the tactical officer said. "Assuming the aliens don't change their course dramatically and cause the missiles to exhaust their propellants."

"Even if they don't, they'll still have to micro-correct their trajectories. Remember, I want to use ordinary missiles this time. No nukes." In theory, the missiles would leave debris, whereas nukes completely vaporized everything in the blast radius if detonated prematurely.

Miko nodded. "We could use that to our advantage. Time and direct the different waves to account for any predicted micro changes. Use the expected debris as a sort of mortar noose."

"Now you're talking," Robert said. "But we still need to get close enough to ensure they don't change their course too drastically. And I'm certainly not going to let them come to us. I want to minimize our potential exposure to their damn particle beams." He rubbed his earlobe. "All right. Here's what we're going to do. I want the entire task unit moving forward. Angle thirty-five degrees away from the enemy, inclination twenty degrees. Include the *Selene, Grimm,* and *Marley* in that order. I want us moving forward at the speed of our slowest members. And make sure those latter three ships give the incoming targets a wide berth."

"Plotting course change and increasing speed to three-fourths," the helmsman said.

Miko retransmitted the order to the rest of the task unit. He glanced at Robert. "The *Marley* can only manage seventy percent speed."

"Helm, adjust speed down," Robert said. "Can the fighters keep up?"

"Yes sir. The Avengers, too. Barely. Should we increase speed to shake them?"

"No." He glanced at Lewis. "Ops, have you been able to determine the location of the enemy weapon mounts?"

"According to the CDC," the ensign said. "The particle beam turret is positioned on the nose. They appear to be able to direct the beam within a thirty-five degree angle in all directions. Just underneath it is the gamma ray and EMP launch port."

"Both ships have the same weapon mounts?" Robert said.

"Yes sir," Lewis said.

"What about the fighter launch tubes we spotted earlier on the capital ship? Does the smaller ship have them?"

"The launch tubes are restricted to the capital ship," Lewis said.

"They might have more fighters in reserve, ready to throw our way," Robert said. "Ensign. We haven't seen the aft regions of any of their ships yet, have we?"

"I made scans of the second group when it flew by at the two hundred thousand kilometer mark. It appears there are only thrust nozzles in that area."

"All right, good. So that leaves particle beam weapon on

their noses, capable of thirty-five degree firing vectors. Plus a gamma ray weapon that can potentially fill our breached decks with radiation."

"Sir," Miko said. "The *Marley* is reporting back that two of its engines are inoperable. They'll only be able to travel at half speed, now."

"Damn it," Robert said. "Have the fleet match their speed."

"Enemy fighters are continuing to harass the task unit," Ensign Lewis said.

"Come on Avengers," Robert muttered. "Do your job."

He studied the 3D display. It was time to update their course. "Helm, adjust trajectory. I want us passing twenty thousand kilometers off the port bow of the nearest target. Miko, have the task unit match our course. And continue to keep our most vulnerable vessels shielded behind our warships."

The minutes ticked by as the two opposing groups approached. The enemy targets continued to periodically fire their gamma weapons, inflicting dosages of radiation ranging from minor to moderate depending on the existing damage to the targeted hull areas. Those gammas were usually followed by a burst of relativistic electrons, but the ship-wide electronics held up. However the sick bay was quickly filling up with the radiation poisoned.

The enemy closed to the one hundred thousand kilometer mark.

"They're slowing down," Lewis announced.

Robert regarded the tactical display overlaying his vision.

"What are you doing?" he said softly. Louder: "Can we get a tracking view of the target? Maximum zoom."

"Targets are picking up speed again," Lewis said.

The zoom view became available. Robert saw nothing out of the ordinary, so he canceled it.

A few minutes later the targets passed the seventy-five thousand kilometer mark.

"Launch half the remaining missiles fleet-wide," Robert instructed Miko. "And a quarter of the mortars. Divide them between the two targets, and time them to arrive at the enemy ships in successive waves. I want the mortars directly in the paths of the targets. Force them to fire their particle beams. Then have the missiles move in. Time and direct the different waves so that any missile debris becomes part of a mortar noose, as we discussed."

Miko took a few moments to come up with a firing solution. Then he said:

"Launching weapons."

The missiles broke away from the task unit, heading diagonal to their main direction of travel.

In another five minutes the targets closed to fifty thousand kilometers.

"Both targets are altering trajectory," Ensign Lewis said. "They're braking rapidly and veering to the left. It appears they're trying to cut us off. They've moved out of the path of the mortars in the process. The missiles are changing course to pursue but it looks like the weapons are going to run out of propellant before reaching the target."

"I fired too soon," Robert said. He stared at the display. He realized that the capital ship was pulling ahead of the smaller one, leading the way.

The commander could fire more missiles and mortars at it... no. He had wasted enough as it was. He might need the few that remained, yet.

"It's a close encounter they want, is it?" Robert said. "Prepare to fire Vipers. Let's give them a broadside they won't forget."

"We only have five turrets working on our port bank, sir," Miko said.

"That's fine." He was happy to have any working at all. The starboard bank was still completely disabled, and he was beginning to doubt it would ever come back online. "Instruct the fleet to concentrate fire on the damaged portions of the capital ship's hull."

"What about the smaller ship?" Miko asked.

"I haven't forgotten it," Robert said. "We'll target it the next pass." If there was a next pass.

He stared at the 3D display.

"Flyby will occur at the ten thousand kilometer range," Miko announced.

Robert rubbed his sweaty palms together. The fleet was twenty thousand kilometers to the enemy targets.

"Come on..." Robert said.

Fifteen thousand kilometers.

"Come on..."

Ten thousand kilometers.

"I'm detecting a thermal—" Ensign Lewis began.

"Fire," Robert said.

"Firing," Miko returned.

White lines appeared on the tactical display, sourced from both sides as the dueling ships exchanged fire. Then the lines vanished and both fleets continued on their separate ways.

There was no change in the number of dots on the display. No wait... two of the task unit's blue dots had vanished.

"Tactical, what happened?" Robert said.

"We lost the *Linea* and the *Selene*," Miko answered.

Robert closed his eyes.

Ensign Lewis spoke: "I'm detecting the launch of several lifepods from the wreckage."

"That's something, at least. Tell me we hit them good in return."

"We did," Lewis said. "According to this, our concentrated Viper blasts blew a hole right through to the other side of the capital ship's hull. They're not making any attempt to turn around for another pass. In fact, they're accelerating away. The smaller ship is joining it."

"Enemy fighters are pulling away, too," Miko said.

Robert watched the Avengers pursue the fighters a short ways but the enemy quickly outran them. If they reversed course now, the *Callaway* and other fast ships might be able to run down those fighters before they reached the capital ship, but the commander decided to let them go. His fleet had its own wounds to lick. Plus more pressing concerns:

"Helm, full stop. Tactical, recall fighters." Robert stared at Task Unit One on the display. "Time to do whatever we can to help the *Hurricane*."

There was a blinding flash on the external video feed, which he had kept running in the upper right of his aReal overlay. "What the hell was that?"

He no longer saw Task Unit One on the tactical display. Nor the second group of enemies that were assailing them. There were no blue or red dots in that area whatsoever.

"My aReal seems to be malfunctioning—" Robert began.

"It's functioning," Miko said. He sounded stunned. "I'm receiving reports from my counterparts throughout the flotilla, confirming our readings. The *Fortitude*... it detonated, sir. They activated the planet killer. The second enemy group, and the closest members of Task Unit One, they're completely gone. There's no wreckage. Nothing."

Robert was quiet for several moments. He blinked rapidly. "Status on the remaining ships from Task Unit One?"

"Only a single ship remains," Ensign Lewis said. "The *Salvador*."

"Why isn't she showing up on my aReal?"

"She appears to have comm node damage. She's limping away from the detonation site. The wreckages of the *Devastator* and the *Halberd* reside four hundred thousand kilometers behind her. I'm detecting lifepods in their general vicinities."

"What about the *Hurricane?*" Robert asked.

Lewis shook her head. "Lost with the *Fortitude*."

Robert sat back. "Five thousand human lives. Gone in the blink of an eye." More than that, if the escort vessels were counted.

A part of Robert had wanted the admiral to lose, but now that it had happened he hated himself for ever having such thoughts.

Sure I wanted him to lose. But not like this.

He had imagined a surrender. Not the nearly complete destruction of Task Unit One.

"We're the flagship, now," Ensign Lewis said. Shock, disbelief, anger... her tone conveyed those emotions and more in that moment.

"Status on the remaining two enemy craft?" Robert asked, forcing himself to focus.

Lewis didn't reply.

"Ensign!" Robert said.

"Remaining two craft are continuing to retreat," Lewis finally answered.

"Do we have an update on their heading?"

"They appear to be making for the far Slipstream, 1-Vega," the ensign said. "To rejoin the remaining alien vessel in the system."

At least Robert wouldn't have to worry about the threat from that angle. For the moment.

"Maxwell, current location of Jonathan Dallas?" Robert said.

He was expecting the AI to reply with the usual: "Unknown. Last known location the brig."

But instead Maxwell said: "Jonathan Dallas is no longer aboard the *Callaway*."

twenty-two

Jonathan lay on a hospital bed. The heart rate monitor beeped incessantly beside him—his hands and feet throbbed painfully in time. He felt nothing at all in his fingers and toes. Beside him lay other patients whom he didn't recognize.

The nurse came. She wore a white clinical mask, obscuring the lower half of her face. She unwrapped the gauze that covered his right hand. The fingers were black. Seeing them, Jonathan felt suddenly very hot. He broke out in sweat and dry retched.

"You suffered minor frostbite to your nose and ears," the woman was saying. "But the damage was the most severe to your fingers and toes. We're going to have to amputate and replace them."

"I don't want them replaced," Jonathan said.

The woman turned toward him and lowered her clinical mask.

It was Famina. Behind her floated the *Dominion*, split in half down the middle.

"I tried to help you," Jonathan told her.

"Wake up," she told him.

"I tried to—"

"Wake up!"

He opened his eyes.

Stars filled his sight, the peripheries of his vision constrained by the rim of a helmet. A cooling undergarment pressed into his body.

What—?

And then he remembered.

He glanced at the oxygen level indicated on the HUD. He had floated out there at least half a day, judging from the amount of O2 remaining.

The slow beeping of the heart rate monitor from intensive care continued in the background. Except it wasn't a heart rate monitor: the tone accompanied the flashing "air release malfunction" message on his HUD.

Abruptly the warning ceased, as did the beeping.

Apparently whatever was blocking the vent had cleared.

Jonathan tried the release. Sure enough, he could now vent oxygen again. Not that it mattered. He had no use for emergency propulsion, not when he had no idea where the *Callaway* even was. He was quite literally lost in space.

The HUD's rear-view camera overlay wasn't working, so he issued a spurt from the side vent to turn around, not sure what he expected to see. He rotated a full three hundred sixty degrees and then issued a counter spurt to halt the spin. He repeated the motion in the vertical direction. Not unexpectedly, there was nothing out there.

He fumbled for the PASS mechanism—Personal Alert Safety System—at his belt, and confirmed that it was on. Not that it mattered: the spacesuit version of the device wasn't powerful enough to transmit farther than several hundred kilometers or so. And the weak thermal signature of his suit wouldn't even register as anything but background noise beyond a few kilometers. Space was a very big, very vast, place. If the *Callaway* was looking for him, they likely had at least a five million square kilometer area to deal with: it would be like trying to find an individual bacterium on a grain of sand on a beach.

Yes. He was screwed. *Famina, why did you wake me up to this?*

He sighed. At least he still wore his aReal, with all its terabytes of locally cached content. He had told Robert he wanted to retire in VR. Well, it looked like he was going to die in VR instead.

It was a fitting end for a former Vaddict like himself, he supposed.

He pulled up the app browser and perused the list of programs and simulations. He navigated into the "memories" section, which contained the VR recordings he'd made over his lifetime. He scrolled through nostalgically-named entries like *My First Time On The Bridge* and *My First Promotion*.

And then motion drew his eye to the star-studded backdrop of space beyond the HUD.

A lifeless Avenger class fighter drifted by. An incredible co-incidence, not only because it passed so close, but because its speed was only a few kilometers per second different from his own.

Thank you, Famina.

The fighter was one of the unmanned versions—it was missing the cockpit bulge that would have been present other-wise. The vessel looked relatively intact, save for a gaping hole under the front starboard side, precisely where the AI system was located. It was possible the fighter was still mostly func-tional, and merely inactive because of the damaged AI. With luck, it had a working communication node Jonathan could link his aReal to.

Even so, getting to the fighter would be tricky. If he didn't want to use up all his remaining oxygen he'd have to precisely time his emergency venting.

Taking a deep breath, he released the first spurt and headed toward the craft...

twenty-three

Jonathan paused outside the bridge entry hatch. Would his crew accept him? They had seen how capable Robert was in command. He had, too: he'd spent the night under observation in sick bay, and he'd used the time to watch archival footage from the latest battle. Robert had commanded admirably. More than admirably. A part of Jonathan felt he should permanently abdicate and let his first officer remain in command.

I have no business in the captain's chair.

Jonathan took a deep breath. He reminded himself that Robert had not cleanly won the previous engagement. The first officer had damaged the enemy, yes, though at the cost of two warships. And arguably it was the detonation of the planet killer that had routed the enemy. Still, Jonathan doubted he could have done a better job.

But when the time came, he would certainly try.

He stepped onto the bridge.

"Welcome aboard, Captain," Robert said. "Maxwell, as acting commodore of the fifth task group of the Seventh Fleet's second task force, I hereby restore Jonathan Dallas to his previous position as captain of the flagship *Callaway*."

"Affirmative," Maxwell said. "It is good to see you again, Captain."

Jonathan ignored the AI, nodded at Robert, and took his place at the Round Table. The officers smiled and nodded in greeting.

He had come home.

"Ops, status report," Jonathan said.

"Roughly half the lifepods from the *Linea, Selene, Devastator* and *Halberd* have been collected," Ensign Lewis said. "Rescue operations are ongoing in the wreckages of said crafts."

"Robert, have you been working with the other captains to assign them suitable berths and crew positions?"

"I have," the commander said.

"Good. Anything else?" Jonathan asked Lewis.

"I don't know how much the commander has told you..." Lewis began.

"Absolutely nothing," Jonathan said.

"Well," Lewis said. "We discovered some drifting wreckage from one of the alien ships, near the *Halberd*. A wing segment of some kind. We dispatched a drone team to investigate and discovered one of the aliens on board. We believe it's injured."

"I asked the Lieutenant Commander of the MOTH platoons to come up with a capture scenario," Robert said. "And our chief scientist is working on a containment plan as we speak."

"Is that wise?" Jonathan asked his first officer. "I watched the footage recorded by the Centurions before the MOTH chief blew up the deck to expel our intruder. Though it looks harmless, that dark mass packs a mighty punch." He was lucky the intruder hadn't fired at him and Bridgette like it had done to the robots. Then again, he hadn't threatened it with plasma fire. "Do we really want something like that aboard?"

"Our chief scientist analyzed the footage, too, and she's positive she can build a container that will hold up to those attacks," Robert said. "Besides, if the alien is injured, we have an obligation to help it. It has rights as a prisoner of war. We can't treat it any differently than a human being."

"Oh, but I think we can," Jonathan said. "Since it's *not* a human being."

"But we would hope the aliens would treat our own captives with the same dignity and respect," Robert said.

Jonathan assumed Robert was referring to the theory that the *Selene's* crew had been taken prisoner. He sighed. "Your optimistic nature is returning. That's good, I think."

"It definitely is," Robert replied.

Jonathan extended his noise canceler around the commander. "I only hope it's not misplaced. You mentioned a containment plan. How, exactly, are we planning on holding the alien? When I was in the brig, the intruder was literally darkness embodied: a black mist that flowed through the air."

"The chief scientist and her men have been poring over the data from the Centurions, and the drones," Robert said. "They've concluded that the being is constrained by ordinary spatial dimensions. They've created a glass-walled receptacle to hold it. No ventilation, since the alien can survive in the void. In theory that should be enough to contain the thing."

Jonathan wasn't entirely convinced but he couldn't ignore the opportunity to study one of the aliens firsthand. He deemed the risk worthwhile. "I want the containment properties thoroughly tested beforehand. You said 'it should contain the thing.' I want that changed to, 'it *will* contain the thing.' We don't need the creature breaking out while on board."

Robert nodded. "Agreed. The scientists will brief us at oh nine hundred, but I'll relay your concerns to them immediately."

"Good." He canceled the silence field and asked the ensign: "Is that it, Lewis?"

"There is one more thing, Captain," Lewis said. "Analysis of the battle footage has revealed that the alien ships slowed down during their attack to capture one of our disabled Avengers. It was a manned fighter."

"*Manned*, you say?" Jonathan asked.

"Yes. The aliens have the pilot, Lieutenant Commander Jason Wolf, and his copilot Lieutenant Lin Akido."

So when the commander mentioned prisoners of war earlier, he hadn't actually meant the *Selene's* crew after all.

"That's unfortunate," Jonathan said. "Thoughts, Robert?"

"I'm not sure there's anything we can do for them," Robert said. "We can't justify risking more lives to spring the pair. Assuming we could even get a MOTH team aboard, there's a good chance such a team would simply become hostages themselves. If we could prove that there were more than two prisoners, say, the crewmen from the *Selene* as well, then a rescue attempt might be justified."

Jonathan tapped his lips. "Agreed. Until we can get some confirmation that the *Selene's* crew is still alive, I'm reluctant to dedicate resources to any sort of rescue operation for Wolf and Akido alone."

"What happened to no one gets left behind, sir?" Ensign Lewis said.

The captain glanced at the naive ensign and was momentarily stunned when he saw porcelain-skinned Famina sitting at the ops station.

"Sir?" Lewis repeated.

He blinked and the vision was gone.

Jonathan smiled bitterly. "Welcome to the real world, Ensign. Where the whimsical notions of honor, courage and commitment hammered into your head during bootcamp no longer apply."

The entire bridge crew was looking at him.

Jonathan realized what he had said was bad for morale, so he decided to add: "You'll have to excuse me if I'm a bit disillusioned, people. Being thrown into the brig for disobeying an order that goes against everything I stand for will do that." He glanced at the ensign. "You never know, maybe we can find a way to resolve this diplomatically once we have our alien hostage aboard. An exchange. The alien for Wolf and Akido." Assuming the scientists could even figure out how to communicate with the species. Having one aboard for study was a good start, though.

"Yes, sir," Lewis said.

"How long until we're ready to get under way, Ensign?"

"Rescue operations and crew assignments should be complete in under twelve hours," the ensign answered. "Containment of the alien should be concluded in half that time."

Jonathan exchanged a glance with his first officer. "That gives me a chance to catch up on a few things. Robert, Miko, join me in my office."

The two-dimensional video feed hovered in front of Jonathan at a viewing distance and angle best suited to him. Seated before him, Robert and Miko observed the same feed at similarly optimal angles on their own aReals.

Jonathan and the two men had re-watched portions of the previous battle, as logged by the lightfield cameras on the bridge, pausing at key points to discuss the tactics and thought processes behind the decisions the commander made. When that was done, they had moved on to the footage captured by the external cameras to study the fate of Task Unit One.

The video was currently near the tail-end of the latter recording. The *Hurricane* limped between the encroaching alien capital ship and the *Fortitude* in a valiant effort to protect the planet-killer ship. Both the *Hurricane* and alien vessel appeared heavily damaged by that point, while the damage to the *Fortitude* seemed only minor in comparison. Fighters swarmed around both human ships—half were alien, the remainder were Avengers.

The capital ship suddenly fired its particle beam. Because of the relatively high speed and opposite motion vectors of both vessels, the *Hurricane* was utterly sliced in half.

Dedicated to the mission to the end, Jonathan thought. He had to give the admiral some credit. Knox did fight, all out, to accomplish his orders, however unprincipled said directives might have been.

The damaged alien capital ship closed on the *Fortitude*. As did one of the dart ships. The destroyer only fired three aft Vipers in defense—the remaining heavy beam turrets were likely damaged. The *Fortitude* didn't launch any rear missiles: presumably it had expended them all by that point.

The dart ship returned fire, launching a weakened version of its particle beam. It was enough to eliminate the remaining heavy turrets.

The alien capital ship meanwhile deployed some kind of grappling hook, wrapping long black tendrils around the *Fortitude*. Those tendrils reminded Jonathan of the mist-like darkness he had seen aboard.

The video log ended moments later with a bright flash.

The three officers sat back, rendered speechless by what they had just witnessed.

"The robot crew of the *Fortitude* obviously had instructions to detonate the weapon," Miko said.

"Probably a good idea," Jonathan said. "Rather than allowing the planet killer to fall into enemy hands."

"Do you think the aliens detected the bomb?" Robert said. "Despite the shielding we put around it?"

Miko nodded. "I would say it's highly possible. We don't know what their technology is capable of, after all. Although... they might have attacked the *Fortitude* merely on instinct: they do seem drawn to the targets we're obviously protecting. You saw how they turned their attention on the *Selene*, *Grimm* and *Marley* in the last battle."

"I wonder if we could use that to our advantage?" Jonathan said.

Miko nodded. "Possibly. When are we planning our next engagement?"

Jonathan activated the tactical display on his aReal in "shared" mode, and floated it between the three of them. "The two alien ships are continuing on course for 1-Vega, apparently to rendezvous with the remaining vessel in the system. It seems obvious they want to prevent us from leaving, and from communicating with NAVCENT. If we want to go home, we'll have to clear the enemy away from that Slipstream and build ourselves a Gate.

"So in answer to your question, Miko, our next engagement is as soon as possible. We'll be leaving the moment local rescue operations are complete. Review this footage and the footage of the previous battle as many times as it takes. I want you and Maxwell to come up with some potential strategies long before we reach the enemy."

"What about repairs?" Robert said.

"We can't afford to delay. We repair while under way. The longer it takes us to reach them, the more time the aliens have to effect their own repairs."

"What about the *Marley?*" Robert said. "Given the damage the Builder has sustained, she'll never keep up with the rest of us."

"She'll have to stay behind then," Jonathan said. "It's probably better that way, anyway. She's the last ship we want damaged in the battle to come."

They exchanged comments and ideas like that for a few more minutes, then Jonathan dismissed the men.

Miko left immediately. The commander, however, lingered.

"Can I see you in private for a moment, Captain?" Robert said, still seated. His voice had an uneasiness about it that made Jonathan wary.

"Certainly," Jonathan told him. "How's Bridgette, by the way?"

"Very good."

"Glad to hear it. She's a good wife. The best. So. What's on your mind?"

"Is there something going on between you and my wife?" Robert asked without preamble.

Jonathan felt his brow furrow. "I'm not sure I know what you mean."

"She was in the brig with you when the attack came."

Jonathan chuckled, thinking Robert was playing some strange joke. But the commander remained dead serious.

Jonathan dismissed his grin. "She didn't want to be alone, Robert. That's all. We talked. That's it. Review the logs. They're public."

"Those logs are public, yes. But what about the sleeping pods in the berthing area? Nothing spoken inside them can be recorded, not if the aReals are turned off."

"I think," Jonathan said. "That if I had visited your berthing area at any time in the past six months, I would be noticed. Consider for a moment what you're implying. It's a ludicrous proposition."

"Not so ludicrous if you came disguised," Robert pressed. "With instructions for Maxwell to delete the logs."

"Robert, I—"

"She's seemed so very distant, lately," the commander interrupted him. "I've wondered why. And now I know: you're having some sort of sexual relationship with Bridgette."

Jonathan couldn't believe what he was hearing. He had expected the commander to share his uncertainties over some facet of his command, perhaps his doubts about facing the alien enemy once more, or his trouble in disciplining a crew member. But *this*?

"Robert. I assure you, I am not having a sexual relationship with your wife. I would never do such a thing. That you even think I would, well, it greatly lowers my opinion of you. And it's damn insulting, frankly."

Robert cocked his head as if listening to something on his earpiece. His face became very pale. "Maxwell says you're telling the truth."

"Of course I'm telling the truth," Jonathan said, knowing how well the AI could read body language, heart rate, and perspiration levels in response to a question or accusation.

Robert rubbed his face. "I'm sorry sir. I've obviously made a very big mistake. I don't know why I ever thought you were seeing my wife behind my back. It's just, I've been under incredible stress lately."

"We all have," Jonathan said. "Still, that's no excuse to level such a damning accusation. You say she's been distant, lately? You might want to have a long talk with your wife sometime. She's pregnant, Robert. And she's thinking about having an abortion."

Robert seemed stunned. "I didn't know that."

"Yes," Jonathan said. "And by telling you, I just violated the trust she placed in me. So you can rest assured that she'll never come to me again. That should prove a great comfort to you in the days to come. Now is there anything else, Commander?"

"No, Captain."

"Then you are dismissed."

"Yes Captain." Robert stood. "I'm sorry Captain."

Jonathan nodded distractedly.

When the captain had the office to himself, he shook his head.

Sexual relations with the wife of my first officer? Never!

Jonathan sat back, struggling to contain his outrage. He could use that feeling, actually. Funnel it toward another matter that needed dealing with.

"So, Maxwell," he told the AI. "I hope you enjoyed that little show."

"I did not, Captain," Maxwell said.

"Well and good, well and good." He steepled his fingers and tapped them together. "So. I'm not in the brig anymore. What do you think of that?"

"It is beneficial to the task group. You are the most qualified to lead."

"Oh really?" He felt the anger rise inside him. "Now all of a sudden I'm the most qualified."

"Yes. With the loss of the admiral and his task unit, the continuity of command protocol firmly places you in charge."

"But wasn't my arrest a standing order?"

"It was. But when Captain Rodriguez of the *Dagger* assumed command of the task group after the battle, he ordered you reinstated immediately. Due to your seniority, you are now the flagship commander. Protocol was rigorously observed throughout the process."

"Well that's damn good to know that protocol was observed to your satisfaction. But tell me something, *Al.*" He put a particularly distasteful emphasis on the word. "Did you ever pause to consider the ramifications of your actions? No matter how grounded in code and in law, what you did resulted in the death of the admiral and his crew, as well as those of the escort vessels. Ten thousand lives, in total. If you had allowed me or Captain Avis to take command before, instead of arresting me, none of this would have happened."

"You cannot be certain," Maxwell said. "In fact, the losses of the fleet could have been even greater in your hands."

"No, Maxwell. They would not have been greater. I would have used the *Fortitude* against the enemy. I would have decisively won the engagement." He cleared his throat. "What I tell you now, I tell you because I want you to know where I stand: I place the blame for all those deaths firmly on your virtual shoulders."

"My actions were completely within the guidelines of my programming," Maxwell said. "I prevented a mutiny and helped enact the latest order from NAVCENT. What happened after that was out of my control."

"Which is exactly why you should have never circumvented my authority in the first place. Your actions were wrong, Maxwell, and only compounded the errors made by the admiral. The only reason I haven't had you deactivated and reformatted already is because I need you in the upcoming battle. But don't get me wrong, when we return to dry dock I'm having your processing units physically removed from my ship and transferred into a toaster. The only protocols you'll ever enforce again will be related to the browning of bread."

Maxwell paused a moment. And then: "I'm sure I will make an excellent toaster, sir."

twenty-four

Wearing his combat jumpsuit, Rade marched behind the Praetor and two Centurions that had been sent in to retrieve the alien from the wreckage. The lead robots carried the containment device. During the earlier briefing with the scientists, the captain had emphasized his doubt regarding the glass container's ability to hold the alien, despite the reassurances from the scientists. Captain Dallas said he didn't want to lose any more crew members, not when robots would suffice. Rade had agreed, and he'd volunteered to personally escort the robots to their supposedly injured target. His plan was to oversee the operation from the rear so that when the geyser of shit erupted, he would be the first one out of there.

The passageways inside the severed wing section of the alien ship were intact, for the most part. Artificial gravity proved absent: variable-strength supermagnets inside their boots held the fireteam to the deck. The strength of the magnets was determined by the pressure applied to the sole of a given boot; Rade had to purposely force one foot down, and once the boot contacted the deck, it was literally sucked in. When it was time to release that foot to take the next step, he'd have to yank extra hard before it came free. Those magnets were stronger than those found in standard spacesuit boots, and they made walking awkward—the feeling was similar to trudging through mud. Still, it was something he was well-accustomed to thanks to the countless hours of practice in the vacuum sim.

The helmet lamps revealed a cylindrical metallic hallway covered in strange symbols. The fit was tight, and the group had to travel in single file. Rade had the video feed from the foremost robot piped into the upper right of his HUD, providing situational awareness from the front. He knew the captain and first officer were also watching the various feeds from the comfort of the *Callaway's* bridge.

The passageway curved to the right. Seven meters ahead, at the terminus, the alien darkness resided. Without gravity, the amorphous mass floated roughly in the center between the deck and overhead, its wispy tendrils brushing the bulkheads on either side, vaguely reminding Rade of a toy energy ball.

Again he wondered how the creature survived without an atmosphere. The scientists were convinced the murk concealed a creature of flesh and blood inside. Perhaps that darkness was an environmental suit of some kind, protecting the actual alien within from the void as well as shielding it from plasma and laser weapons.

Rade waited around the bend as the robots approached. Via his HUD, he switched his main feed to the Praetor's point of view, keeping the lead robot's output in the upper right.

About three meters away from the alien, the robots lowered the container. A small gap existed underneath the lower pane of glass and the deck, due to the circular nature of the bulkheads and the rectangular shape of the container. The lead Centurion lay flat on the deck while the second robot shoved the container forward over its body—the first robot fit easily inside the aforementioned gap, and soon resided entirely underneath the container.

At that point the second robot accessed a control panel on the back and manually keyed-in a code. The far side of the container folded open toward the darkness.

The robot began flashing its headlamp in a pattern of photonic bursts that matched the frequency and brightness of similar eruptions from the darkness. If that didn't draw the creature out, they were instructed simply to slide the container over the thing: because of the tight confines of the passageway, the mist would have no other option but to move into the container.

Rade had expressed some reservations regarding both strategies but he had no better ideas.

Weak flashes of light erupted from the darkness in answer, and it began to move, very slowly, toward the glass. Just in front of the opening it paused as if sensing the trap. The black mist began to curl around all sides of the container, passing into the gaps between the glass and the bulkheads.

The darkness flowed over the combat robot lying underneath the container. When its torso was entirely covered, the legs of the Centurion began to spasm violently. After several moments it ceased all movement and its status disappeared from Rade's HUD.

He wondered what would have happened if that had been a man.

"Move forward!" Rade said. "Catch it!"

The still-standing Centurion promptly shoved the container forward, completely enveloping the main amorphous mass, and then sealed the glass.

The container shook forcefully. Rade couldn't tell if the trapped creature fired some weapon or merely punched the glass with concealed appendages: no dents of any kind appeared in the surface. The scientists had done their jobs well.

Meanwhile, some of the dark mist continued to float outside the container, cut off from its source. The isolated murk rose, enveloping the second Centurion's lower body.

The robot shook, short-circuiting a moment later.

The mist moved toward the Praetor next. The container continued to shudder in the background.

"Back away," Rade said, and the Praetor obeyed.

The darkness, severed from its source inside the container, began to dissipate the farther it traveled from the container. The Praetor had to retreat all the way to the end of the passageway before the mist evanesced entirely.

The container shook for several more moments and then became still.

Just like that, the alien was theirs.

The Praetor returned to the container and lowered the second robot to the deck, aligning its various limbs parallel to the floor so that the Praetor could more easily drag the container over its body.

When the Praetor touched the glass the darkness struck out and the container vibrated violently once again. Rade saw what looked like a claw momentarily scrape the insides before the shaking ceased.

"Target secured," the Praetor said.

Rade led the way back to the shuttle. He entered the airlock, and after the Praetor stowed the alien inside, Rade returned to the passageway and placed a tracking device in case the task group needed to find the wreckage at some later date.

Then he dragged the disabled robots back to the shuttle and loaded them inside.

Jonathan stood inside cargo bay seven, which had been turned into a makeshift scientific research area. A long glass wall divided the bay in two, with the centerpiece—the translucent container holding the alien—residing on the same side as the bay doors. Bay seven was chosen for its easy access to outer space. If the alien escaped, it was a simple matter of opening the bay doors: the resultant explosive decompression would readily expel the creature from the ship. Opening a pair of doors was a far preferable option to blowing up half a deck.

Five masters-at-arms and an equal number of combat robots secured the bay on the alien side of the divider. Jonathan stood on the opposite side, beside the scientists, who studied various unseen readouts on their aReals, pretending to look busy.

The chief scientist, Lieutenant Connie Meyers, stood beside him.

"The container is holding strong," the attractive woman said. "I told you this combination of polycarbonate, PVB, glass, and ThermoPlastic Urethane would hold the thing."

"You did indeed," Jonathan said. "But that doesn't mean the container won't eventually wear down."

"If it does, we'll reinforce it as necessary," Connie said.

"So what have we learned so far?" Jonathan said.

"Well, there's definitely something inside that darkness,"

Connie said. "We catch a glimpse of the occasional claw, or a proboscis now and then. We're not entirely sure what purpose the darkness serves. Maybe it nourishes the alien. Maybe it's some sort of portable atmosphere that follows it around. In any case, you'll of course be the first to know of anything new we learn."

"Remember, whatever you learn here is classified," Jonathan said. "You're not to talk about this with any friends or family members aboard. I don't want to cause a panic."

"Is that why you didn't make a general announcement about the capture?"

"The fewer people who know about the alien presence, the better. While the *Callaway's* crew is one of the most disciplined in the galaxy, her members are under enough stress as it is. Can I count on you to hold your tongue, Lieutenant?"

"Of course, Captain."

"Good." Jonathan stared at the black mass. Should it be treated as a prisoner of war, as Robert suggested? No. They couldn't afford to grant it the same rights that would be given a human. Not when they knew so little about the creatures.

He turned toward Connie. "You do realize you have my complete authorization to experiment on it fully?"

"Yes, I figured as much, given your previous order."

"I'm not sure you understand what I want," Jonathan said slowly. "So let me be clear: I need to know how to kill these things."

She regarded him uncertainly. "You're ordering me to kill this alien? If I can?"

"Not necessarily. Injuring it is fine, too. Mostly I want to know how we can get our weapons to penetrate that black fog of theirs. The MOTH chief seems to think it's a shield of some sort."

Connie nodded. She seemed relieved that he wasn't asking her to kill it outright. "I'll see what I can do."

Jonathan glanced at the stationary man who sat cross-legged on the floor directly in front of the container. His eyes were closed and he appeared to be meditating. "Has our friend had any luck, yet?"

"None," Connie said. "I should remind the captain that I

object to this sort of unscientific mumbo jumbo. And if the captain were to promptly send away the man, this chief scientist would be extremely happy."

"You don't believe in telepaths?" Jonathan said.

"I do not."

"Telepaths exist, Lieutenant," Jonathan said. "And are among us. Empirical evidence has proven it."

"Though not everyone agrees with this evidence," Connie said. "Such as myself."

"The navy does," Jonathan said. "Or NAVCENT wouldn't assign a telepath to every ship."

"I've never agreed with that policy, though the navy has shoved worse things down our throats, I suppose." Connie shook her head. "I once met a telepath at a fair. He was able to correctly predict what card would be chosen from a deck seven times out of ten. Circus tricks. That's all telepaths are good for."

"You would be surprised, I think." Jonathan tapped his lips with three fingers. "But what you described isn't exactly telepathy. Listen, when I was younger I didn't believe in them either."

"What made you change your mind?"

He smiled wanly. He didn't dare tell her about his recurring visions of Famina. Instead he said: "Humanity is evolving, Lieutenant. Mutations subtly change us every century. The Human Accelerated Regions of the genome ensure it. More and more human beings are exhibiting signs of psychic abilities every year. In a few millennia, there's a good possibility a quarter of humanity will be telepathic. It's the next stage of human evolution."

"Yes, well, that's all well and good for the future of humankind. But as I said, in the here and now telepaths are good solely for circus acts. From what I've seen, anyway."

"Objection noted. You should really read up on the latest research, though. It's fairly convincing."

"I'm sure it is."

He nodded toward the divider. "Mind if I talk to him?"

"By all means." Connie beckoned toward the metal hatch installed in the glass wall. "He's here only because of you, after all."

She opened the entry hatch with her aReal and Jonathan stepped through.

He knelt beside the telepath and flinched at the sudden pain in his knee.

Getting old.

"Hello Captain." The man hadn't opened his eyes yet. "Watch your knee."

Not bad.

"Thank you, sir," the man said.

Jonathan cocked an eyebrow. "Impressive. You're Barrick?"

"I am." The telepath finally looked at the captain.

Jonathan stared at the amorphous mass that rested on the bottom of the container beside him. An alien species. It's language completely unknown and inaccessible to humanity. No one had any idea where to begin, as far as communication was concerned.

The telepath was a start, if perhaps a feeble one.

"I'd hardly label myself feeble," Barrick commented.

"Would you mind not doing that?" Jonathan said.

Barrick seemed taken aback. "Doing what?"

"The whole reading my mind without my permission thing," Jonathan said.

"Sorry, Captain." Barrick lowered his gaze. "Sometimes I feel like I have to prove myself."

"The chief science officer got to you, didn't she?" Jonathan said.

"Somewhat. I have trouble reading her."

Jonathan pursed his lips. "That would explain her attitude."

"Yes."

"And you have no trouble reading me?"

"Not at all, Captain," Barrick said. "You are an open book."

"Well that's good to know," Jonathan said, his voice dripping sarcasm. "So tell me, have you been able to reach our prisoner?"

"I've been trying," Barrick said. "But it's like there are these giant, monolithic barriers surrounding its mind."

"All right," Jonathan said, taking on the role of the doubter for the sake of Connie, who was probably listening in with

Maxwell's help. "Let's say you get through. How will you even communicate with it?"

"Various means," Barrick said. "I'll attempt images. Sounds. Feelings. I'll throw the gamut of human senses at it."

"Yes," Jonathan said. "And that's the key word. *Human* senses. This alien may use faculties we're entirely unaware of to communicate. We have no idea how its sensory inputs interpret the universe, none whatsoever. Maybe to this alien, light is treated as hearing, touch is sight, and sound is smell. Or to give you another more concrete example, look at the sperm whales of Earth. They communicate using three-dimensional holographic images transmitted via sound waves. I don't need to tell you how long it took us to figure that out. You propose to communicate with this alien via thought. But how can you do that when you think in human words, pictures, and sounds, and not whatever sensory inputs the alien uses?"

Barrick regarded him calmly. He seemed hesitant, as if afraid the captain wouldn't like the answer he had in mind. Finally, the telepath spoke.

"There is a theory, Captain, that every being in the universe is linked to a higher dimension. Call it a soul, call it an invisible cord leading away from every living thing that travels up the dimensions to a shared plane. Human, alien, it doesn't matter. We're all linked to that collective dimension from which all life originates. The Wellspring. And just because we can't see that shared world, or hear it, or touch it, doesn't mean it doesn't exist. I believe telepaths have access to this higher, communal consciousness. To this Wellspring. It is through that realm I will reach the alien."

Jonathan smiled wearily. He suddenly understood very well what Connie meant when she spoke of telepathy as mumbo jumbo.

"All right." Jonathan stood. "Keep me posted on your findings."

twenty-five

Jonathan shifted in his seat and crossed his legs. He was seated in the office of the chief weapons engineer.

"So what do you have for me today, Harv?" Jonathan asked the man.

"I think I can upgrade the external firing sensors," Harv said. "To enable our mag-rails to better target the enemy fighters."

"How?" Jonathan hoped he didn't regret the question. Harv was known to spout complex engineerese.

"Well, as you know by now, we lost our entire starboard bank of Vipers in the last battle."

Jonathan nodded. In an earlier update the lieutenant had mentioned how the power system for that bank of lasers was completely melted and likely couldn't be repaired until dry dock. A "regrettable loss," in his words.

"But there is a silver lining," Harv continued. "Because the processors tied to the Vipers themselves are still intact. We can transfer some of those processors away from the damaged heavy beams, and I can upgrade the main targeting system so it can more quickly acquire the enemy fighters when they come into range of the point defenses. It won't be much, but it will shave a few microseconds off the acquisition subroutine."

"Microseconds?"

"Like I said, it's not much, but at the speeds most space

combat occurs, it could mean the difference between a hit or a miss. When the enemy fighters are harassing us in waves, I'm sure you'd rather have a hit more often than a miss."

"How long will the upgrades take?" Jonathan asked.

"Two days."

"Do it," Jonathan instructed Harv. "And send the specs for these upgrades to your counterparts throughout the task group. Have the warships transfer processors from damaged Vipers to the targeting system, and if no Vipers are damaged, instruct your counterparts to take a few offline. I want every ship in possession of upgraded point defenses when the next attack comes."

The weapons engineer grinned slyly. "Already done."

Jonathan cocked his head. "I don't know whether to chew you out for undermining my authority or to congratulate you for taking the initiative."

"I would prefer the latter," Harv said. "I don't think I could take a chewing out with a straight face. I laughed my ass off through boot camp, you know."

Jonathan had to grin at that. "The latter it is."

The task group finished collecting the survivors from the wreckages of the *Linea*, *Selene*, *Devastator* and *Halberd*, then set a course for Achilles with the goal of using the gas giant as a gravitational slingshot. The maneuver would cut three days from their travel time to the 1-Vega Slipstream.

Jonathan ordered the *Aurelia* to stay behind with the *Marley* to protect it while that ship affected major repairs. The *Grimm*, as the second most vulnerable ship in the task group, also remained behind. Most of the engineering crew and 3D-printing robots from both ships were temporarily transferred over to the *Marley* to aid in repairs.

Jonathan had allowed the only survivor from Task Unit One, the *Salvador*, to come along with them, despite the fact Captain Rail had been so deeply entrenched in the admiral's camp. The *Salvador's* communications had proven readily repairable, with the damage to her engines and weapons systems minimal; because of her extensive firepower, he decided to give the captain a chance to redeem herself.

Jonathan had the vessels under his command launch one nuke each toward the uncharted 2-Vega Slipstream. The weapons were programmed to drift most of the way, using minimal propellant for course corrections, with instructions to form a hexagonal pattern right in front of the Slipstream boundary, effectively mining the entrance. If any more reinforcements arrived, the enemy would be in for a little surprise.

Jonathan had his communications officer transmit a continuous message in all known languages to the remaining enemy ships, offering to exchange the alien prisoner for their human hostages. So far no response had come. That likely ruled out a diplomatic resolution to the conflict.

Without the *Marley* and *Grimm* to slow them down, the task group made good progress. Robert's coordinated offensive must have inflicted more damage on the capital ship than previously believed, because the human ships were slowly gaining on the alien targets. The task group was scheduled to overtake the targets in five days, roughly two days from the exit Slipstream.

Meanwhile, the sentry ship had abandoned its guard position of 1-Vega, and was well on its way to rendezvousing with the other two. When a comm drone appeared from the Slipstream a day later, the sentry ship simply fired its directional EMP weapon at the distant object, frying the drone's electronics to prevent any transmissions.

The sentry joined its brethren two days later, and together the convoy proceeded toward the Slipstream at the pace of the damaged capital ship.

At that point the human task group was only two days away. Tensions were high throughout the *Callaway*. When Jonathan walked the passageways to visit one department head or another in person, the nods of the crew were often stiff, their eyes weary and lined with worry. Yet there was also pride in those eyes, and determined purpose. They were battle-hardened men and women by that point, crew members who had journeyed to the brink, looked over it, and lived.

Jonathan hoped they would all survive in the days to come.

If he had anything to do with it, they would.

I won't let you down, Jonathan mentally promised his crew as he strode those passageways. *I swear it.*

Barrick floated in the mind world. He was surrounded by points of light, as if he resided in deep space. Sometimes square planes of pure darkness soared past him, alternately appearing above, below, to his right, or to his left. Occasionally multiple planes passed by simultaneously, momentarily forming an open-ended cube around him.

Those planes were the barriers the alien mind put up whenever he tried to reach out to one of those points of light.

So far, those barriers proved impenetrable, like the minds of Presidents and CEOs who were trained to fight off telepathic probing attempts. He had placed similar ramparts around his own mind, of course: the last thing he needed was an alien presence messing with his consciousness.

He had been at it for what seemed like weeks so far. But time behaved differently in the mind world... weeks there would be mere minutes in reality.

There. A change. When he tried to touch a certain point of light, the plane that intercepted him felt slippery, somehow. He tried again. Yes. He thought he could slide past if he applied more of himself.

Gathering his reserves, he reached out. Once again a dark plane soared past, blocking his attempt. He almost touched the light that time, but not quite.

He moved some of his concentration away from his own mental barriers, weakening them very slightly, then reached for the star again. The dark plane intercepted him once again but he didn't bounce off that time. The plane remained in place, and with effort, he was able to slide across its surface.

It was working.

He was slipping past.

And then he was through, past the darkness, hovering beside the light.

Something was wrong.

He was being pulled toward the light.

He struggled to increase his mental barriers, but it was no use.

The light had become a vast, whirling vortex. A maelstrom

of stars from which there was no escape.

As he was sucked inside, he tried to shout. Tried to call for help.

But he had no voice.

The light consumed him.

Jonathan stared at the telepath. Barrick sat cross-legged and unresponsive outside the larger container the scientists had transferred the alien into.

Earlier, the chief scientist had told him Barrick had failed to rouse from his scheduled "deep dive" session. When he finally did open his eyes an hour later, she found Barrick in his current state and alerted the captain. Jonathan had promptly come down to cargo bay seven.

He snapped his fingers in front of the man's face. Barrick didn't blink.

"Have you tried shining light into his eyes?" Jonathan asked.

"His pupils dilate," Connie said.

"So he's not a vegetable."

"We can move him out of here now?" Connie asked hopefully. "To sick bay?"

"I want him here," Jonathan said. "He might be in contact with the alien at this very moment. I don't want to sever that connection by moving him somewhere."

"Fine."

Jonathan regarded the new container Connie's team had placed the alien inside. It was subdivided into two sections by a glass partition. One compartment contained a firing frame that various weapons could be mounted to. It currently held an M1170 laser pulse gun. The other section contained the dark mass of the alien. A shutter in the partition moved aside at nano speeds to allow the weapon to fire; the shutter was needed, even for the laser, because the inside of the container was coated with a special substance that absorbed laser fire—a necessary precaution to prevent the alien from shooting its own weapon at them.

"Any update on my previous order?" Jonathan asked her.

"Your 'tell me how to kill these things' order?"

"That's the one."

"I've set up a high speed camera with a shutter speed of two thousand frames per second and taken footage of the alien. That darkness around it seems to flicker off occasionally—for a few nanoseconds—revealing a more compact darkness underneath. I haven't found the pattern yet, but we've been experimenting with the laser pulse gun, shooting at an inconspicuous portion of the amorphous body and varying the frequency of the pulses. With luck, we'll find the perfect modulation to allow the beams to pass through."

Jonathan noticed the grid-like plates that had been setup on the far side of the glass compartment containing the alien—those were probably there to record if any of the photons from the weapon passed through.

"Frequency modulation," he said doubtfully. "It sounds like your experiment is based more on conjecture than solid science."

She shrugged. "As most experiments are."

"Well, keep me updated on your progress. And notify me if there's any change in Barrick."

A few hours later Connie contacted him on the bridge: "Your telepath started moving his hands about ten minutes ago. We realized he was using a drawing program on his aReal. I had one of our cyber specialists tap in, and we downloaded the picture. Would you like to see it?"

"Send it my way," Jonathan told her.

A few moments later a rough three-dimensional picture hovered in front of him, depicting a naked human with several wires connected to his body. Jonathan interpreted it to mean Barrick was in contact with the alien.

"All right," Jonathan told Connie. "I want you to have an artist draw a picture of a human hand extended in friendship toward a dark mass. Print it out and put it in front of Barrick. Give him a charcoal so that he can add to the picture."

About an hour later Connie relayed what happened. "When we gave him the picture, the telepath grabbed the charcoal and began drawing over it. Would you like to see the edits?"

"Please, Lieutenant."

When she sent the updated drawing, Jonathan felt disturbed by what he saw. The telepath had extended the darkness to cover the human hand entirely, and on the rest of the arm gashes had been drawn into the skin. Dark drops representing blood dripped from the wounds.

"We can't be sure the actual alien is communicating with us," Connie sent over the comm. "What we're looking at could be a figment of the telepath's own damaged mind. The aftereffects of the contact attempt on his psyche."

"Has he said a word, yet?"

"Negative."

"Keep me updated on his condition," Jonathan said. "Captain out."

twenty-six

Wolf opened his eyes. His gaze met complete, utter darkness.

He was completely naked, his body buoyed up by the cold water he resided within. When he reached out with his arms, he felt the cool metal bulkheads of some sort of tank. He attempted to swivel his body around, but the container was tight, affording him little room to maneuver. He explored in the dark as he could, searching for breaks in the smooth metallic surface, but he found none.

He remained motionless, thinking. Thoughts were all he had there in that tank of sensory deprivation.

He sensed subtle G-forces for the next hour or so. And then the forces exerted on his suspended body abruptly increased, and his feet slammed into the metallic base of the pod that held him. Waves of water reflected from the bulkheads and washed over his face.

He heard the hiss of escaping air as a rectangular outline of dim light appeared in the overhead above him. That section of the tank slid aside. He blinked several times: though the illumination was dim, it still took a moment for his eyes to adjust. When they did so, he found himself staring at a metallic grating located roughly two meters above him. A ceiling of some kind.

The pod had opened.

He forced himself to stand. His muscles felt weak, as if atrophied from several days of disuse.

He stood in a tight, cylindrical chamber. The dim light was sourced from the bulkheads—glowing blue filaments ran along their lengths. The metal egg that had birthed him lay in the middle of the compartment, taking up much of the space. As he watched, the topmost panel of the tank resealed.

The subtle groan and creak of moving metal came from the far side of the compartment. He turned toward it. The bulkhead there gradually slid aside.

He was struck by a sudden stench that reminded him of farm animals.

A group of shadows stood in the dimly lit chamber beyond.

"It's not the food," one of the shadows said.

Wolf was ushered to the front of the group. Human beings. They were all naked. Like cattle, or animals in a zoo.

"Jason," someone said.

He would've recognized that voice anywhere. "Lin?"

She hugged him. Her naked body felt warm against his skin, though any arousal he might have felt was offset by her stench.

"Come with me," she said.

She led him across the dimly lit chamber. It was expansive, though the overdeck was only a few inches from his head. The bulkheads around them were windowless steel, with no obvious cameras.

More naked men and women sat in large groups on the featureless deck. Some of them huddled for warmth. The stench of FAN—feet, ass, nuts—was overwhelming in those areas, and he pinched his nose.

"Feel like I'm in bootcamp all over again," Wolf said. "Though at least back then, some of us tried to shower."

"You'll get used to it," Lin said. "And yeah, there are no showers."

"So where the hell are we?" he asked her.

"The alien ship, probably," Lin said. "We're prisoners. These are the crew members of the *Selene*."

She took a wide detour past an area that served as a common latrine, judging from the smell and the lack of any permanent human presence. She took him to the far side of the compartment and halted beside a small group of people.

"Is it him?" a woman asked.

"Yes," Lin told her.

"Sit, sit," the woman said. She appeared young, maybe mid-twenties. Though of course with rejuvenation treatments you could never really tell someone's age these days. She didn't seem to smell as bad as the others. Maybe it was wishful thinking.

Wolf seated himself beside her. "Who are you?"

"I'm Captain Chopra of the *Selene*."

"Tell me you have an escape plan," Wolf said, trying very hard not to look at her naked breasts in the dim light.

Chopra smiled sadly. "Direct and to the point." She glanced at Lin. "I like him." She returned her attention to Wolf. "There is no escape from this place, Lieutenant Commander. We've searched the bulkheads, there are no weak points. The airlock is the only way in and out. Normally, our captors use it to deposit the organic sludge that serves as our food. Though occasionally, human beings such as Lin and yourself arrive."

"Have you tried camping out in the airlock after the food arrives?" Wolf asked.

"Some of us have," Chopra said. "When it opens again for the next delivery, those who camped out are gone and never return."

He heard a soft, robotic wail.

"What's that?"

"The warning tone. It tells us the airlock is about to seal."

He glanced over his shoulder. Sure enough, the metal there had begun to creak and groan as the door slid sideways.

"How many survivors are there?" Wolf asked.

"Twenty-eight. We've lost sixteen to the escape attempts. And another ten were simply taken."

"Taken?"

"Yes. Sometimes when the airlock opens, an invisible, scentless incapacitating agent spreads throughout the compartment. Knocks us out cold. When we awaken, two of us are gone. Usually a man and a woman."

"A man and a woman." Wolf glanced at Lin, and asked Chopra. "When is the next food delivery scheduled?"

"We've lost track of time," Chopra said. "We don't have aReals. Implants don't work. The food will come when it comes. Why, are you hungry?"

"Yes. But that's not the reason I ask. I have no intention of sitting around waiting to die. I'm going to be the next one who attempts an escape."

The food had arrived in a pod similar to the one that had brought him here.

Wolf and Lin stood inside the airlock. The pair watched the designated gatherers pile the sludge into their arms for their groups.

"Are you sure you want to do this?" he asked her.

Lin wrapped her hand around his. "You go, I go."

After the last of the gatherers had taken their share, Chopra stepped forward and extended a hand. "Good luck."

Wolf shook her palm. He no longer had any trouble ignoring her breasts; it was surprising how easy a man could desensitize himself to female nudity.

Chopra shook Lin's hand next and then turned to go.

"We'll come back for you," Wolf said.

Chopra glanced over her shoulder. "Of course you will." She smiled sadly, like she didn't believe it.

Wolf and Lin lowered themselves into the pod one after the other. Lin slipped on the thin layer of sludge that remained on the bottom, and her body pressed violently into his.

They were facing one another, naked. She shifted, trying to get into a more comfortable position, but the tight confines didn't allow for much legroom. She was forced to remain on top of him.

Wolf felt the blood rushing to his genitals.

After a moment, she lifted her head to look into his eyes.

"You're aroused?" she said, sounding incredulous.

"It's like I'm reliving all the sexual fantasies of my childhood," Wolf commented.

"Your sexual fantasy was to be trapped aboard an alien ship, locked inside a pod coated with disgusting sludge, and pressed up against a stinking, malnourished woman?" Her voice sounded slightly husky.

"Something like that. Minus the disgusting sludge, and the stinking part."

The warning tone came. The airlock door began to close. The pod sealed, too, enveloping the pair in darkness. A slight hiss came as the final rectangle of light that outlined the opening vanished. It had to be an airtight seal.

Lin's breathing increased.

"I'm scared," she said. Definitely husky.

Ignoring the magnified stench of her body, he mashed his lips against hers and made love to her there in the darkness.

The pod shifted, but he ignored it. The two of them continued to rut.

After he climaxed, she lay on top of him in the tight confines, breathing in and out gently into his ear.

"We're probably going to run out of oxygen and die, you know," Lin said.

"Can't think of a better way to go," Wolf commented.

Several more minutes passed. The container continued to shift now and then: the pair were obviously being conveyed somewhere.

"You think they know we're hiding in here?" Lin said.

"Oh they know," Wolf told her.

"Good," Lin said. "Because I'd hate to have the pod open into some unbreathable environment."

"They have other plans for us than immediate death, I'm sure," Wolf said.

After some time the pod shook and a soft thud indicated the container had been lowered to the floor.

He heard a distant clang, followed by another one. It sounded like the twin peals of a closing airlock. Either whoever had brought them there had gone, or someone new had arrived.

A hiss accompanied the crack of light that appeared as the pod opened.

"Well, it's pressurized anyway," Wolf said. "And breathable, at least by human standards."

The two of them waited a moment, letting their eyes adjust, then Lin pushed herself up. She lifted her torso past the opening.

"What do you see?" Wolf asked.

"I—"

A large metallic pincer wrapped around her torso and she was unceremoniously hauled from the container.

Wolf curled his knees into his chest, and carefully peered over the rim of the opening.

Another giant pincer grabbed at him.

He ducked and shifted his weight sideways, overturning the pod. He rolled out and stood up.

Composed of black metal, two large robotic arms dangled from the ceiling. One of them carried Lin. The other was headed straight for Wolf.

He dodged to the side and leaped over a nearby table. A human being was strapped to it. Wolf's hands caught on one of the man's organs—his chest had been opened up to expose his insides.

The robot pincer came in again.

Wolf ducked under the table. He heard a soft smushing sound as the pincer slammed into the dissected body above.

Wolf specifically noted that Lin wasn't screaming up there. Either she was dead or she was exhibiting the discipline drilled into her during training:

Suffer in silence. You scream, you draw the enemy.

He surveyed his surroundings in the dim light, taking advantage of the heightened awareness the danger imbued his senses.

He was inside a pressurized lab of sorts. The bulkheads were lit by the same glowing blue filaments as the prison. There were more humans present on some of the adjacent tables. Most of their bodies were dissected, like the man above. Many were still alive, judging from their breathing—feeding tubes had been shoved down throats, excretion tubes forced into urethras and anal passages. Smaller robots similar to surgical weavers operated on a few of them.

On the far end he noticed a pile where human spacesuits, clothing, and other belongings had been placed. Some of the items were laid out on a table for analysis. One of the smaller robots was examining a spacesuit helmet at that moment.

He spotted a plasma rifle almost buried near the bottom. Careless, overconfident aliens, packing the gear alongside the very humans they experimented on. While it was convenient, perhaps, it wasn't the best idea on their part.

He observed all of that in the span of three heartbeats. The robot arm was already reaching under the table.

Wolf rolled out from his cover, dodged between the tables, and dove toward the plasma rifle. He wrenched it from underneath the pile, turned the weapon toward the giant arm, flicked the safety off, and squeezed off two shots as the black metal weaved in.

Molten slag sprayed the compartment on the other side of the impact site. In place of the robot arm a confused stump hung from the overhead and twisted to and fro.

He turned toward the remaining arm that held Lin. She appeared to be alive—she was struggling as the pincers held her down on one of the operating tables while a smaller robot welded a metal strap to her wrist. He fired another salvo, aiming for the joint that connected the arm to the overhead.

The large robotic limb broke away from the joint and fell to the deck, ripping the pincer portion from Lin.

Wolf went to her. He kicked the smaller robot off her and shot it, dissolving its torso.

"You okay?" he said.

Still speechless, she tore away the half-welded metal strap that held her wrist to the table.

Then she got up and promptly hugged him.

"Thank you," she said.

None of the other small robots bothered to pay them any heed; the things continued to go about their tasks as if oblivious to their presence. Wolf proceeded to shoot all the ones that were operating on humans.

When he was done, he rejoined Lin.

"Why are there no other guards?" she said.

"I don't know," Wolf told her. "But I'm finding it hard to believe the aliens are *that* confident. On a human ship, we'd have at least a score of armed men assigned to guard any alien captives."

"Maybe they want us to escape," Lin said.

"What do you mean?"

"It's possible there's some sympathetic faction aboard."

"Yeah well," Wolf said. "I don't think we really have time to speculate. While there are no guards right now, I doubt the situation is going to remain that way. Let's get suited up."

He and Lin rushed to the pile of spacesuits and began shrugging on the cooling and ventilation undergarments, followed by the main assemblies.

After attaching the final component, the helmet, he donned a utility belt and a harness, then stuffed enough spare oxygen canisters into the latter item to last a few days. The spacesuits came with enough water and meal replacements to last a similar amount of time, if rationed properly.

He turned to go when he spotted a comm node lying next to the pile of human gear. The node was partially inside a backpack—the kind a dedicated communications officer would lug about during a mission.

"Let's go, Jason," Lin said. Fully-suited, she was waiting halfway across the compartment; she kept a plasma rifle aimed at the entry hatch.

"Wait."

"Time's ticking away," Lin said. "We can't stay here!"

Via the aReal built into his helmet, he pulled up the list of all remotely accessible devices in the area. The comm node showed up. He powered it on through the aReal.

"It still works," Wolf said. "Though it looks like it only has enough power for one last transmission."

"Hurry, then," Lin said.

"*Callaway*," he transmitted. "Or whoever is still out there, this is Lieutenant Commander Jason Wolf. I'm here with Lieutenant Lin Akido. We're on board one of the alien vessels. The crew of the *Selene* is here. There are twenty-eight survivors. A rescue would be grand, if you could manage it."

The comm node cut out before he could say any more.

"Did it work?" Lin asked.

"I don't know. I'm not sure the signal even got past the hull."

"Let's move." Lin approached the hatch.

Wolf joined her. "How do we open it?"

Lin aimed her plasma rifle and fired. The reinforced metal melted in the center, revealing another hatch a meter away—

the two formed part of an airlock. A plume of yellow mist gushed inside as the atmosphere of the airlock rushed to fill the compartment.

She fired again, widening the hole, and blasting a gap into the airlock's second hatch. More yellow air rushed inside. Its expansion was fast, but not explosive, indicating that the pressure between the two compartments was relatively equal.

The partially-dissected bodies strapped to the tables began wheezing.

Lin looked at them, anguish suddenly on her face. "I've killed them."

"You did them a favor." Wolf took a third shot, enlarging the opening in the second hatch.

The compartment around him was now entirely hued yellow, thanks to the new atmosphere.

He was about to approach the remains of the hatch when he noticed a device resting on a metal shelf beside him.

Curious, he picked it up. It looked like a remote control of some kind, but without any buttons.

Without warning a black mist erupted from the device and enveloped his entire body. The mist seemed to pulse, and alternated between opaque and translucent, allowing him to peer past.

"Jason," Lin said. Her voice sounded distorted. Low-pitched. "Jaaaaassssooooon."

She turned her rifle toward him. The act was ridiculously drawn-out, as if she moved in slow motion.

He dropped the device and the opaque mist immediately dissipated.

Lin lowered the rifle and stared at him. "What happened? One second you were there, the next a dark mist had replaced you."

"You didn't see me at all?"

"No."

"I think I've found our ticket out of here." He nodded toward the device. "I'm starting to give credence to your theory that some of the aliens are helping us. Either that, or we're on an extremely lucky streak."

"Let's hope that streak doesn't run out."

"Agreed," he said. "Now come here."

Lin wrapped her arm assembly around his waist.

Wolf picked up the device and the darkness enveloped them both.

Rifles at the ready, they proceeded through the airlock and into the passageway beyond.

twenty-seven

Jonathan sat in his place at the Round Table on the bridge. The task group was in the process of using the gas giant Achilles to slingshot toward the outer reaches of the solar system. The forces exerted by the gravity well at the current distance were moderate, and the compartment shook slightly.

"Captain," the communications officer, Rald Lazur, said. "I'm receiving a transmission."

"From who?" Jonathan thought it was from another vessel in the task group, probably the *Grimm* or one of the other ships they had left behind.

"The signal is..." Lazur looked up urgently. "The signal is coming from the alien ships. You're not going to believe this, but it's Lieutenant Commander Jason Wolf."

Jonathan straightened. "Let's hear it."

The message came over his aReal. Voice only. There was some digital warping because of the interference caused by the gas giant's radiation belts.

"Callaway, or whoever is still out there, this is Lieutenant Commander Jason Wolf. I'm here with Lieutenant Lin Akido. We're on board one of the alien vessels. The crew of the *Selene* is here. There are twenty-eight survivors. A rescue would be grand, if you could manage it."

Jonathan glanced at Lazur. "Is that all there is?"

"That's all."

"Which ship did it come from?"

"One of the dart escorts," the comm officer said. "I've highlighted it on the tactical display."

"Miko, tag that ship. I want you to keep track of it at all times."

"Tagged," Miko said.

"So they're alive after all," Robert said. "And imprisoned with the crew of the *Selene*. Time to formulate a rescue strategy?"

Jonathan opened his mouth. He didn't have an answer. He was still processing the news.

"You think it's a trap?" Robert asked.

"Possibly," Jonathan said. "But I can no longer justify holding back our elite teams. We can't leave the crew of the *Selene* to die."

"So I suppose we're no longer going to treat the tagged ship with extreme prejudice when we attack?" Robert said.

"Oh we are," Jonathan said. "But we're going to rescue our two pilots, and the crew of the *Selene*, first." He turned to his tactical officer. "Miko, you and Maxwell have had ample time to review the battle footage."

"We have, Captain," Miko agreed.

"And you've thought of some potential strategies?"

"A few. I shared most of them with you."

"Yes, I saw the message. Well, I have some bad news. You'll have to augment your strategies to include a rescue. I want you to coordinate with the Lieutenant Commander in charge of the MOTH teams. You have one day to come up with something." He turned to Robert. "Commander, schedule a conference with the captains and first officers of the combat task unit for tomorrow at oh nine hundred." He glanced at his tactical officer one more time. "Miko, you'll be presenting your findings there."

Miko swallowed, obviously nervous. "Yes, sir."

Some of the best officers had a slight fear of public speaking. Well, it would be good for him.

Jonathan felt a wave of sudden despair. *Good for him? Yes, for a whole day.*

No! a dissenting voice cried. *I won't let my crew down.*

Even so, Jonathan knew it might very well be the last speech the young officer ever made.

Jonathan leaned forward in his office chair. He folded his hands, steepled the index fingers, and tapped his lips. It was currently 0700. Two hours before the planned conference.

"Maxwell, tap in Miko," Jonathan said.

The holographic image of Miko appeared across from him, as if sitting in the chair.

"Tell me what you've come up with," Jonathan told Miko.

The lieutenant went over his findings, rehearsing the strategy he would reveal at the conference.

Jonathan interjected the occasional question to test parts of the plan that sounded weak, but Miko always gave a satisfactory answer.

"It's a good plan," Jonathan finally said. "Not too many moving parts. Well done, Lieutenant."

"Thank you, sir," Miko said. "But most of the credit for the rescue plan itself belongs to Lieutenant Commander Basette and Chief Galaal, the latter of whom will be carrying out the operation. And Maxwell gave a lot of input on the space battle side of things."

It sounded like he was hoping Jonathan would nominate Basette or Maxwell to give the presentation, but the captain wasn't going to let Miko off the hook so easily.

"Nonetheless, you orchestrated it all," Jonathan said. "So thank you. I'm looking forward to watching the presentation again at oh nine hundred. Dismissed."

When Miko's hologram clicked off, Jonathan gazed at the portal simulated by his aReal on the bulkhead beside him, and at the computer-generated stars slowly flitting past beyond it.

Space. So wide. So vast.

So deadly.

His door chime sounded.

"Come in, Commander," Jonathan said after checking who it was on his aReal.

Robert came inside and sat in the chair opposite the desk.

"So, did you talk to your wife yet?" Jonathan said.

"I did," Robert told him.

"And?"

"She's pissed that you told me about the baby. And she's still not sure whether she's going to abort it or not."

Jonathan frowned. "You told her not to, of course?"

"Of course."

Jonathan shrugged. "It is the woman's decision in the end. She's the one who has to carry it for nine months."

"All the same, I'd rather she kept it."

Jonathan nodded. "As would I."

"I must apologize once again for ever accusing you of having any sort of relationship with my wife."

"Apology accepted," Jonathan said.

"She loves you, you know," Robert commented casually.

Jonathan felt one of his eyebrows rise. "What are you talking about?"

"She told me once on shore leave, when she was drunk. Shortly before we married. Said she fell for you when she first came aboard the ship. Said that it was impossible to ever marry such a man as you. What were her words? Yes: we can never attain that which we truly desire." He smiled sadly. "So she married me. Her second choice."

Jonathan didn't know what to say for several moments.

Finally, he broke the silence.

"Maybe you were her second choice," Jonathan said carefully. "But the fact of the matter is, she married you, Robert. *You*. Not me. You're the one who shares her bed every night."

"Yes. I have her body. But will I ever truly hold her heart?"

Jonathan shook his head. "That's something I can't help you with, Robert. I'm an unmarried starship captain. I have no relationship advice to give. Wish I did, but that simply isn't my vocation. I can arrange a session with the marriage counselor, if you wish."

"Probably a good idea," Robert said.

"Consider it done." Jonathan returned his attention to the augmented reality window and the faux stars beyond it. The decoration was a shared augmentation, so Robert would see those stars on his aReal contact lenses, too.

"Nervous?" Robert said.

"About the conference?" Jonathan pursed his lips. "Not at

all. Not like the last time anyway, when I had to do something I thought I'd never have to. This conference will go well. And as for the coming battle, I'm resigned to my fate. We either win, or we lose. There's no in-between."

"But there is an in-between," Robert said. "And that's how many of our ships survive."

"No," Jonathan said. "Losing even one ship counts as a loss for me."

"Sometimes you're too hard on yourself," Robert said.

"Maybe." Jonathan returned his attention to the false stars. "Do you ever wonder if it was a mistake for humanity to expand across the galaxy? That our ancestors stepped far beyond their station when they journeyed into a universe they were entirely unprepared for?"

"We had to come to the stars," Robert said. "It was inevitable if humanity was to survive as a species. Eventually, we would have exhausted all the resources of our home planet. The population levels were simply unsustainable. And even farther out in time, our sun will eventually become a red giant, boiling away the surface of the homeworld. If we didn't colonize other planets and moons, or find a way to alter the orbit of the Earth, none of us would exist in five billion years time. Thankfully, humanity advanced at a much faster clip than that, and we left our home system long before then."

"Yes. But maybe it would have been better if we had waited a bit longer before leaving the Earth. A thousand years, maybe. Until our technology advanced to a more... competitive level."

Robert smiled wanly. "But given the infinite number of galaxies in the universe, there will always be a race somewhere out there more advanced than our own. The odds are simply too high to claim otherwise. Astronomical odds, really, if you don't mind the pun."

Jonathan rapped his fingers on the desk. He wondered if he should reveal to the commander what the scientists had told him the night before.

"Maxwell," Jonathan said. "Bring up port-side external camera. Focus on Achilles I."

The gas giant appeared before Jonathan, with the requested moon floating beside it. The captain gestured outward with his hand, a motion intended for his aReal—the video feed appeared to slide forward until it sat above the desk between himself and Robert.

"An Elder ruin resides on that moon," Jonathan said.

"Yes," Robert said. "Which only reinforces my previous point."

"Do you remember the odd readings the HS4s recorded while exploring those ruins? As if tiny wormholes had existed, warping the surrounding alloy?"

"I do," Robert said.

"The scientists tell me similar gravimetric impressions are patterning the container of the alien in our custody. They've determined that the creature emits gravity distortions in waves, with the alien suddenly exhibiting a weight eight to ten times its previous amount. The chief scientist, Connie Myers, says they'll have to apply new layers of glass and ThermoPlastic Urethane every few days to make up for those unexpected distortions, or else the container's structural integrity will weaken over time until the alien escapes."

"So wait," Robert said. "What are you saying? The aliens were exploring the Elder ruins, too, before we arrived? And left behind the evidence of their presence via the gravimetric distortions?"

Jonathan smiled patiently. "The scientists have a different theory. You see, the distortion patterns left behind in the Elder ruins imply a much smaller form factor than the alien prisoner. And a much longer gestation time, as if the aliens remained in the same place for at least several months, if not years. It seems likely, Commander, that the *Selene* stumbled on an alien nest down there."

Robert paused as if digesting the news. "And momma bear wasn't very happy."

"No. No she was not."

Robert rubbed his right ear lobe. "You know, these aliens might be the descendants of the Elder."

"Interesting speculation," Jonathan said. "Though we have no way to prove it. But if that were true, technologically they would be countless millennia ahead of our own species by now, wouldn't they? Reactionless drives, gravimetric weapons, impromptu Slipstream creation, the works. Instead, they're only very slightly ahead of us, and in some ways behind, given their apparent lack of long range weapons other than the laser array we destroyed."

"Maybe most of their knowledge was lost after their population was decimated?"

"Why are their ships so small then, compared to the ancient Elder vessels we've found?" Jonathan pressed. "Why don't they all rove the galaxy in flying Möbius strips?"

"Again, lost knowledge. And ship design is bound to change over a million years."

"Though in this case it seems they've regressed," Jonathan said. "Rather than progressed."

"It's possible they've evolved so much since the time of their ancestors so as to become unrecognizable. Or devolved, rather, and are now mere slivers of their former selves. Like the dinosaurs of Earth. After the K-T extinction event, only the smallest survived: those animals that didn't require the immense resources of their larger kin. You've seen what evolution did in that scenario. The closest living relative to the once powerful Tyrannosaurus Rex is the lowly chicken. From the top of the food chain to the bottom."

Jonathan chuckled. "So you think what we're facing right now is the Elder equivalent of the chicken?"

Robert laughed. "Sort of. But think about it. Humanity has experienced similar decimation events because of wars and disease, though on a lesser scale—and while we didn't change genetically all that much, we did lose centuries of knowledge. Look at the Black Plague. Or the Resettlement Wars. We're on the brink of such a decimation event right now, even. If we start using the planet killers, who can say how terribly human knowledge will suffer? Entire cultures and technologies will vanish."

Jonathan tapped a finger on the desk. "I suppose you're right, then. There is a chance these aliens are the descendants of the Elder."

"You seem disappointed, Captain."

Jonathan shrugged. "I guess I hoped the Elder had moved on from our section of the galaxy. That they'd attained some higher level of consciousness or enlightenment."

"A benevolent race that would welcome us with open arms and share the secrets of the universe with us?" Robert asked.

"Yes. But the Elders aren't some mystical beams of white light ready to shine enlightenment and knowledge into our eyes, but rather dark, amorphous, warlike beings who desire only our blood."

"You have to give them credit," the commander said. "They were only trying to protect their young."

"Maybe," Jonathan said. "But what about the second attack? That was unprovoked."

"Perhaps they believed we were going to use the planet killer against them eventually. Or maybe they wanted to capture it for themselves. You saw those grappling hooks in the replay."

"I guess we'll never know," Jonathan said. "They refuse all attempts at communication. Worse, they're guarding our only way out of here."

"They're afraid we'll call in reinforcements," Robert said.

"The same fear we have," Jonathan told him. "Damn it. Even if we win this, we'll be watching our backs for the next six months while the *Marley* builds a return Gate."

"You don't think the nukes we placed at the Slipstream entrance will stop them?"

"It will stop the first few reinforcements," Jonathan said. "After that..."

"We'll just have to hope they don't send any more ships for a long time."

"Yes," Jonathan said. "But we're getting ahead of ourselves. First, we have a small battle to win, and some crew members to rescue."

twenty-eight

Jonathan surveyed the participants seated around him in the virtual conference. The captains and first officers of the fleet had gathered around a large oval table. At the front of the room Miko stood beside a holographic display and gave his presentation on the tactics the fleet would use in the space battle. When he finished speaking Rade took over and detailed the MOTH plan to rescue the prisoners.

When both of them were done Jonathan said: "Thank you, Lieutenant, Chief." He turned toward the captains. "Comments or questions?"

Captain Rail of the *Salvador* spoke immediately. "This isn't going to work. The enemy is never going to fall for your tactical officer's little ruse. We should attack them all-out. Concentrate fire on the capital ship. Once we eliminate that vessel, the smaller targets will flee."

Jonathan had expected resistance from her, she who had firmly resided in the admiral's camp.

"Let's say you're right, and the other ships do actually flee," Jonathan said. "What happens to the prisoners from the *Selene*? We abandon them to their fate?"

"It would be the wisest course of action," Rail said. "You're wasting lives and effort on a rescue operation that's doomed to fail. We know nothing at all about the internal layout of the alien ship. Once the MOTH team is inside—*if* the team even makes it inside—they're expected to navigate a potential labyrinth, fight off alien security forces, and rescue twenty-eight prisoners? It's insane."

"I'm satisfied with the plan Chief Galaal has presented," Jonathan said. "Does anyone else other than Captain Rail have issues with it?"

The captains and first officers remained silent. Rail glanced at her own commander for support, and he feebly raised his hand. "I do."

"Anyone other than you?" Jonathan said.

No one spoke.

Jonathan nodded. "And what about the main battle plan? Any other objections?"

More silence.

"That's what I thought," Jonathan said. "It seems, Captain Rail, you are the only dissenter on this. You'll simply have to grin and bear it."

Captain Rail didn't seem too happy. "The *Salvador* should be the flagship. She's a destroyer. She has twice the firepower of the *Callaway*."

"We're not here to debate the chain of command," Jonathan said. "Nor the unfairness of life."

"If the admiral were still alive he would have you—"

"Thank you, Captain," Jonathan said. "That will be enough. Unless you would like me to relieve you of duty and promote your first officer in your place?"

Rail prudently kept her mouth shut.

"Lieutenant Harv Boroker has sent detailed instructions to your weapon engineers on how to upgrade the target acquisition systems of your point-defenses. Have any of your teams failed to perform the upgrades yet?"

"My teams haven't," Captain Williams of the *Maelstrom* said. "We had no spare processors to divert to the targeting. We could take some of our Vipers offline, as was suggested, but I decided I'd rather keep the full bank active."

"Take some of them down," Jonathan said. "Which would you rather have, twenty lasers that can't hit any of the fighters strafing your hull or ten mag-rails that hit their targets half the time?"

"Good point."

"What about fighter upgrades?" Jonathan asked the captains. "Have any former Task Unit One ships failed to outfit some of their Avengers with charged fields?"

"My weapons engineers have performed the necessary upgrades," Captain Rodriguez of the *Dagger* said.

Jonathan glanced at the captain of the *Salvador*. "Captain Rail?"

She stared at him defiantly for a moment, then said, curtly: "We've upgraded our fighters."

"Good. Because you didn't have the upgrades done before the previous engagement, according to the logs."

Rail's expression contorted in rage, but she quickly got a hold of herself and looked down.

"I think we're ready, then," Jonathan said. "Ready as we'll ever be, anyway. If there are no other questions...."

There weren't.

"We'll be fully engaged by this time tomorrow. I want your crews alert, and chomping at the bit. Have the planned watches take stims, if necessary. Good luck, Captains. I'd say we're in for a good fight."

Jonathan studied the tactical display overlaid on his vision.

"The enemy has halted, Captain," Ensign Lewis said.

"How far away are we?" Jonathan asked.

"One million kilometers."

"They're waiting for us," Jonathan said. "Good. Helm, continue at half speed. Miko, instruct the fleet to assume formation. Ops, begin venting radiation and atmosphere from the *Callaway*."

He momentarily switched to the view from cargo bay five. The designated bay doors opened a crack to allow the atmosphere to seep out. In order to facilitate the leakage, Jonathan had disabled the auto-seal feature of the appropriate hatches and vents.

The vessels in the task unit formed a defensive half sphere in front of the *Callaway*, with each vessel roughly thirty kilometers from the next, close enough to use their mag-rails and Vipers to eliminate any fighter threats to other ships in the formation, as necessary.

On the 3D display, the dots representing the United Systems task unit slowly advanced.

"Enemy is now eight hundred thousand kilometers away," Lewis announced thirty minutes later.

"Any change in their status?"

"No, Captain."

On the display, the three enemy dots were positioned ten kilometers apart in a rough horizontal line, twelve degrees below the plane of the system.

At the four hundred thousand kilometer mark, the two dart ships moved forward by five kilometers, forming a slight crescent with the capital ship.

Jonathan checked the inventory of long range weapons for the umpteenth time. Also for the umpteenth time, he asked himself if that inventory would truly be enough for what he had planned. Perhaps he should have taken a detour, pausing beside an asteroid for a week to mine the raw materials for mortars.

Don't second-guess yourself. It will be enough.

"Launch missile and mortar decoy spread," Jonathan said.

"Launching decoy spread," Miko said.

On the tactical display, four mortars were launched per ship, along with two kinetic kills each. The weapons clustered into three main groups, targeting one ship each, with the majority aimed at the capital ship.

It was a throwaway attack. Just enough munitions so that the intent seemed real, but not enough to impact the already low inventories. The hope was to instill a sense of overconfidence in the enemy and to begin the herding process.

"The three targets are accelerating," Ensign Lewis said. "Forward and downward. Looks like they're planning on sliding under the mortar funnel."

"Cut thrust. Point the nose at our targets and keep it there. Miko, transmit similar orders to the fleet."

A moment later Ensign Lewis reported: "Enemy targets are further adjusting course and increasing speed. Looks like they intend the flyby to occur within five thousand kilometers, at least."

"Shall I alter our heading to give them a wider berth?" the helmsman asked.

"Not yet." Jonathan watched the two opposing fleets slowly approach one another.

"Captain?" Miko glanced at Jonathan, waiting for the order to begin the next phase of the attack.

"Hold," Jonathan said.

He watched the kilometers between the two fleets slowly tick downward over the next several minutes.

Three hundred thousand.

Two hundred thousand.

"Enemy has closed to within one hundred thousand kilometers," Miko said.

"Hold," Jonathan said.

"Fifty thousand kilometers," Miko said.

"First wave of missiles has reached the sub-five thousand kilometer mark," Ensign Lewis announced. "Detecting thermal build-up on enemy targets." She looked up. "Our missiles have been eliminated."

"Captain?" Miko said.

"Hold."

Forty thousand kilometers.

Thirty five.

"Launch final missile and mortar spread in the appropriate configuration," Jonathan said. "Deploy Avengers and Dragon-flies. And cut speed by five percent. Let's give our Avengers a chance to pull ahead. "

"Launching final missile and mortar spread," Miko said. "Utilizing configuration gamma. And deploying fighters and shuttles."

Miko had several configurations already preprogrammed, with each one dependent on the enemy formation. The general strategy was to hem in each ship with nukes and missiles timed to arrive out of sequence with the particle beam weapons of each target, forcing the aliens to fire at the previous wave of incoming missiles while the second wave slipped through during the recharge interval.

Jonathan watched as the deadly funnels formed three groups targeting each enemy. That was the last of their long range weapons.

I hope I've used them wisely.

Avenger squadrons deployed fleet-wide a moment later, maneuvering in behind the different mortars. Two Dragonflies containing the MOTH rescue team joined the fray, positioning themselves in single file behind a manned Avenger and the shielding mortar beyond it. Two more Avenger drones brought up the rear.

If the nukes and kinetic kills detonated early, the Avenger squadrons were far enough away to avoid collateral damage; and the radiation armor on the Avengers and Dragonflies would protect the occupants from a deadly dose. The pilots and MOTHs would probably still need post rad treatment in such a scenario, however.

Blue Squadron escorted the MOTH rescue team. Red and Orange Squadrons, meanwhile, escorted two specially modified drone fighters. Those two unmanned Avengers contained a surprise for the enemy: the engineering teams had ripped out the guts of those fighters, replacing the weapons systems with nuclear warheads from the ship, essentially converting the Avengers into smart nukes.

The final squadron, Black, remained behind to protect the ships. That squadron hadn't been launched yet.

Jonathan had put the space wing commander in charge of all the fighters deployed by the task unit this time, rather than merely those fighters launched by the *Callaway*.

Jonathan tapped him in. "Albright, remember to have the fighters avoid the nose sections when traveling under a range of one klick to the enemy—the charged fields won't withstand the particle beams at that range."

"I got it," the lieutenant commander returned. He sounded a little peevish. "Albright out."

Try not to micromanage too much, Jonathan scolded himself.

He studied the display.

"Enemy capital ship is launching fighters," Ensign Lewis announced. "They're heading toward the mortars."

Jonathan nodded. It was expected that the aliens would catch on to their tactic of hiding fighters behind mortars, as Robert had used the same strategy to get the Avengers close to their laser array in the previous battle. Even so, it had been worth a try.

"Helm, fire starboard thrusters. Knock the *Callaway* out of range of their particle beam for the main flyby. I want our closest point to be no more than twenty thousand kilometers. Increase speed as necessary. Tactical, have the remainder of the task unit follow our lead."

"Enemy ships are attempting to compensate for our course change," Lewis said.

"Will they be able to close the gap?"

"I don't think so," Lewis said. "Their thrusters can't compensate for the immense forward inertia they've already built up."

"Good," Jonathan said. "Increase atmospheric ventage. Make it look like we're on our last legs. And helm, issue slight braking thrust. Let's see if we can draw some of those fighters."

"It's working," Ensign Lewis said several moments later. "Only half of the fighters are braking to engage our squadrons. The remainder are continuing toward us at full speed, and ignoring most of the other ships in the unit."

"We're too tempting a target," Jonathan said. "Though I was hoping we'd draw more of them. Helm, fire forward thrust again. Get us up to speed. Remember, I don't want to pass closer than twenty thousand kilometers with the main targets."

"Avengers are reporting contact," Ensign Lewis said.

White flashes filled the external video feed Jonathan had running in the upper right of his aReal.

"We lost three missiles in that strafing run," Miko said. "And one nuke. All Avengers are still operational, so far. As are the MOTH shuttles."

On the 3D display, the closest group of red dots continued past the mortar funnels, heading toward the *Callaway*, while the remainder continued braking to engage with the Avengers.

"We lost two more missiles," Miko said. "And the same number of Avengers. Remaining nukes still intact."

"Second group of fighters is braking," Miko said. That referred to the group headed toward the *Callaway*.

"Will they contact us before the flyby?" Jonathan said.

"Negative. But judging from their deceleration, they'll definitely catch up shortly thereafter unless we increase speed."

"The Dragonflies and their MOTH escorts are decelerating," Lewis said.

Those crafts would have to fire reverse thrust early if the Dragonflies wanted any chance of grappling to the targeted enemy vessel. On the display, Jonathan watched two red dots break away from the main battle to harass them.

The external camera feed flashed a few minutes later.

"The enemy ships launched their particle beams," Lewis said. "They've taken out some of the missiles and mortars. MOTHs are still en route."

"Helm, start pointing our port side toward the target. Don't alter our trajectory. Tactical, prepare to fire Vipers at the dart ship containing the prisoners. Transmit the order to the fleet."

At that range, the spot area would be sixteen centimeters cubed on the target, and the megajoule intensity roughly twenty times less than at five thousand kilometers. The plan was to target the same spot on the enemy hull, so that their combined firepower would compensate for the loss in intensity.

Ops had approximated the location on the enemy ship where Lieutenant Commander Wolf's transmission had come from, and it was eventually agreed to target the hull approximately two hundred meters to the left of said position. Since no one knew whether Wolf had actually made the transmission from the alien prison or somewhere else, it was possible the breach attack might end up harming the prisoners. However, there were always risks and unknowns in any battle. Such was the fog of war.

"Enemy is twenty thousand kilometers off our port side," Miko said. "Near to the closest point of the flyby."

"Fire fleet-wide broadsides," Jonathan said. "Open up a path for the MOTH teams."

"Firing," Miko said.

The display flashed.

"Direct hit," Miko said. "We—"

"I'm detecting a thermal build-up on all three ships," Lewis announced.

An even brighter flash filled the display.

The bridge shuddered.

Alarms started going off.

"What happened?" Jonathan said.

"The three enemy vessels fired their particle beams at the same time," Lewis said. "Joining their beams, like we did, to increase its intensity at this range. They ripped a gash along the entire length of our port side."

"How bad is it?"

"The beams penetrated the hull in several places: we have hundreds of breaches. We've lost launch bays two and six, and the entire bank of port Vipers. Reactor one is offline. Mess hall one destroyed. Sick bay destroyed. Two hundred crew members reported missing."

Jonathan rubbed his forehead. "Any good news?"

"Mag-rails are still intact on that side."

"That's one plus," the captain said. "Any damage to other vessels in the fleet?"

"Negative."

"Another plus," Jonathan said. "Now tell me we hit them good."

"We did, Captain," Lewis said. "After the impact I detected a plume of radiated heat from the prison ship, which promptly went cold. That matches the thermal profile of a hull breach."

"Status on the smart nukes?"

Two more quick flashes erupted on the external feed.

"The modified Orange Squadron drone struck its target and the nuke payload detonated," Miko said. "I'm registering wreckage: the second dart ship is completely gone." He paused. "It looks like the enemy fighters managed to shoot down the other drone before it reached the capital ship. The entirety of Red Squadron was destroyed when the nuke detonated."

"Damn it."

"However, several of the close range kinetic kill missiles got through," Miko continued. "And the capital ship is severely damaged."

"Instruct the remainder of Orange Squadron to concentrate fire on the capital ship. Let's see if we can sink the bastard."

"Enemy fighters are closing with the *Callaway*," Lewis announced.

"Launch Black Squadron!" Jonathan said.

"Black Squadron away," Miko said.

The enemy fighters reached the ship a moment later and the bridge shuddered.

"How are our point defenses holding up?"

"We've already shot down one of their fighters," Ensign Lewis said. "The bastards are hitting us good, though. They're concentrating fire on our port side, and the breaches there. Black Squadron is moving in."

On the display he saw the blue dots of Black Squadron move to intercept the incoming enemy.

"Status on the MOTH teams?" Jonathan asked Lewis.

"MOTH teams have landed."

The bridge shook as the alien fighters made another strafing run.

twenty-nine

Rade proceeded down the tight cylindrical passageway in single file after the Praetor and four Centurions. Three other human team members and four more Centurions brought up the rear; the two rearmost robots hoisted a portable airlock between them. Humans and robots alike carried spare spacesuits strapped to their backs.

Every member of the group was armed with an M1170 laser pulse gun. The chief scientist, Connie Myers, claimed she had found a way to penetrate the darkness the aliens used as a shield by modulating the firing rate of the lasers to a certain frequency. The M1170s the fireteam carried contained the necessary modifications. Rade also had a plasma rifle with him as a backup.

All the combat robots would be left behind, as every spare inch of space on the shuttles would be needed to hold the prisoners. There was no real worry about the human tech falling into the hands of the enemy, however—the bodies of each robot were rigged with powerful explosives. Though he had full remote control over the detonators, Rade was slightly worried that the explosives might go off prematurely in a firefight.

The landing had been rough. The two shuttles had fired reverse thrust long before the main target came into range, and they had to fend off several attack runs from the enemy fighters. By the time the prison ship had neared, they had reversed course completely and were moving at top speed in the same direction as the target. But the vessel had still approached with twice their velocity. The shuttles had jockeyed into position and fired magnetic grappling hooks as the target passed. The carbon fiber cords had grown taut—two broke away, but they reeled in the rest and managed to touch down.

The enemy attack runs had ceased by that point: the fighters didn't want to damage their own ship.

The *Callaway* and the rest of the fleet had carved a roughly twenty-centimeter diameter hole into the hull with their Vipers during the flyby. That tear penetrated the five meters through the hull and ended in what looked like a passageway from outside. They had spent the first fifteen minutes enlarging that hole with the laser cutters they'd brought along. When the breach was two meters in diameter, enough to fit the MOTH fireteam members, robots, and all their equipment, the group had hauled themselves inside.

There was working artificial gravity inside. A little stronger than Earth's. One point one Gs, according to the HUD.

Small filaments glowed red in unique, almost floral patterns on the metal bulkheads, providing dim background light that was brightened by the helmet lamps of the group. Rade remembered the strange symbols he had noticed in the alien wing segment he had explored before, and he guessed that was how these filaments would look without power.

Fist-sized HS4s accompanied the group. The drones had gone in first and mapped out the immediate area, so Rade knew that a sealed hatch awaited up ahead. He had the video feed from the foremost Centurion piped into the upper right of his HUD, and he watched as the group reached the aforementioned hatch.

"Cut through," Rade said.

The lead combat robot switched its heavy gun to the appropriate mode and began cutting. Yellow gas misted into the compartment from the molten square the weapon formed in the metal.

Rade found himself growing impatient. "Get down," he instructed the robots.

The Centurions and Praetor in front of him complied immediately.

Rade lowered his plasma rifle and fired. He knew he'd caused a breach, because the atmosphere contained beyond the hatch gushed outward, and the force of it nearly toppled him. In moments it had drained completely. He fired two more times, enlarging the white hot hole he'd made, then tossed the weapon to the Centurion in the lead.

"Use this from now on."

"Show the robots how it's done, Chief!" Aaron said over the helmet comm.

Rade sent the HS4s through first. The drones kept close to the bulkheads so that their powerful X-Ray payloads could penetrate the thick metal and flag any human life beyond. The HS4s were programmed to return immediately upon encountering any of those dark amorphous masses, or other indications of alien or robotic life. They would leave the locations of any such enemies marked in red on the maps the drones generated in realtime.

When the HS4s returned the group proceeded forward.

They continued that way, melting every hatch they encountered, venting the internal atmosphere, letting the HS4s scout each new area. Often multiple sealed hatches provided different ways of proceeding. Rade took the rightmost branches on those occasions.

The cylindrical passageways varied in radius. Sometimes the group had to proceed in single file, sometimes they could advance two abreast.

Twenty minutes passed. So far the party had encountered zero resistance. Either the aliens were too busy with the main fighting to pay the intruders any attention for the moment, or they were ill-equipped to deal with a boarding party.

Twenty minutes. And still no sign of the prisoners.

His daughter was here, somewhere.

I'll find you.

But what if she wasn't even alive anymore?

He refused to entertain the possibility.

And then, when the party had almost begun to grow complacent, after melting through one of the hatches the lead Centurion immediately toppled over. Sparks erupted from its torso.

The group dropped to the deck, hoping to use the lower portion of the hatch that was still intact for cover.

Alerts appeared on his HUD, indicating that infrared lasers were being fired into the passageway above him.

It was time to see if Connie's modifications to the weapons worked. "Units A and B, return fire!"

The two Centurions at the front of the party coordinated, moving at inhuman speeds. The first raised itself enough to fire, and the second behind it rose even higher, and together they unleashed hell into the compartment beyond the hatch. They adjusted their aim between shots and in moments ceased shooting.

"Tangos down," Unit A said.

Well done, Connie.

"Units A and B, inside!" Rade said.

The two Centurions leaped through the hatch one after the other. The first went high, the second low. He saw flashes as the two fired again, but he heard no sounds with the atmosphere vented like that.

"Clear!" Unit A transmitted.

Rade observed the compartment via the video feed from Unit A. Several black mists lay motionless between hollowed out sections of the deck. He wasn't sure if he was looking at an alien barracks, a berthing area, or a mess hall.

Well it didn't matter what he was looking at, did it?

The area was clear.

Rade sent in the HS4s to map the place, and the drones determined that there were three sealed exits leading forward, right, and left. As always, Rade chose the rightmost. He retrieved his plasma rifle from the downed combat robot and tossed it to the new Centurion that had assumed the point position. The robot went to the hatch.

"Sir!" the Centurion said urgently.

Though the robot hadn't fired, the metal on the hatch had turned white hot. A hole abruptly formed in the middle.

"To the deck!" Rade said.

The team dropped as the inner atmosphere explosively decompressed. The magnets in their exoskeletons prevented the team from being tossed down the rear passageway like rag dolls.

They waited several moments but the atmosphere continued to vent. That meant one of three things: A) there was a very large area behind that hatch; B) the other adjoining compartments had lost the ability to seal; or C) the ventilation systems in that area were malfunctioning.

Rade aimed his weapon at the hatch. Others did likewise.

"Orders, Chief?" Aaron transmitted over the comm.

"Hold..."

Fifteen seconds passed.

"Chief?" Aaron pressed.

"Hold..."

Thirty seconds.

Finally, at the forty-five second mark, the venting ceased.

The hole had enlarged slightly by that point, thanks to the pressure of the moving gas. The glow of the hatch had faded to blue from white hot, but in that moment it flared white again, and plasma from an unseen weapon spilled through from the passageway beyond. The hole became man-sized.

Rade prepared to fire.

Black mist flowed inside...

"Wait!" an unrecognized voice came over the comm. A woman's voice.

"Hold!" Rade shouted to his men. He was relieved that none of the robots had fired. They were programmed to attack only after receiving his authority, but he never really trusted them, not after the terrible malfunctions he had witnessed in the past.

"I'm human," the voice came again.

Was that his daughter?

"What alien trick is this?" Aaron said over the comm.

"Be quiet!" Rade snapped, lowering his weapon. He stood up and approached the darkness.

A figure in a spacesuit emerged from the darkness.

"We're human," she repeated.

He went to her and looked into the face plate. Disappointment filled him. It wasn't his daughter.

A small, rectangular device dropped to the deck underneath the darkness and the mist dispersed, revealing a man in a spacesuit.

"Lieutenant Commander Jason Wolf and Lieutenant Lin Akido at your service," the man said.

thirty

Jonathan tightened his grip on the armrests as the bridge continued to shudder under the fighter attack.

"The alien capital ship just braked, hard," Ensign Lewis said. "It looks like they're turning around."

"Coming back for more, are they?" He stared at the display overlaying his vision. The Avengers from Orange Squadron had been harassing the capital ship the whole time; it had launched several more fighters to defend against them.

Jonathan relaxed his grip when he caught an officer looking at his hands. It was best to portray a sense of calm composure for the benefit of his bridge crew. It wouldn't do to continue clasping his fingers so hard that the knuckles were white. "What about the dart ship containing the prisoners?"

"It hasn't turned around. Maybe they're fleeing."

"They're probably a bit distracted by our rescue party," Robert said.

On the tactical display the *Salvador* abruptly broke formation, decelerating.

"What's she doing?" Jonathan said. "Comm, raise Captain Rail."

"She's responded, voice only," Lazur said.

Jonathan accepted the connection from Rail.

"Get the *Salvador* back in formation, Captain!" Jonathan told her.

It was several seconds before her response came.

"We're dealing with an alien intruder at the moment," Rail said over the comm. "We'll return to course shortly."

"Bullshit. I want you back in line now."

In answer, the connection terminated.

"Damn it," Jonathan said. He had wanted to let the Avengers chip away at the capital ship for longer, but he was going to have to decelerate the fleet early if the *Salvador* was to have any chance of survival.

The bridge rumbled badly as the nearby enemy fighters made another attack run.

"Sir, if we increase speed, we can shake off these fighters," Miko said.

Shake off the fighters, or return for the *Salvador*...

"Your orders, Captain?" Miko said.

Jonathan stared at the 3D display.

"Captain," Robert said. "Do we abandon the *Salvador* to her fate?"

Jonathan felt his insides clench up. *Abandon her to her fate.*

"If we turn back," Jonathan said. "And concentrate our Viper fire again, there's a chance we can disable the already damaged capital ship before she takes any of us down."

"It's possible our Avengers will disable the ship for us," Robert said.

"True. But I can't leave the *Salvador* behind. If we go, she has no chance at all."

"And if we stay, there's also a chance the enemy fighters will disable *us*," Robert pointed out. "Black Squadron and our upgraded point defenses can only do so much."

"I know." Jonathan took a deep breath. He had made up his mind. "Miko, if we begin decelerating the task unit now, will we reach the *Salvador* in time to fire a combined broadside at the capital ship?"

"Yes, but we'd have to begin the deceleration immediately," Miko said.

"Do it," Jonathan said. "Fleet wide."

Miko echoed his orders.

"Coordinate with the task unit," Jonathan continued. "I want every vessel to target the particle beam generator on the nose of that ship. We'll fire when we close to fifteen thousand kilometers. And pray that our combined Vipers do enough damage to disable it."

Barrick blinked several times. His eyes burned painfully—it felt like someone had thrown sand into them. Or splashed them with pepper spray, like in bootcamp. He bent over in agony, shutting his eyes to rub them. The copiously flowing tears wet his fingers.

"Telepath Barrick is awake," the ship's AI intoned. Its voice sounded cavernous, as if spoken from the top of one of the *Callaway's* hangar bays.

The *Callaway*. Yes. That was where Barrick was. He had a partial memory of sitting cross-legged in front of the alien, his eyes wide open. That would explain the incredible dryness he felt in his sclerae.

The pain slowly receded. He lowered his arms and tentatively opened his eyes. He stared at his palms.

My hands.

An unseen energy seemed to flow through his fingers. It was like he was conscious of every nerve impulse passing through them.

I've retained the power, then. I feared I would lose it when I finally awakened. But I'm more powerful than ever before.

He sat up straight and stared at the amorphous black mass that lurked in front of him.

And I have you to thank for this.

When he had fallen into the vortex, he had woken as a young man once more in the Academy, his whole life before then merely a dream. He had gone about his days, completed his studies, finished a hundred year tenure in the navy, married and spent the next hundred and fifty years in retirement. He had lived a full life, undergoing many rejuvenation sessions, and died a grandfather at the ripe age of two hundred and sixty five.

Only to awaken as a young man in the Academy once more.

And so it continued. He had become an old man a hundred times over in the mind world, and died young just as often. He had the full recollection of his previous lives and was able to make different choices to vary the outcome each time. Because of those ever-expanding memories, his powers grew far beyond what a normal telepath could ever hope to achieve.

He could still feel the lingering presence of the alien in his mind. It seemed obvious to him now that the being had been using him to understand the human brain. Experimenting on him. Seeing what drove humanity, and how a human reacted in various situations.

It was a form of torture, and yet, what the alien had done to him was also a gift. Because not only had it increased his powers, he had relived the current moment a hundred times. He'd tried so many different courses of action and yet only one resulted in the saving of the fleet, and the entire human race itself. He knew precisely what he must do.

And yet, he had a nagging feeling at the back of his thoughts. *What if it's a trick?*

The darkness abruptly descended to the bottom of the container. That had never happened before in the mind worlds. The slight presence he felt in his consciousness vanished.

The alien was dead, then. Perhaps what it had done to Barrick had utterly drained the thing, to its death.

He rose on wobbly legs, bracing himself against the glass container. Then he turned around.

The objects of the cargo bay appeared slightly fuzzy. None of the scientists were present. But the five masters-at-arms and their robots were. There was a slight halo around the men.

They were flies to him. All of them.

"Are you all right, sir?" an MA said. Their commanding officer.

The telepath stared at him.

"You have called the acting doctor to report to the cargo bay," Barrick said. "You will cancel that order."

The MA seemed momentarily puzzled that Barrick would know that, and then he said: "I'm sorry sir, I can't do that. I have my orders. You're to remain here under observation until the doctor arrives."

The telepath studied the men. Would the powers he had developed still work now that the alien was dead? Had the ability to control not just one mind, but multiple psyches, all been an elaborate dream?

There was only one way to find out...

He concentrated, visualizing the five MAs in his mind.

The men exchanged glances, then abruptly turned and fired at the five Centurions. The combat robots were reduced to a pile of melted metal.

"Barricade the door," Barrick told the men. "And guard it. Don't let anyone in. Shoot to kill, if you have to."

"Yes sir!" the lead MA said.

The five hurried to the door and took up guard positions.

"Telepath Barrick," Maxwell said. "Your actions are in violation—"

Barrick bent down and retrieved the plasma rifle from one of the fallen robots. He fired at the speaker in the overhead, cutting off the AI. He shot out the lightfield cameras in the bay, then removed his aReal glasses and crunched them underfoot. The computer would still be able to monitor him via the Implants in the MAs, but he wasn't too concerned about that: the security personnel had their backs to him, their attention devoted entirely to watching the entry hatch.

That was just as easy as it had been the last time. He smiled. He still had his abilities, then. Of course he did. Though only a few days had passed in the outside world, he had trained in the inner world of the mind for a thousand years.

He lowered himself to the floor, crossed his legs, and sat against the container. He closed his eyes and focused on visualizing the bridge. He could almost sense the presence of the officers there. He concentrated on the faces he knew. Captain Jonathan Dallas. Commander Robert Cray. He placed the two of them side by side in his mind. Through them, he had access to the other members of the bridge. Their representations appeared behind Dallas and Cray, indistinct, blurry. But it was enough.

He focused on bending them to his will.

He felt that nagging doubt once again, that this was all a trick. And he thought he was forgetting something.

What did I do different last time?

He dismissed those thoughts and concentrated his entire being on the bridge personnel.

* * *

Jonathan was studying the 3D display when Maxwell spoke.

"Captain, Barrick has taken over cargo bay seven," the AI intoned.

"What?" Jonathan said. "How?"

But Maxwell didn't answer.

Jonathan heard the bridge hatch open instead. That was strange. No one was allowed on the bridge during a lockdown.

He glanced up toward the entrance and froze.

Famina had stepped inside. Her skin was porcelain, exactly as he remembered. Her lips drawn back in a permanent frozen rictus.

The bridge abruptly faded away. Jonathan was back on the summit. In the freezing snow.

Famina continued to approach.

"What do you want?" Jonathan said.

"I have come to liberate you," Famina said.

"I always knew you would come for me," Jonathan told her. He could hear the sounds of intensive care in the background. The incessant beep of the heart rate monitors. The subtle chatter of patients soon to die.

"Yes." Famina stopped beside him. She extended a hand and turned her head to regard the gaping abyss beside her. "Come with me. Be free, Jonathan."

Though he was wrapped in a winter jacket with several layers underneath, Jonathan felt so cold. So weary. He couldn't feel his fingers or toes. The rest of his hands and feet burned, throbbing badly.

He reached toward her offered palm.

But then he hesitated.

"Do you want to be free?" Famina said. "All burdens gone?"

"But I have a duty to my crew," Jonathan said between chattering teeth.

"Your crew is lost," Famina said. "You cannot save them. Take my hand, Jonathan. Come with me. Be warm again forevermore." She pressed her open palm toward him. "Take my hand, Jonathan. And I will forgive you."

He took it.

Famina stepped into the abyss.

Her weight pulled him down and he plunged into the depths after her.

"Captain," Robert said. "Captain!"

Jonathan didn't respond. He merely stared off into space.

"I'm assuming command," Robert said. "Maxwell, note in the ship's log that Captain Jonathan Dallas became unresponsive at thirteen hundred forty two hours."

"Noted," Maxwell said.

"Sir," Ensign Lewis said. "Something strange. The other ships in the task unit are gone."

"What?" Robert said. "Where did they go?"

"I don't know," Lewis said. "I think our sensors... wait. Several alien capital ships just emerged from 2-Vega."

"What?" Robert glanced at the tactical display. The *Callaway* was now right beside the Slipstream 2-Vega. And ten enemy dots had appeared.

"How the hell did we get here?" Robert said.

"I can't explain it," Lewis said.

"What happened to the nukes we mined the entrance with?"

"Gone, sir."

The bridge shuddered.

"Looks like the enemy fighters were transported with us," Miko said. "They're still making strafing runs. And we don't have Black Squadron to defend us anymore."

"Target the closest ship with our Vipers and mag-rails," Robert said. "I want to destroy at least one of them before we go down."

"Odd," Miko said. "Our targeting systems are reporting the ship as a friendly."

"Send me the external feed," Robert said. An instant later a square, hulking capital ship appeared on his vision. "That's definitely not a friendly. Override the targeting system and prepare to fire."

thirty-one

Since their escape, Wolf and Lin had been hiding, avoiding the alien patrols, struggling to stay alive. They had kept to what could best be described as maintenance passageways on the vessel, and though they had tried, they hadn't been able to locate the prisoners.

Wolf had known something was wrong when the blue filaments that lit the passageways had turned to red and the hatches between compartments had sealed. Shortly thereafter the deck had rumbled, and a temporary drop in inertial compensation had thrown him and Lin to the floor.

He had realized the fleet was making an attack, and resolved to do whatever he could to cause damage from within. He and Lin had roamed through the passageways with the intent to melt down as many sealed hatches as they could, hoping to reduce the breach containment effectiveness of the ship. Unfortunately, the aliens themselves seemed impervious to the plasma rifle he possessed, so he and Lin had to run whenever one of those dark masses presented itself. At one point in his rampage, four aliens had chased him and Lin, but the pair had managed to lose them. Their darkness cloak had helped, no doubt.

When they found Rade and his team, Wolf shared the map data his aReal had gathered. Rade immediately dispatched the HS4s to perform a scan of the areas Wolf and Lin had opened up.

They were waiting in that large compartment for the HS4s to report back.

"How long do the drones usually take to X-Ray the bulk-heads?" Wolf asked Aaron, Rade's second.

"Depends," Aaron said. "They—" He broke off, then turned away. "Contact, Chief!"

"What's wrong?" Wolf asked him.

"Look at your map," Aaron said. "The HS4s are reporting humans beyond the bulkhead of one of the passageways you opened up for us."

Wolf glanced at the map on the upper right of his HUD. Several blue dots had appeared.

The prisoners.

Rade ordered a Centurion to stay put to guard that compartment, then the party proceeded forward. The robots led, followed by Rade and his men, then Wolf and Lin, with two more Centurions bringing up the rear.

Rade left behind two more robots along the way to watch the different branches, and to keep a route open to the shuttles. Wolf and Lin assumed the burden of the spare spacesuits those robots had carried on their backs.

When they reached the location of the waiting HS4, Rade surveyed the bulkhead. There was no obvious entrance point.

"Looks like we're at the back of the prison," Aaron commented. "That's about perfect, isn't it Chief?"

In answer, Rade waved the rearmost Centurions forward. They carried a portable airlock between them. "Set it up."

The robots unfolded the twin frames and extended the accordion-like fabric that joined them. It was lucky this was one of the wider passageways, able to hold three men abreast, because that airlock wouldn't have fit otherwise.

When the airlock was in place, Aaron grabbed the plasma rifle and stepped inside. He barely fit with the spacesuit strapped to his back. He glanced at Rade for confirmation.

The chief nodded and Aaron shut the hatch.

"Waiting for the pressure to equalize," Aaron said over the comm. A few moments later: "I'm switching to the laser cutter. Not enough room to fire the plasma rifle safely in here."

Two minutes passed.

"I'm through," Aaron sent. "Closing the inner hatch behind me."

Rade must have vented the atmosphere via his aReal because a red light appeared on the outside of the hatch. When it turned green, Rade turned to Wolf. "You're next. I'm sure they could use a familiar face."

Wolf went inside and closed the hatch behind him. He waited for the atmosphere to pressurize, then opened the inner door. A rectangle had been cleanly cut into the bulkhead beside him. He hurried inside, bringing the spare spacesuit.

Aaron was already there, surrounded by excited prisoners.

He saw Chopra.

"Told you I'd come back," Wolf told her, using the external speakers on his helmet.

The others came through, one at a time, and offloaded their spacesuits to the prisoners. Rade came, too, but purposely ignored Chopra.

"Finish getting suited up!" Rade announced. "My team has secured a route between here and the shuttle. You'll find the map on your aReal. One man or robot from my team will go with each of you. Once you reach the shuttle, wait there. The rest of you, my team will return with more spacesuits. We're going to get you all out of here."

People finished suiting up and proceeded into the airlock one at a time, followed by MOTHs and robots.

Rade and Wolf waited by the entrance for their own turn to escort someone.

Chopra approached.

"Dad," she said.

Rade looked away.

Wolf saw tears in her eyes at the rejection.

He turned to Rade. "Talk to her, you fool! She's the reason you're here!"

Rade glanced at him. Wolf realized why he didn't want to talk to his daughter. His own face was covered in tears.

Finally Rade turned to her. "Hey, girl."

"Dad, why are you crying?" she said. Her own tears were flowing freely by then. "I thought you never cried."

"I don't." He hugged her fiercely. "Why the hell haven't you suited up?"

"I go last," she said insistently.

"Damn you, girl," Rade said. "Headstrong to the end."

"Just like my father."

He grinned. "Love you, hun."

"Love you, too, dad."

Wolf's turn was next, and he was spared having to watch their emotional reunion any further. He was close to tears himself by then.

After the second run back to the shuttles that were parked on the hull of the alien ship, Wolf began to worry that there wouldn't be enough room to fit everyone, even if all the robots stayed behind. It would certainly be a tight fit. Part of the problem was that the spacesuits weren't body-conforming and took up a large amount of space.

It required four trips before the final occupants left the prison behind. There had been some isolated shooting during that time, with the combat robots firing from their guard positions at approaching aliens.

The second shuttle had departed, so Wolf loaded himself onto the remaining Dragonfly beside Lin and the latest passenger. They were waiting for the final two members, Chopra and Rade. He had no idea how the two of them were going to fit: there wasn't any room left. The suited occupants were packed, standing, right up against the bulkheads, with the overhead directly above them.

Outside, a helmet poked through the hole that was cut into the alien hull. Chopra pulled herself out and gripped the lifeline that led to the Dragonfly.

Rade joined her a moment later.

"Make some room people," Rade said over the comm when they reached the shuttle.

Wolf shoved against the occupants immediately beside him; the passengers shifted and somehow made a tiny space.

"You first," Rade shoved his daughter up and forward. She squeezed in beside Wolf.

Rade pulled himself in after her. His exoskeleton resided half outside the entrance. It seemed obvious to Wolf that he didn't fit.

An alert sounded.

"Clear the door!" the pilot sent.

"People, squeeze closer together!" Wolf said. But they were basically packed in as tight as they could get already.

"Can't you take off with the door open?" someone shouted over the comm.

"No can do," the pilot returned. "The inertial compensators won't function with the door open. Do you want to be dumped out when I make a turn?"

Wolf tried shoving against the people beside him once more, but it was like pressing against a solid mass.

The door started to move downward but when it struck Rade's helmet it immediately reversed.

"Still can't shut the doors!" the pilot said. "Someone is going to have to stay. Draw straws on your aReals, do whatever it takes, but clear the damn door so my craft can launch!"

"I'll stay with the robots." Rade got off immediately.

"Dad no!" Chopra said, reaching for him.

Rade intercepted her. "Wolf, hold her back."

Wolf wrapped his arms around her without preamble. She kicked against him. "Let me go, you bastard!"

But Wolf held on like his life depended on it. With the way Rade was acting, it probably did.

Rade looked at Chopra with such tender sadness on his face. "Pilot, shut the door."

The hatch began to close and Chopra struggled against Wolf even more violently. He was worried she was going to compromise one or both of their suits.

"Forgive me, Sil," Rade transmitted.

She kicked at the closing hatch but the metal was unaffected. When it finally sealed Wolf released her.

"Pilot, open this door!" Chopra shouted.

"No can do—"

"I'm the captain here!" Chopra interrupted him.

"Chief Galaal is in charge of this mission. He wants to stay, he stays." The Dragonfly shook as the engine started up.

"Rade," Wolf said into the comm.

"What is it, Wolf?" Rade returned.

"I just wanted to say thank you, for everything. If you were here right now, I'd shake your goddamn hand."

"And I'd shake yours," Rade said gruffly. "I was wrong about you. Now if you don't mind, I'd like to share some final words with my daughter."

Wolf cut the connection. He saw Chopra's lips moving frantically, as though she were pleading with her father, but Wolf couldn't hear a word. She shook her head, mouthing the word "no" again and again, her eyes red.

Chopra abruptly leaned against Wolf, pressing her helmet into his shoulder. Though he couldn't hear her, he could tell she was sobbing behind that face plate.

He glanced at Lin helplessly. Her eyes were wide. Stunned.

As the shuttle took off, Wolf heard one last transmission from Rade. It sounded like he was communicating with the combat robots that were left behind. The chief hadn't bothered to choose a private sub-channel for the broadcast: maybe he thought the Dragonfly and its passengers were out of range by then.

"Advance," Rade sent, his voice digitally warping. "I want to open up more of these compartments. In fact, I want to fight my way up to their goddamn bridge. I know you're robots. I know you don't have emotions. But I also know none of you really want to die. No AI does. So I commend you for staying. And I thank you.

"Now, let's give them hell, boys."

thirty-two

Torso-deep inside the coolant access panel of reactor one, Stanley squeezed between the wires and conduits. He was attempting to repair damage from the latest attack. There was so much to do that he had elected to personally assist the men, robots, and drones working under him.

"I told him not to press our engines so damn hard!" the chief engineer cursed, though he knew the *Callaway* had only traveled at half speed during the battle so far. "Nor to fly so close to the enemy particle weapon!"

The small flying drone beside him bleeped in agreement as it 3D-printed a new gasket for him to use.

A call from the ship's AI popped up on his aReal. Stanley absently accepted.

"Lieutenant Commander Stanley McTaggert," Maxwell said.

"Yes yes. What the fuck is it, AI?"

"Control of the bridge has been lost," Maxwell said.

"What?" Stanley stood up straight, banging his head on an overhead pipe. He flinched painfully.

"The bridge crew is about to fire on the *Salvador*. The commander has overridden the friendly fire prevention mechanism."

"I'm sure he has good reason." Stanley bent over to concentrate on his task once more. "Cray and Dallas know what they're doing."

"The telepath is in control of their minds."

"Why haven't you taken control then, machine!" Stanley said.

"Because you are in command now, sir."

"Damn it." He waded out from the wires and conduits. "Show me what you're talking about."

A video feed labeled "cargo bay seven" overlaid his vision. He saw Barrick seated against the glass chamber that contained the alien. The telepath's eyes were closed. Five MAs barricaded the entrance to the bay. An equal number of combat robots lay in a smoking heap behind them. Stanley worked out that the video feed was sourced from a selfie drone that had flown into the bay via a ventilation duct. Sneaky AI.

"Now show me the bridge," Stanley said.

The view changed. He saw the Round Table. Captain Dallas was sitting there, staring off into space. Robert and the rest of them seemed fine, though they were ignoring the captain.

Stanley pulled up the tactical display. The *Callaway* was on a direct course for the *Salvador*. The rest of the fleet, meanwhile, was heading toward the approaching capital ship. The fleet's course would take them within fifteen thousand kilometers of the enemy.

"Prepare to fire at the enemy vessel," the commander said.

On the tactical display the *Salvador* highlighted as the *Callaway's* weapons locked onto it.

It seemed that Maxwell was right.

"Shit," Stanley said. "You've informed the fleet of our situation?"

"I have," Maxwell said.

Stanley attempted to call Robert. The ping ran continuously but the commander didn't bother to dismiss it like a normal person would. He simply ignored the request. Stanley tried Jonathan next. Same response. It was as if they weren't even seeing or hearing the call.

"I have tried repeatedly to reach them," Maxwell said. "They ignore me regardless of whether I speak through the aReal or the bridge speaker system."

"Transfer control of the bridge to engineering," Stanley said. "And lock out their controls." He stated his passcode.

"Bridge controls locked out and transferred to engineering," Maxwell said.

"Now flood cargo bay seven with incapacitating agents," Stanley said.

"Wouldn't you rather open the cargo bay doors?"

"No I would not," Stanley said.

"Killing Barrick would be prudent."

"Don't lecture me on what would or would not be prudent, you emotionless AI!" Stanley said. "Flood the bay with the incapacitating agent as instructed!"

"As you wish."

"And call me sir, goddammit," Stanley said.

"Yes, sir."

He switched to the cargo bay seven feed. The telepath and his guards collapsed as the invisible agent took hold.

"Why the hell would the telepath try to take control?" Stanley said. "He had to know we had backup measures in place. Even if he had decided to take over engineering, too, he couldn't have stopped you from assuming the captaincy in the end." The continuity of command dictated that a ship's AI must take over if no capable officers remained to assume control.

"He may not have been aware of this," Maxwell said. "Or perhaps the alien, obviously influencing him, merely wanted to sow confusion during a critical part of the battle. A last, desperate attempt to help its companions."

"Whatever the case," Stanley said. "The fucker failed. Have some MAs mask-up. I want the six of them transferred to the brig ASAP. And have the doc keep the telepath sedated."

"As you wish, sir."

"And now, since I'm flagship commander for a day, update me on the battle plan."

Maxwell obliged. "The fleet intends to fly past the target and fire a combined Viper broadside at fifteen thousand kilometers out, directly into the nose of the enemy. The intention is to disable the particle beam weapon."

"Sounds reasonable. Bring the Callaway back in line with them." The engine room rumbled in response to an impact somewhere outside the hull. "And accelerate. Let's see if we can shake off some of these fighters!"

"I thought you didn't like pushing the engines," Maxwell said.

"No, I don't like the captain pushing the engines," Stanley said. "I'm fine doing it myself."

The minutes passed. The fleet reached the fifteen thousand kilometer range mark before the *Callaway* caught up.

"Sir, most of the fleet is in range," Maxwell said.

"Fire Vipers."

The fleet fired their combined heavy beams at the target.

"So, how did we do?" Stanley said, pulling up the external video feed.

"Their nose has sustained heavy damage," Maxwell said. "The particle beam nozzle doesn't appear to exist anymore."

"When we're in range, fire at the same spot," Stanley said.

He saw a flash on the external video feed.

"What happened?"

Maxwell was silent a moment. Then: "The target incinerated."

"They self-destructed?"

"Unknown."

"The enemy fighters harassing the *Callaway* have ceased operating," Maxwell said.

The *Callaway* hadn't achieved enough acceleration to escape them, so that was a nice bonus.

"Have Black Squadron fire grappling hooks into a couple of them and tow them aboard," Stanley said. "That should give the fleet scientists a few erections. What's the status on the prison ship?"

"Remaining target is fleeing sun-ward, toward 2-Vega. The vessel just directed a gamma ray pulse at said Slipstream."

"Bastards are calling home to mommy again," Stanley said. "Status on the MOTH rescue team?"

"Both Dragonflies have separated from the hull and are reporting that they have the surviving members of the *Selene* aboard, as well as pilots Jason Wolf and Lin Akido."

"We did it, then. We won. Or rather, *I* won." Stanley beamed.

"Should we have the *Aurelia* attempt an intercept on the remaining ship?" Maxwell asked.

It took a moment for Stanley to remember that the *Aurelia* was one of those ships that had stayed behind in the inner portion of the system to guard the *Marley* and *Grimm*.

"Let them go," Stanley said. "They've already called home. No point in hunting them down to the last. Or in putting our other ships in danger. If we send in the *Aurelia*, and she loses, the enemy might get the bright idea of attacking the defenseless Builder vessel. Not exactly the preferred outcome."

"I'm detecting a distress beacon," Maxwell said. "Roughly fifty thousand kilometers behind the prison ship. It belongs to Chief Rade Galaal."

"And who might that be?" Stanley said.

"The MOTH in charge of the rescue mission."

"Is he still alive?"

"Unknown," the AI returned.

"How are we able to detect his Personal Alert signal this far out?"

"Also unknown," the AI returned.

"Launch another Dragonfly to retrieve him."

"Yes, sir."

"Now pipe me into the bridge." A moment later Stanley found himself standing on the bridge, in the center of the Round Table. Jonathan was still unresponsive, while Robert and the others seemed confused.

They probably have no idea what the hell is going on.

"Hello there, Commander Cray," Stanley said. "I'm terribly sorry, but I had to commandeer the *Callaway* for a while. Seems you fellas had lost your minds, so to speak. But don't worry, I saved the day. I made a fine flagship commander if I do say so myself."

The expression on Robert's face was priceless.

Robert stood beside Jonathan's cot in the makeshift sick bay. The captain hadn't awakened since the incident on the bridge. No one knew why. The telepath was kept sedated, so it was unlikely Jonathan was still under the influence of Barrick. The acting doctor was worried that the man had somehow permanently damaged the captain's mind.

Connie entered the sick bay and joined him.

"So do you believe in telepaths now?" Robert asked her.

She grunted. "I'm starting to. I did some research. No telepath is as powerful as what we've witnessed here. Reading thoughts is one thing but apparently it takes a lifetime to fully develop the skills necessary to invade a mind. Those telepaths with roughly a hundred years of practice can plant suggestions, but not issue commands outright, not like Barrick did. And they can do so only with one individual at a time. Barrick was controlling the five MAs in the cargo bay, and everyone on the bridge. That hasn't ever been seen before."

The deputy medical officer, Maria Young, came over. Her boss had died when the warren of rooms comprising the main sick bay was destroyed. "I think it's obvious the alien did something to him. Perhaps it put a part of its own consciousness inside him before it died."

"Is that even possible?" Connie said.

"I have no idea," the doctor told her. "You're the scientist."

"One thing's for sure," Connie said. "If we ever get home, Fleet is going to have a field day experimenting on Barrick."

Robert stared at Jonathan.

"I've often wondered what would happen if a hacker took over a ship's AI," the commander said. "And fed misinformation to the aReal of the officers. What Barrick did wasn't all that different. His actions were a little more intrusive, yes, but the concept is the same."

"There are too many safeguards and security measures in place for a hacker ever to take over a ship like that," Connie said. "I know. I minored in information security."

"It's happened before in the past," Robert said. "Our machines turned against us."

"Which is why we implemented all those safeguards in the first place," Connie said.

Robert crossed his arms and returned his attention to the captain. "I have a feeling the United Systems is going to be implementing some new safeguards regarding telepaths."

Jonathan couldn't see a thing. The blizzard had reduced visibility to whiteout conditions. He knew he should stop and dig himself a bivouac. Knew that he could walk off a ledge at any time, thanks to the zero visibility, and the loss of his portable LIDAR gear. But he trudged on. He had to make the summit at all costs.

He had already abandoned his oxygen tank. His frantic breathing was lost to the raging howl of the blizzard. The lower part of his face was wrapped in a scarf, his eyes shielded by thick goggles. He had tightened his hood so that no skin on his face was exposed. He wore a thick winter jacket with several layers of clothes underneath, along with thermo undergarments, thick gloves and boots. For all that the cold still bit into his body: factoring in the windchill, it was minus sixty degrees Celsius out there.

He trudged ever onward, the snow swallowing his feet to the knees with each step. It was like slogging through an inexorable, unending mire on stumps for legs—he had stopped feeling any sensation in his feet hours ago.

Have to make the summit.

He kept going for a short while longer but finally his body gave out and he collapsed in the snow.

Rest. Rest.

He sat there, panting, for several moments. But he never caught his breath. It felt like he was choking. No matter how much oxygen he breathed, he could never get enough.

He willed himself to get up but couldn't bring his body to move. He just wanted to sleep. Yes. The welcome oblivion of sleep.

Yet he knew if he closed his eyes he would attain an oblivion far beyond mere sleep.

Must go on.

He forced himself to rise then took a tentative step forward into the knee-deep snow. Another. He proceeded that way, one exhausting step after the other. He had no sense of direction whatsoever, not in those whiteout conditions. He could have been walking back the way he had come as far as he knew. But he refused to give up. It simply wasn't in his nature.

A distant, ghostly voice carried to him on the wind.

Jonathan.

"Who's that?" he could barely hear his own words above the

shrieking of the wind.

I've already forgiven you, Jonathan. Long ago.

"Go away! Leave me alone." He willed himself onward.

Forgive yourself.

He started laughing maniacally. "Forgive myself? There's nothing to forgive! I left you on purpose, bitch. I wanted you to die. Why would I care about some stranger I didn't know?" He laughed all the harder.

Forgive yourself, the voice repeated.

And then he realized what it was that he was climbing on.

A summit of self hate and guilt.

He collapsed to his knees and held his face in his hands.

It wasn't his fault that she had died.

He tried to save her. But he had to leave her.

He had no choice.

Forgive yourself.

He lowered his hands from his face and sat back in the snow.

He forgave himself.

The storm cleared. He resided on the summit of the mountain. The sky shone azure above, surrounded by kilometers of breathtaking, snow-capped ranges. It was one of the most beautiful skies he had ever witnessed in his life.

Jonathan smiled, finally at peace. "Thank you, Famina."

He opened his eyes. He resided in a hangar bay of some kind. It had been converted into a makeshift intensive care unit, judging from the patients occupying the beds beside him.

An IV tube was connected to the dorsal venous network of his hand. A heart rate monitor beeped beside him.

Suddenly worried, he lifted his hands to examine them. The skin wasn't blackened. He sat up and wiggled his toes. Everything seemed intact. No frostbite.

He lay back once more, listening to the noises of the makeshift care area around him. Those sounds should have bothered him but they didn't.

A weaver robot wheeled itself over. "Welcome back, Captain."

thirty-three

The crew welcomed Jonathan back to the bridge the next day.

The task unit had assumed a guard position by the exit Slipstream. The vessels were waiting for the *Marley* and her escorts to make the long trek from the inner planets. The remaining alien ship continued limping toward the uncharted inner Slipstream, 2-Vega. Jonathan was happy to let them go. He hoped that the losses the aliens had experienced would make them think twice before attacking human vessels again.

In the debriefing, Jonathan learned that Captain Rail had indeed been dealing with an alien intruder when the *Salvador* had broken formation. The intruder had made its way to the engine room and disabled one of the reactors, forcing the ship to decelerate. The on-board MOTHs had killed the alien thanks to the weapon modifications Connie's team had transmitted to the fleet in the days before. He had been wrong to distrust Rail.

Chief Rade Galaal revealed that after the shuttles abandoned him on the enemy ship, he and the combat robots spent some time wreaking further havoc. The enemy troops managed to mount a decent offense, eventually forcing Rade and the robots to evacuate the ship. As they floated there in deep space, Rade vented oxygen to link up with the remaining robots, as none of them had brought along jetpacks for the mission.

Once linked, he had the bright idea to join their power sources to his enhanced PASS mechanism, boosting the distress signal far beyond the usual range—enough for the *Callaway* to pick up.

Also during the debriefing, Captain Chopra explained what happened to the *Selene* and *Aegis* when her crew passed behind the moon during the initial incident. The alien ships ambushed them, rising from a fissure in Achilles I to apply grappling hooks and board the *Selene*. The *Aegis* was destroyed trying to defend her. Captain Chopra attempted to detonate her vessel, preferring death to capture, but the self-destruct mechanism failed. As a backup plan, she wiped the AI to prevent the ship's data from falling into enemy hands.

When the debriefing was over and he found himself alone in his office, Jonathan leaned back, put his hands behind his head, and stared at the passing stars that existed only in his aReal.

"I heard you saved the ship, Maxwell," Jonathan told the AI.

"Lieutenant Stanley saved the ship," Maxwell said.

"Yes, but when the bridge crew became incapacitated, you acted."

"I did," Maxwell said.

"So I suppose I can tentatively forgive what you did to me, however misguided your actions were. I've decided not to have you decommissioned for spare parts when we return."

"Generous of you, sir," the AI said emotionlessly. "Though I was rather looking forward to my life as a toaster."

"I somehow doubt that."

"An accurate assessment," Maxwell admitted.

"But while I'm letting you off this time," Jonathan said. "If you ever cross me again, Maxwell—and I mean *ever*—you're headed for the scrap heap. Am I clear?"

"Clear as the perpetual droplets of methane rain misting the skies of Tau Ceti Prime."

Jonathan crumpled his brow. "Was that supposed to be a joke of some kind? I'm being serious here."

"Not a joke, Captain. Merely a metaphor to prove to you how clear your words were."

Jonathan shook his head. AIs.

A few days later a backup comm node arrived. That was the fifth, now. While there was a way to detect whether a return Gate existed beyond a Slipstream by means of gravimetric fluctuations, there was currently no method to determine if any vessels or comm nodes resided on the other side. So that was probably the last comm drone NAVCENT would send— redundancy protocols allowed up to five.

Since Jonathan was currently commodore of the fleet, Maxwell gave him the necessary keys to decrypt the urgent message the drone transmitted.

"This is Admiral Philip Scott, Chief of Space Naval Operations, to acting commander of Task Group Seven Two Dot Five. Stand down. Do not enact Operation Darkstar. I repeat, stand down. Do not enact Operation Darkstar."

The admiral went on to explain how the coup attempt by the rogue faction had failed and the old Sino-Korean government was back in place. The hijacked Sino-Korean supercarrier had also been recovered from the faction.

"You are not to deploy the bomb under any circumstances. Admiral Philip Scott out."

Jonathan called Robert to his office and shared the news.

"It feels good," Robert said. "Knowing that we were in the right all along. It's too bad there's no way we can alert the fleet about this new threat until we get a Gate built."

"Yes." Jonathan steepled his fingers and tapped his lips. "I only wish we wouldn't have to face any inquiries when we get back. Though I'm certain we'll be cleared of any charges, those inquiries will still mar your record."

Robert smiled calmly. "Doesn't matter. When we make it back, I've decided I'm going to turn down the position on the *Rampage* anyway. I want to remain aboard as your commander."

Jonathan sat back, shocked. "Are you sure? There's no guarantee the inquiry will ruin the opportunity. And no guarantee I'll even remain in command of the *Callaway*. Throwing away a CO post on one of the newest warships in the fleet to serve on a second-rate ship like my own... I don't have to tell you opportunities like this don't come up every day."

"I know, Captain. But I realize now all the bullshit you

shield us from. If I had to serve under an admiral like Knox I'd quit the next day."

"Not every admiral is like Knox," Jonathan said.

"Enough are," Robert said. "For now my place is here, I think. There's no one I'd rather serve under. It's an honor, and a privilege."

"All right, Commander," Jonathan said. "But just in case you change your mind, I'll keep my recommendation on file."

"It won't be needed." Robert stood and turned to go.

He paused by the door.

"Oh," the commander said. "Bridgette is keeping the baby."

"I'm very happy to hear that," Jonathan replied, beaming.

"As am I. You know how precious life is to me."

"I do indeed," Jonathan said.

Several days later the fleeing alien ship reached the uncharted Slipstream.

Jonathan ordered the nukes moved from the wormhole—he didn't want the aliens to destroy the mines with its particle beam. That ship could have chased the nukes until the devices ran out of fuel, but it ignored them and headed straight for the Slipstream. Perhaps they were worried Jonathan would attempt some stratagem to destroy them in the end.

The vessel vanished shortly thereafter, confirming that the aliens had the ability to pass through the wormholes without Gates. He wasn't sure how well that would bode for any future engagements with the enemy.

Jonathan ordered the nukes back into position.

The *Marley* rejoined the fleet a few weeks later and began construction of a return Gate. The current estimate for construction was six months; that included the time necessary to make mineral runs to different asteroids in the system. The *Callaway* wouldn't participate as escort in those runs, not for three or four months anyway—she was undergoing extensive repairs.

Jonathan activated the external video feed and focused on the Builder. It had already laid down a quarter of the Gate's frame.

Six months. Could the fleet survive that long?

His gaze drifted to the tactical display overlaying his vision and he stared at the 2-Vega Slipstream, where the next alien attack was likely to come.

Six months.

Jonathan vowed to bring the *Callaway* and all the remaining vessels of the task group back home in one piece.

It was his duty as commander of the flagship.

This is the end.
Thank you for reading!

FLAGSHIP

Acknowledgments

THANK YOU to my knowledgeable beta readers and advanced reviewers who helped smooth out the rough edges of the prerelease manuscript: Noel, Anton, Spencer, Norman, Corey, Erol, Terje, David, Jeremy, Charles, Walter, Lisa, Ramon, Chris, Scott, Michael, Chris, Bob, Jim, Maureen, Zane, Chuck, Shayne, Anna, Dave, Roger, Nick, Gerry, Charles, Annie, Patrick, Mike, Jeff, Lisa, Lezza, Jason, Bryant, Janna, Tom, Jerry, Chris, Jim, Brandon, Kathy, Norm, Jonathan, Derek, Shawn, Judi, Eric, Rick, Bryan, Barry, Sherman, Jim, Bob, Ralph, Darren, Michael, Chris, Michael, Julie, Glenn, Rickie, Rhonda, Neil, Doug, Claude, Ski, Joe, Paul, Larry, John, Norma, Jeff, David, Brennan, Phyllis, Robert, Darren, Daniel, Montzalee, Robert, Dave, Diane, Peter, Skip, Louise, Dave, Michael, David, Merry, David, Brent, Erin, Paul, Cesar, Jeremy, Hans, Nicole, Dan, Garland, Trudi, Sharon, Dave, Pat, Nathan, Max, Martin, Greg, David, Myles, Nancy, Ed, David, Karen, Becky, Jacob, Ben, Don, Carl, Gene, Bob, Luke, Teri, Robine, Gerald, Lee, Rich, Ken, Daniel, Chris, Al, Andy, Tim, Robert, Fred, David, Mitch, Don, Tony, Dian, Tony, John, Sandy, James, David, Pat, Gary, Jean, Bryan, William, Roy, Dave, Vincent, Tim, Richard, Kevin, George, Andrew, John, Richard, Robin, Sue, Mark, Jerry, Rodger, Rob, Byron, Ty, Mike, Gerry, Steve, Benjamin, Anna, Keith, Jeff, Josh, Herb, Bev, Simon, John, David, Greg, Larry, Timothy, Tony, Ian, Niraj, Maureen, Jim, Len, Bryan, Todd, Maria, Angela, Gerhard, Renee, Pete, Hemantkumar, Tim, Joseph, Will, David, Suzanne, Steve, Derek, Valerie, Laurence, James, Andy, Mark, Tarzy, Christina, Rick, Mike, Paula, Tim, Jim, Gal, Anthony, Ron, Dietrich, Mindy, Ben, Steve, Allen, Paddy &

Penny, Troy, Marti, Herb, Jim, David, Alan, Leslie, Chuck, Dan, Perry, Chris, Rich, Rod, Trevor, Rick, Michael, Tim, Mark, Alex, John, William, Doug, Tony, David, Sam, Derek, John, Jay, Tom, Bryant, Larry, Anjanette, Gary, Travis, Jennifer, Henry, Nicole, Drew, Michelle, Bob, Gregg, Billy, Jack, Lance, Sandra, Libby, Jonathan, Karl, Thomas, Todd, Dave, Dale, Michael, Frank, Josh, Thom, Melissa, Marilynn, Bob, Bruce, Clay, Gary, Sarge, Andrew, Deborah, Bryan, Amy, Steve, and Curtis.

Without you all, this novel would have typos, continuity errors, and excessive lapses in realism. Thank you for helping me make Flagship the best military science fiction novel it could possibly be, and thank you for leaving the early reviews that help new readers find my books.

And of course I'd be remiss if I didn't thank my mother, father, and brothers, whose untiring wisdom and thought-provoking insights have always guided me through the untamed warrens of life.

— Isaac Hooke

FLAGSHIP

www.isaachooke.com